THE
ROAD
TO
HEAVEN

A PATRICK BIRD MYSTERY

THE ROAD TO HEAVEN

ALEXIS STEFANOVICH-THOMSON

DUNDURN
PRESS

Publisher: Meghan Macdonald | Acquiring editor: Megan Beadle
Cover designer: Laura Boyle
Cover image: detective: istock.com/breakermaximus; streetcar: Roger Puta

Library and Archives Canada Cataloguing in Publication

Title: The road to heaven : a Patrick Bird mystery / Alexis Stefanovich-Thomson.
Names: Stefanovich-Thomson, Alexis, author.
Identifiers: Canadiana (print) 20230566553 | Canadiana (ebook) 20230566618
 | ISBN 9781459753723 (softcover) | ISBN 9781459753747 (EPUB) | ISBN
 9781459753730 (PDF)
Classification: LCC PS8637.T4335 R63 2024 | DDC C813/.6—dc23

We acknowledge the support of the Canada Council for the Arts and the Ontario Arts Council for our publishing program. We also acknowledge the financial support of the Government of Ontario, through the Ontario Book Publishing Tax Credit and Ontario Creates, and the Government of Canada.

Care has been taken to trace the ownership of copyright material used in this book. The author and the publisher welcome any information enabling them to rectify any references or credits in subsequent editions.

The publisher is not responsible for websites or their content unless they are owned by the publisher.

Printed and bound in Canada.

Dundurn Press
1382 Queen Street East
Toronto, Ontario, Canada M4L 1C9
dundurn.com, @dundurnpress

for Lara with all my love

TUESDAY,
JULY 13, 1965

I

THE HALLWAY STRETCHED out before me, the bright lights held in sconces, the closed doors on either side, the carpet's orange, black, and blue quadrilaterals overlapping in a hophead's nightmare. Around a corner and still more carpet reaching into the distance, still more doors on the right and left, still the sharp lights burning on the walls. An ice machine clunked and gurgled in an alcove to the left. My watch read 12:04 a.m. I was late; but how could I have known the hallway was this long? The numbers on the doors were counting up with each step. Here it was, room 724. My fist made two sharp raps on the panel. I reached for the knob, turned it, and pushed.

There was darkness, and movement in the darkness, rustling, the sharp intake of breath, and the smell of sweat and skin. The opening door threw an oblong of yellow on the floor that widened as it swung inward. I felt for the light switch with my left hand and raised the camera with the right. The flashbulb popped just before the light came on and the scene appeared frozen. The pale back lifting off the bed, a second body underneath, the limbs once intertwined, now disentangling, a flay of dark hair spread out on the pillow, her face obscured beneath his torso. His neck swivelled at the noise of my entrance, and his bulging eyes, caught in the freeze-frame of the flash, were wide, staring, surprised. In that frozen moment, it was possible to see the change in his expression as lust leaked out, and anger and fear filled the vacuum. The bulb popped again, and he blinked as he turned and rose off the bed, the sheets falling from him, his salt-and-pepper hair glinting in the light, her hands holding on to his shoulders as she was pulled up by his movement. He emerged from the bed, the roar of fury on his face, the sagging flesh of his chest under a growth of grey moss. The woman was naked too, younger — much younger — her black hair falling onto her shoulders as she sat up. He pulled free from her grasp before the third flash flared. With his feet on the floor, he came at me, quick for an old guy and swiped at the camera.

"Easy, this is my livelihood."

"You bastard. I'll kill you."

"Not in front of a lady."

"She's no lady, she's a fucking —"

"I guess we can agree on one thing" — I cut him off — "she's not your wife."

"This was a set-up."

The whole time he was grabbing at the camera and I was holding him off with the other hand.

"I put the chain on the door." He turned to look at her, beginning to figure it out.

The camera was held high, trying for a couple more pictures of his pathetic attempts — these ones not of the deed but strictly for entertainment value. There wasn't much you could do in no clothes without looking like a fool, and he looked like one, trying to rip the Kodak out of my hand while I, in my nattiest Tip Top Tailor duds, stood just inside the door frame.

The camera was up out of his reach. It clicked, and time stood still again as the light flooded the interior, capturing the wounded animal, blinking, and sweating, secreting some noxious fear that crawled up my nose. The flash stoked his rage. He stopped swiping at the camera and tried a wild hook to my chin. I rolled to my right, stepped back, and watched it sail by with a grin.

He gave up on me and turned to the woman in the bed. She'd pulled the sheet up and held it over her chest with crossed arms.

"You bitch."

She didn't yawn, but her sleepy eyes didn't express much interest.

"Leave the lady alone." I stepped into the room.

"I told you before she's no lady. She's a two-bit tramp." His anger was petering out; his bark had lost the teeth behind it. Shame and defeat showed in his eyes as he reached toward the floor, scooped up a handful of clothes, and retreated behind the bathroom door. The lock clicked. I agreed: getting dressed was best done at a table for one. Hopping around on one foot trying to find a pant leg wasn't a pretty spectacle.

Victoria stepped out of the bed. She knew how it was done; she picked up the minidress — the pattern of orange, yellow, and red rectangles on a maroon background wasn't so far off the fever-dream carpet on the other side of the door — slipped it over her head, pulled it down, smoothed the front, slid her feet into plain black pumps, scooped her panties and bra off the floor, dropped them into her purse, looked at me, and mouthed, "Let's go."

I held the door for her, and she made a two-step detour to scoop some bills off the dresser, before passing into the hall and turning left, away from the direction I'd come.

"Elevator's the other way," I said.

"Stairs," she said.

I followed behind. It was the first time I'd been in the Royal York; she knew the routine. She reached the fire door and didn't wait on me, but pulled it open. Once we were in the cement stairwell, I said, "Did you see the look on his face? I can't wait for the photos."

She shushed me, and I shushed. Seven floors down, round and round, eleven steps on each run. Beige walls and a pale grey handrail, fluorescent lighting and chips in the paint. It was eleven minutes past midnight and the lobby was quiet, even quieter in the corner where we emerged back into a world of lush colour. Victoria never broke stride. Six steps led us down to a back door that opened on Piper Street, the short service road that ran behind the hotel. She stopped on the sidewalk, looked at her reflection in the window of a parked vehicle, and adjusted stray strands of hair. "I need a ride. Where's your car?"

Coming out the back door, it took me a minute to orient myself. "It's on Station Street, across Front."

Victoria nodded her head, reached for my elbow, and pulled me beside her. "Pretty safe now, but if anyone asks, we're heading home after a night at the theatre followed by a nightcap." We walked out to York and turned south. Red brake lights, the angry blare of a horn, and the truncated rainbow of the traffic signal brought the world alive.

"Good idea. We could make it real. What do you say to a drink?"

"No."

"What'd we see?"

"What?"

"At the theatre."

"*Guys and Dolls*. It just opened."

"A musical?"

"That's right, Patrick."

"No, I can't do it."

"You don't have to watch it. You just say you did."

"I don't know. Singing and dancing."

"It's about your world, Detective Bird: hustlers, molls on the make, low-life dives, PIs like you, the whole bit."

"Maybe."

We lapsed into silence as we passed onto the dark stretch of Station Street, parked cars, yellow pools beneath street lamps, and the half-darkness of night in the city. I opened her door, and she sat on the bench and swung her legs in.

I went around the other side and dropped the camera on the back seat. She slid over and cozied up to me, and I put the car in gear and my arm around her shoulder.

"Don't get frisky," she said. "It's all for show."

"I'm a method actor."

She poked a finger in my ribs, and it backed me up a little.

"You still living in the same place?"

"I've moved." She named a western suburb that was a distance away and I asked about cross streets, and she recommended the highway they'd just built along the lake. I retrieved my arm from around her shoulders and used it to crank the wheel and turn south. I gave the engine some gas up the on-ramp and there we were on the new expressway, elevated above the city, with the lake on our left and tall new buildings sprouting up on our right.

"You were late."

"Just a minute or two."

"More than that. Let me see your watch."

I held my wrist out for her to examine.

"It's fine — which means the fault is yours. Every minute matters. It's not easy to choreograph that kind of dance. It's just about hell. Slow down, speed up, hurry up and wait. Everyone's got their own timetable. Most guys think they can't wait. Some of them really can't. Next time, be on time. That's all I'm saying."

"Yes, ma'am."

"Don't be sarcastic." She dug around in her purse and found a stick of gum, peeled the wrapper, and dropped it in the ashtray.

"Everything was okay?" I asked.

"Fine. I just need to know you're going to be there when you're supposed to be there."

"Sid'll give you a call in the morning and settle up."

"I know how this works. I've been at it a good lot longer than you."

The highway was still under construction and didn't make it all the way to her neighbourhood. The car decelerated as we came onto the service road that ended in a traffic light. She guided me through the dark streets lined by bungalows and we stopped in front of a low-rise apartment on a dead-end that ran down to the lake.

"I'll see you to the door," I said as I put the car in park.

"Nice try, but no thanks. You're cute and all, but that's not how it works."

"Sometimes it is."

"Not this time, Junior."

"I'm not that young."

She stood on the curb, speaking through the open door, "Keep telling yourself that, and one day you'll be right. But why fight it? Enjoy it while you can." The car door slammed and I watched her back as she progressed into the lighted vestibule. She dug in her purse for keys and the bright red of her panties made a brief appearance in the tumble. The second glass door swung wide and she disappeared into the interior of the building.

She wasn't up for a drink, but I still had time to make last call. Somewhere. Who knows, maybe I'd find someone as lonely as me. So, I got to bed a little later than I'd expected, which explains why when Sid called just after seven that morning I was still asleep and in no mood to join the day; which explains why I was rushed getting out to the mansion on High Park Boulevard that the *Telegram* later called "the house of blood"; which explains why I wasn't in my most sympathetic mood when I first met Linklater and learned about his missing daughter.

I RANG THE bell and the sound of steps approached; I wasn't surprised to see Linklater answer the door. Sid had warned me about the need for discretion and confidentiality in the early morning phone call — Linklater was likely doing his best to keep the help out of the picture. He was a tall man in a nondescript charcoal suit. His square glasses, wedged onto the bridge of his nose, magnified his already large eyes. And while his words welcomed me — "Bird? You're from the agency? Come in" — his glance at the watch on his wrist took it back. He closed the door quickly behind me; his long nose looked as if it might be smelling something he'd stepped in. This was what discretion looked like. "The agency assured me you're their top man." It was the pitch made to clients, but considering there were only three of us working full-time — Sid, his wife, Rachel, and me — it wasn't a high fence to scale. "They said you're the number-one missing-person man they had."

"I do my best."

"Hmm." He seemed unsatisfied. "Come this way." He led me into the living room; we were greeted by a cold fireplace and a square archway leading into the dining room where an oval table gleamed in the morning light. Looking around, he gestured to an armchair and sat down in its partner across from me. The silence of the house was oppressive and not fully explained by the absence of the missing girl. He offered me a cigarette, which I declined, and lit one for himself. "I'm sorry, Bird," he said, shaking the match and dropping it into the cut-glass ashtray, "I haven't introduced myself properly. I'm Trent. Trent Linklater." The smoke from the spent match curled upward.

"Pleased to meet you. Patrick Bird, private investigator."

"Well, thank you for coming out so quickly. And on such short notice. I imagine the agency gave you the details — about Abigail."

"I understand she's missing — but why don't you tell me what's happened and what you'd like to see happen. That's usually a good place to start."

He hesitated.

"I'd offer you a cup of coffee, but we don't keep help during the morning — and my wife, Jane, is out. She's become very serious about her tennis. Four days a week — doubles partners can be as tyrannical as a job. And I'm not much good in the kitchen."

"It's fine. Why don't you get started?"

"But what more is there to know. Abbie's missing. She didn't come home on Sunday night. And yesterday, we spent phoning around to her friends, trying to learn what was going on. And now this morning we couldn't wait any longer. I called the agency first thing."

"Have you called the police?"

"No."

"Do you mind my asking why not?"

"I don't mind, although I think your business model isn't very good if you're trying to push your clients to your competitors."

"We don't think of the police like that; we do different things. And when we investigate, we ask questions. You might not like the questions, but we need as much information as possible to move forward. What I want to know is if there's a reason the police weren't called? They're a bigger organization than us; they have the ability to cast a wider net. They have more resources and a broader system when searching for a missing person."

"No. I'm not involving the police. This should be a simple and straightforward case of finding Abbie and bringing her home. She isn't a criminal — she's a teenage girl. I don't know if she is into this peace and love that the so-called hippies are espousing, but I imagine with a little digging you could find her in one of these coffee houses that young people seem so enamoured with. I don't think it should be difficult."

"All right, if you suppose it's so easy, why don't you do it yourself? Just go down to Yorkville and pull her out of the Riverboat." Something about Linklater's mixture of self-importance and helplessness grated against my fatigue. Sid had spent the last six months trying to slay this raw impulsiveness, to teach me a gentler approach to interrogation, for use with the clients, but to my ears it sounded like PR and not investigation.

I'd succeeded in making him huffy. "I'm a busy man. I don't have time for these diversions. I was supposed to have left for the office," he said, checking his wrist again, "five minutes ago. I'm too old to search these establishments for Abbie — you might have a certain understanding of teenagers, being younger yourself." There was a pause — the threat of a standoff — before he capitulated. "The agency told me you'd come and get a photo and be on your way. I wasn't expecting to be put through the third degree."

I ignored his plea to end the conversation. "But is this what you think; that Abbie is acting and dressing like a hippie — that she's part of this youth movement, hanging out in Yorkville, smoking pot?"

He flinched. "No, I wouldn't say that." He stared at the cold fireplace, lost in his own mind, but not sharing his thoughts with me.

He was a busy man, I knew that. Sid, in the call that morning, had told me about his firm, TGL Building and Design, Architectural Engineering and Construction, which had taken him from work as a partner on the Seaway Bridge, to the building of the Gardiner Expressway, and now in 1965 had stepped into the breach to support the construction of the new city hall after the death of the original architect. Yes, he was a big wheel, and I'd just met him and I didn't like him. "So, you've got nothing for me?"

"This picture." He pushed a colour photograph, the kind a professional does, across the table. I picked it up and took a look at a young girl, becoming a woman, and depending on which angle you held it, you felt that you could see either, but not both at the same time. She had straight, dark hair that flowed over her shoulders; beneath her bangs were a pair of blue eyes, incongruous under the black fringe. A wide mouth with thin lips was frozen in a self-conscious smile. Her young face, in this unfortunate pose, couldn't fully dispel the possibility of beauty once she turned the corner and left adolescence behind. "So, you've got everything you need?" asked Linklater.

"No." I was tiring of his desire to rush me out the door. "I think if you have a real interest in getting your daughter back, you'd take the time to answer my questions. For all you know right now, your little girl could be greasing some guy up at a body-rub parlour on Yonge Street. If you —"

"I ought to throw you out." He rose from his chair and stood above me.

"Why don't you?" I had a good thirty pounds over him and was close to half his age.

He worked his jaw as his cigarette smouldered in the ashtray between us. It was good to feel a little of the fire — to know he was capable of it. But through the thick lenses of his glasses, he still had the dispassionate eyes of an insect looking down on some unsatisfactory picnic crumbs. His collar hung loose on his thin neck, and the mottled flush on his skin climbed to his chin.

I let him wait, giving him as much rope as he needed. "Listen, Linklater. You don't need to physically throw me out. Tell me to leave, and I'll walk, and you can get someone else to find your daughter. It's up to you. But if you keep me, you have me. Love me, love my dog —"

"What the hell are you talking about?"

"If you want a public relations firm, someone to hold your hand and tell you that everything's going to be okay, then that's who you should have hired. It's not how I work, and I'm not about to change. The decision is yours." There was nothing I could do to control the voice that spoke. It would've helped if he wasn't such an arrogant blowhard. I stood, and we had our stare down from closer quarters. The smoke on his breath mixed with the sour smell of anger. I made a movement for my hat, which I'd placed on a side table, and he stepped back into his chair and sat down as if retreating from a threat.

"Sit down, Bird. Sit down." He looked at his watch for the third time. "I don't mind telling you I don't like your style. You need some customer service skills. Goddamn it, I'm the client. I'm paying the bills. You can't talk to me like this. At the very least you should have a modicum of compassion considering the stress and worry I'm under. This is my daughter we're talking about. I concede that we might need to consider some difficult scenarios, but I need to say, I find your approach crude. But ask me your questions and then get started. I know I'm rushing this interview. I understand this takes time, but I'm impatient. I've hired you to solve the problem. I don't have the time to do it myself. That's why I'm paying you."

I placed my hat back on the table and lowered myself into the armchair; brocaded cranberry curlicues covered wooden arms that ended in the carved rolls of clenched fists. I found a notepad in the pocket of my jacket and thumbed it open to a blank page. "Let's start with the immediate family; there's you and your wife. I'll need to talk to her of course. Are there any other children?"

"Abbie has a twin brother, Nelson. He's at work right now."

"And is he close to Abbie?"

He paused. "They're twins. When they were younger, they were closer, but as they get older, it seems they've grown apart. I suppose Abbie matured first and became interested in grown-up things and left him behind. I don't think they share a friend group at this stage, but they get along well enough, I suppose."

"And where can I reach him?"

"He works as a lifeguard at the Boulevard Club. This is his second summer there. He's very dedicated to the job."

"Does Abbie have a summer job?"

He shook his head.

"Has she ever held a job?"

"No. I wouldn't say work interests her."

"Have there been any changes here at home?"

"Look, Bird — she's off on a jag. Teenage girls do this sort of thing. I am asking you to find her quietly — no publicity — and bring her home. I worry that at this age, children are impulsive; she could make a mistake that could have long-lasting consequences. It's easy to have a tantrum and run off — but it needn't ruin one's life."

"Was there a tantrum? A scene that precipitated this disappearance."

"No. Nothing." He opened his palms wide.

"Boyfriend?"

"Not that she confides in me, but it's possible. I suppose she's at that age, but she has a good head on her shoulders. You could try asking her friends. Lena Moore is the friend she's closest to. I'd start with her." He rooted around in a side table and came up with an address book and found her number.

"Servants?"

"We don't have anyone who lives in." That was a surprise considering the size of the house, but it explained the silence we were able to talk in. "The cook comes in some time before noon and makes lunch and dinner and tidies up afterward; we have an old Scot who does the gardening two days a week in the summer — Mondays and Thursdays, and is on call for shovelling in the winter. And the cleaning woman, she's Irish, same as the cook, is here once a week, Mondays, I think. My wife can tell you more about them. The domestic isn't my domain."

"I'd like to look at Abbie's room."

He frowned in displeasure. "This really seems to be an invasion of privacy. This is one of the reasons I didn't call the police. I don't like the feeling of others going through our house —"

"You're worried I'm going to be pawing through her personal belongings? That's what we do; it's how we might find her."

He flinched. "You don't make this easy, Bird. I told you before I don't like your tone. This is my daughter we're talking about."

"She's not your little girl anymore. She's growing up and you need to wrap your head around that."

"And you need to wrap your head around your manners," he flared back. I'd succeeded in getting the blood pumping in his body; there was some fight in there after all. We mounted a broad central staircase that branched off at right angles as it approached the second floor. "The children's rooms are over here," he said as we came out on a landing facing three doors. "This one," he spoke as if to himself, approaching a closed door.

"Has anyone been in here since she left?"

He paused. "She didn't come home Sunday night. I haven't been in the room since. Eileen, our cook, was here on Sunday while we were out, but she doesn't come upstairs. The cleaning woman was here on Monday — she would have been in, I think. I hope so. You'll have to check with Jane, my wife. I was busy at the office yesterday. My impression is that Abbie was here in the morning on Sunday and part of the afternoon; she went out with friends later in the day, and later still, phoned to say she wouldn't be home for dinner, and that's the last that we heard from her."

"So, who was the last person to see Abbie?"

"Sunday. Sunday morning, we were at church together and then we dropped Abbie at home before going off to play a round of golf. Eileen was in that day — perhaps they had an interaction. I don't know." He stopped, pinched his brow in thought, and said, "Eileen usually stays in the kitchen. I don't know if she would have talked with Abbie. Another question for Jane."

"Eileen, the Irish cook," I repeated, seeing if I could provoke any reaction from him.

He frowned at me and pushed the door open. There was a single made bed with two stuffed animals on the pillow, wallpaper with broad stripes in subdued colours, frills on the curtains and the bedskirts, and a few pictures of mop-topped singers tacked to the wall. The desk was clean, the lampshade fringed, the closet door closed, the dresser tidy. I pulled a desk drawer open and looked down into a hodgepodge: a brush, thick with black hair, pencil crayons, shoelaces, jars of face cream, bright bottles of nail polish, and a tangle of hair bands. The next drawer held unused lined paper and the bottom one was empty. The closet and dresser were equally ordered and set. I could feel Linklater flinch behind me as I pushed through the folded squares of clothing to rummage beneath the surface. There was nothing here to tell me anything about this girl — and that, in itself, was a little disturbing.

"Do you see anything missing? Any idea what Abigail was wearing when she left — or what she took with her."

He shook his head no, looking lost and clueless in the vacuum of the missing girl's room.

III

LINKLATER PHONED AHEAD to the Boulevard Club to let them know to expect me and we parted in the uneasy truce of him wanting discretion and me wanting to do the job. He thought you could investigate without asking questions, but he needed to know I wasn't going to tiptoe around and talk in a hushed voice until his daughter was found. That wasn't how it worked, and it wasn't how I worked.

The club was in full summer swing; the drone of the new highway that ran along its north side like a border wall couldn't diminish the zest of summer in the city. The tennis courts were filled with white people in white skirts and shorts. I admired a fresh set of legs that ran to the baseline to catch up to what had looked like a winning lob; somehow the woman chasing the ball down caught up to it, and,

with her back to the net, hit the return on the short bounce
between her legs. The unorthodox shot didn't make it over,
and the woman with the legs dissolved in laughter while the
rest of her foursome roundly applauded the effort. The pool
was through a further fence, full of kids and teens, moms
on the deck, sunning themselves in bikinis, their husbands
farther back on the patio, drinking coffee, and checking out
each other's wives. I studied the lifeguard from a distance,
trying to get a handle on the boy in the chair, wondering if
he was the son, Nelson, but just as in the girl's room, nothing clicked.

Going through the front door, I stopped at the desk to
make myself known and clear that Linklater had vouched
for me. The concierge, a thin moustache over a weak mouth,
was full of faux obsequiousness that let me know that while
I might be the guest of a member, at the same time, I was a
working stiff, just like him. "I need to see Nelson Linklater,"
I told him. "I think he works as a guard at the pool." Funny
Face made an expression to make it clear I'd never understand the complexities of his world, reviewed a piece of paper
on the desk in front of him, and pronounced, "Nelson's pin-
setting today, down in the bowling alley. There's a rotating
schedule for the boys here." He provided me with directions
through the maze of corridors to reach the basement.

I came down the stairs and pushed through a door into
the alley to be met by a wall of thunder as the balls crashed
and rattled in the low-ceilinged space. There were four lanes,
and each pair had a pin boy who stood in the limited space
behind the skittles as the ball came down the hardwood. A
hotshot in the first lane dragged his left leg behind his body
at release to put a sweeping spin on his shot. The ball took
off like a rocket and exploded for a strike against the pins.

The boy in the back jumped to avoid the detonation of skittles and scrambled to set them back up. Most of the world had moved to mechanical pinsetters, but the Boulevard Club seemed to pride itself on retaining this archaic practice as if it could temper the leaders of tomorrow in this basement forge.

A pimply young man in a short-sleeved shirt looked at me with curiosity. I moved to where he stood over a glass countertop and said against the din, "I'm looking for Nelson Linklater. His father sent me down here to find him."

"That's Nelson." He pushed the end of his chin toward lanes three and four, where the pin boy sat in a chair behind the skittles. Only one of the two lanes was in action, and Nelson sat in a strange peace, heedless of the cacophony surrounding him. He had dark hair, like his sister, and looked tall and thin like his father, but there was a certain slack quality to his appearance — the untucked company shirt, straggling locks, and his baggy khakis — that set him aside from them. "Good timing; he goes on break in ten minutes." The peons were scheduling my life, but there was something about the boy manager in his two-tone shirt that made me curious, so I decided to wait.

"I'll take a beer."

He glanced at the clock on the wall behind him. "It's not eleven yet." It wasn't ten.

"Do you think I care?" I indicated the brand I wanted and he pulled a bottle from the fridge and poured the liquid into a mug. "You want to join me?"

"I couldn't. No. Thank you."

"Put it on the Linklater tab. This is for you." I took a dollar bill out of my fold and passed it across the counter to him. "I'm doing some work for them and you can help me. Let's go sit down." We moved to a circular table behind the lanes. THAD — it was written on the badge pinned to his shirt front — made the tip disappear somewhere into a pocket of his slacks. "They phoned down from the front desk to tell you I was coming?"

He nodded.

"Good. I want you to feel comfortable. I imagine a sharp like you doesn't miss too much."

He squinted as the mechanism behind his face tried to work out what he hadn't missed and picked at a pimple on his chin.

"You know the family?"

"Little bit. Good people."

"Do they come in a lot?"

"Nelson's worked here for the past two years — so he's in a lot. He works five days a week over the summer and then picks up some weekend shifts during the school year. Abbie used to be here all the time. She's a good swimmer and I think she curls in season. But she hasn't been around this year. She used to train almost every day but not lately. Maybe she got a job somewhere else. And they play tennis. I think Mrs. Linklater was on the court this morning."

"She's a good tennis player, then?"

The question perplexed him: "I wouldn't say she's a natural. I'm not sure ..." His voice trailed off. "She might have taken lessons as an adult, and she's certainly improved her game, which is a little unorthodox."

"She play singles? Or doubles?"

"Both. I think she's part of a lady's doubles group."

"Mixed doubles?"

His eyes came up from the tabletop as if I'd suggested there was a wife-swapping ring operating from the club. "Not that I'm aware of," he said stiffly.

"All right. But it can happen." His innocence was painful; luckily my work didn't include the education of the city's youth. "And the mister — the guy who's paying for this beer — how often is he in?"

"I think he's pretty busy. We don't see him so much; he shows for the gala events. Or if there's a tournament —"

"Like a mixed-doubles tournament?" I suggested.

"Yes." He flushed under the bright lights of the basement. "He usually finds the time for those."

The beer was giving me a little lift, clearing the fog out of my brain, and pumping a pep into my tired skin. "Thad, you look like a guy I can trust, so I'm going to tell you what's going on and ask for your help."

He looked at me unhappily.

"Abbie's disappeared."

His eyes widened and his mouth pushed out.

"It might be a little exploratory runaway and she'll be back tomorrow; it might be an extended sleepover at a girl-friend's; it could be an older boy who has his own place; it could be one tea stick too many; or maybe something different. I know you've said she hasn't been around a lot this year, but you sound like you know her and you know this place. Any thoughts?"

He was slow to answer. "I'm surprised. I don't think of Abbie like that. She always seemed pretty straight. My impression is she's happy, but stable — not as giddy or silly as some of the other girls. Into her training. Serious. There are some I can see getting into trouble, but not her."

"When was the last time you saw her?"

"Maybe in the early spring. I was working in the curling club and she was there with some friends. It was like she was part of the life of the club, on teams, training here one week, and then the next she just dropped out and disappeared. Like something changed for her."

"Early spring — say April."

"That sounds about right."

"Anything else I should know?"

He shook his head and I passed my card across the table. "Thanks for your help, Thad. Keep your eyes open, and if she shows up, or you see her, give me a call." I drained the last of my beer and used the cuff of my jacket to wipe my chin.

"Yes, sir." He looked at the clock, eager to escape my questioning. I was a pariah to be avoided; even the dollar carrot he'd gobbled up couldn't help to make me likeable. "I need to give Nelson his break. I'll send him over."

I nodded.

He tightrope-walked along the ridge between the gutters to relieve Nelson; they had a brief conversation against the clash of pins and the rumble of the balls with Thad gesturing back at me. Nelson walked up the middle of the unused lane in his bowling shoes and sat at my table. "Thad says you want to talk with me."

"That's right." I let a pause hang in the air, waiting to see where he might take it, what he might know about the situation.

"He said it's about Abbie. I guess everyone at home's worried she's run away."

"Yeah." I noted his choice of words: she wasn't missing, she hadn't disappeared, it wasn't a question of abduction — she'd been the active agent in this situation. He might have been parroting what Thad had said to him, but judging by the way he'd walked up the alley, he didn't look like he took his cues from anyone. "She's missing and your father asked me to look for her. Where do you think she could be? Sometimes twins have an intuition about the other half."

He watched the bowlers while he spoke. "It's a little crazy, but I haven't seen Abbie much this summer. I've been working a ton. Usually up in the pool. I'm a lifeguard. They were short today and stuck me down here as a pin boy. I hate it. I did my time down here last summer, but …" He looked down at the table, his anger creating a stillness of focus, before he came back with: "If it happens too much, I'll quit. This isn't the only pool in the city."

It sounded to me like he had this complaint in his head every third day when he was down in the alley, working himself up to a pitch; but he never did anything about it. He met my eyes and realized he'd lost the thread of the conversation and was talking about himself, not his sister. There was a sort of selfishness that so many of these postwar kids had; this generation born into the golden age of prosperity who'd never wanted for anything. I was less than ten years older, but felt like I was living on a different planet.

He recalibrated and pushed on — at least he had the wherewithal to be embarrassed at being caught staring in the mirror. "I saw her on Saturday night, when I got home from my shift, her door was open and I said, 'Hi,' but she was busy and we didn't talk much. I left Sunday morning, back here, before she was up."

"Busy with what?"

"She has some project she's been working on all summer." That might be, but she hadn't left a trace of it behind in her room. "I don't know what it is, but she didn't take a job, and she's stopped her swimming; she used to train all the time. I don't know if she still goes out with her friends, but she's working on something. During the spring,

I thought it was school work — that she wanted to be a top student or something stupid like that. But I don't think that's it. Her marks aren't so special, but she spends all her time at the library."

Far be it for me to be worried about this girl devolving into reefer madness or being held against her will in a Yonge Street massage room — I just needed to check the library.

"Maybe she's writing a novel or something," he said.

"You ask her what she's doing?"

"Not much. When I did, she just called it 'her project'; and if I try to ask more she clams up and acts like she knows something I don't, and I don't need that bullshit at home. I get enough of it here." He shot a look at me, a challenge to see if I was going to respond to the swearing. He seemed like the kind of kid who was trying to grow up by picking a fight with anyone older than twenty. But even his failed attempts at maturity were transparent gestures. I stared at a ball that veered into the gutter just before the pins and wondered if his sister had the same ugly chip in her makeup. "She says something about research or history and tries to look superior, like she's better than me or something."

"So, if I'm looking for her, your suggestion is the library? Which branch?"

"The local one on Roncesvalles. Just down the corner from our house. She's always in there, getting help from the staff."

"Okay. I'll look. Any friends I should be aware of? Boys?"

He gave me the same name that his father had given, the Moore girl, and confirmed that the two had been close, but he thought they were drifting apart now — but still worth a try. No boys he knew of.

"I have to talk to your mother as well. Do you know what time she gets back to the house?"

There was a smoulder of life under his slack demeanour and he flared. "She's not my mother."

"Then according to my calculations, she wouldn't be Abbie's mother, either."

"Very funny."

"I studied a little biology in school."

"She's my stepmother."

"Uh-oh, the evil stepmother. I like how this is shaping up, a ready-made suspect."

"It's not that. It's just, you're the investigator — you should get your facts straight."

"I appreciate the information. Do you know when I might find her at home?"

"No idea. I don't know her schedule. She gave me a ride down in the morning; she plays tennis, but I don't know her plans after that." The family was remarkable in their collective ignorance; it was hard to believe they all lived under the same slate roof.

He surprised me by asking a question: "And you? How's the life of a PI? Is it like it is in the books?"

I wasn't so sure about books, but I'd seen *The Maltese Falcon* on TV. "Like Sam Spade, you mean."

"Or even his partner? Archer."

"Archer?"

"You don't remember him?" He smirked.

"No, I don't. It's been while since I've seen it."

"Yeah, he doesn't have a big part. He gets it right at the beginning."

"That doesn't sound so good."

"Not for him."

I wasn't so happy with the way the conversation ended, but Thad appeared back at the table and my fifteen minutes with Nelson had come to an end. I shook his hand, which had the same inconsistent tension as his manner, and let him know we might need to talk again.

IV

IT WAS TIME to circle back to the stone mansion with its dim interior and reluctant family. The father and the brother had stonewalled me; now it was time to talk to the stepmother. I took the double underpass beneath the highway and the train tracks, and then ran up the hill on Parkside to come at the Linklater home from the other direction. Across the street, in the car, my eyes were drawn to the house: the gunmetal grey of the slates on the roof, the almost black of reflected nothingness from the symmetrical windows, the weight of the rough-cut stones that formed the wall. It was an imposing monolith, an obelisk distilled to an uncompromising block. My hand was on the car's door handle, ready to pop it open when I was brought to a pause by a man turning up the walk to the front door. His back was to me, but he didn't look like a friendly neighbour coming to borrow a measuring tape or ratchet set. His full head of hair sprang in unruly coils, and the first signs of grey streaked his locks, visible even across the distance of the road. A double-breasted suit, a good number of years out of fashion, and a good number of months out of the cleaners, flapped open on his thin frame. He rang the bell and hiked the pants, adjusting his belt as he stood on the porch. His body, turned ninety degrees to the door, showed his profile, his nose coming down in a straight line before making a friendly turn into his upper lip. On his feet he had a pair of scuffed boots with the tongues hanging loose under the cuffs of his trousers. He rang again, before giving up and turning to come back down the stone walkway. His white shirt wasn't too white, and in lieu of a tie he had a couple of buttons undone and wore his chest hair as an ascot. He had a handsome face that close-set eyes could not spoil, his high cheekbones caught the sunlight as he came toward me, and he smiled to himself, creating dimples at the corners of his mouth. I was ready to pop out of the car and introduce myself when he turned away to cross the garden; he skipped over an orange dahlia and cut around the side of the house. His back was to me now, and I didn't need an invitation to follow.

I crossed the residential street, and when Handsome disappeared behind the corner of the building, I started to jog, the morning beer sloshing in my stomach. I got him back in my sightline in time to see him reach up and unlatch the gate to the yard. He stepped through and closed it. I came up the driveway and peered through the latticework of the fence and vines to see him on the back deck that ran the length of the house, moving from window to window, with his eyes pressed against the glass, his hand shading the glare. I clicked the latch and swung the creaky door while his back was to me.

"Hello, stranger," I said. "I don't think we've —"

He turned quickly and without waiting to introduce himself, vaulted like a gymnast, both legs together, hands on the rail of the porch. His feet, in their cracked boots, swept toward my head, and I stepped back and loosened my neck, ready to roll with it; a rush of air whooshed by. He bolted into the gap my retreat had created. I lunged forward and got my hands on him, one on his arm and the other on the tail of his jacket, and we tussled in the gateway, me grunting and sweating, him silent and wiry. He wriggled like an eel and slipped his arm through the jacket's sleeve. I tried to use my weight to pin him against the post, and his unsheathed right arm drove a short shot into my gut that knocked the wind out of me. He squirmed a few more times against my fading strength and the next thing I knew I was on my knees gasping for air and holding the greasy coat, and he was running around the corner and down the hill toward the park. I gave chase, but my breath was gone before I began, and he widened the gap right from the get-go. Determined to keep him in sight, I kept after him, huffing and puffing down the sidewalk. One of his boots came loose and he kicked it off. I wasn't going to be beaten by a one-legged man and ran harder. He kicked the second boot off at the corner of Parkside and dodged the cars as he crossed into High Park. I let the boots lie, passing on to the red light on the corner; traffic had picked up and I needed to wait for it to turn green before entering the park. In the distance, running in his sock feet, down the hill to the pond, he followed the winding road toward the petting zoo. I belched an unhappy belch and turned back to the car; I could take a drive through the park and see what I could see, but I was pretty sure I'd missed my chance. Finding a shoeless man in five hundred acres wasn't impossible, but he could sit in the bush as long as he needed and wait me out. The father and son had been almost taciturn; the shoeless man had set the bar of resistance even higher.

I stooped to pick up the first half of the discarded footwear and a mouthful of stomach bile jumped up my throat; I spat it onto the curb. The old leather workboot in my hand had been resoled at least once; on the inside of the tongue was the ink stamp of a repair shop, smudged and bleary through years of sweat and friction. Straining my eyes, I could see the phrase SHOES AND BOOTS, but what came before was a smear of a word — maybe ELEGANT, maybe MELVIILE, maybe something else. I couldn't tell. Out of breath, I stumped back toward the Linklater home, stopping to pick up the boot's lonely partner on the way. This one didn't have any identifying marks; I knotted the two together and threw them into the trunk of the car as my heart began to return to slow and steady. Morning was no time for running. The backyard gate hung open, and I stepped through, to find the abandoned jacket lying like a dead man on the flagstones of the patio. Bending to scoop it up, there was a second minor insurrection in my gut that I successfully suppressed. The two front pockets of the jacket were fakes, but the inside one held some paper folded around an object. My fingers were just in the process of extracting the package when a beige Coupe de Ville pulled into the driveway. I held my hand still as a woman in tennis whites slid out of the car and walked around to the trunk to retrieve her racquet. This time I was looking through the latticework of the ivied fence from the inside out. I had a good view of Mrs. Linklater, if it was indeed her; she was the same woman I'd seen at the club make the failed, but adventurous, back to the net, return of the lob. Her skirt and white top highlighted the tan on her arms and legs, and down the V of her chest. Her long hair, a mix of brown and blond highlights, hung loose to frame a pretty face. She was younger than Linklater, younger than I'd expected, closer to my age, but men taking youthful women for their second wives was hardly news — it was what kept the agency in business. I stuffed the envelope I'd found into my pocket, pushed the gate, and came out from where I'd been hiding, the jacket in my hand. "Mrs. Linklater."

She startled as she turned toward the sound of my voice. "Who are you?"

"My name's Bird. I was hired by your husband this morning — to look for Abbie. I'm a private investigator."

"You scared me." She put a hand on my arm to steady herself.

"Apologies. Just snooping."

"Let me get my breath. What's that?" She gestured at the greasy pinstripe in my hand.

"A jacket I found in your backyard."

"It's terrible," she said, focusing on the appearance of the sports coat. "The neighbourhood. It's getting worse, ever since they put the highway in and closed us off from the lake. There are people on the streets that were never there before and now they're in my backyard." She frowned at the thought. "But I'm being rude. Let me introduce myself. Trent told me he was hiring a man. I'm Jane Linklater." She extended a long-fingered hand that was still warm and moist from her morning's exertions. "Thank you for coming to help us." By the time she'd finished talking, she'd regained some composure and taken the first steps to lead us around the house to the front door.

"Let me just throw this in my car."

She wrinkled her nose.

"It could be evidence."

"You take your job seriously." She laughed.

She slid the key into the lock, turned it, pushed the door open, and stepped across the threshold, as I returned from the car. "What have you found out so far?"

I couldn't tell if she was making conversation, or, true to the stereotype of the moneyed client, busy checking on the help and making sure she got full value for her money. "I've been running around. I was at the club and spoke to Nelson down in the bowling alley, and had a few other conversations too." I was padding my resumé but held back on the silent stranger who had been wandering in the backyard. "I was hoping we might have some time to talk."

"And I need to shower. I hate to sit on the sofa after tennis." She drew a finger across the sheen of moisture on the triangle of skin the open collar exposed. "But I suppose there's no helping it. We could sit on the back porch, but I'm sure Trent would never forgive me airing our dirty laundry to the whole neighbourhood. The couch will have to make do. Come in, won't you." I entered the grey mansion for the second time that day and was led farther into the interior. Through an open door there was a large den, with two couches forming a right angle, some prints hanging on the wall over the striped paper, a big square television, and a cream-coloured carpet underfoot. She indicated a couch while saying, "I'm going to have a glass of water; can I get you something?"

"Nothing for me, thank you."

She returned with a tall glass and sat at the other end of the couch, leaning back against its corner. "Well, it's about Abbie. We need to do something. I'm sorry about this morning. I should have been here to talk with you, but to tell the truth, these doubles partners can be little fascists; they don't take it well when you no-show. And, I hate to say this, but I thought it might be better to see you without Trent. He's wound so tight, and has such a mania for privacy that one can't quite talk freely, can one?" She looked at me over the glass of water, with eyes the same shade as the grey stones of the house.

I was delaying asking that first question, hoping my silence might be the doorway that allowed her permission to enter into the free flow of conversation. Our eyes held until I felt uncomfortable; her face cracked into a disarming smile that fell like a sunbeam. "We can't sit here staring at each other all day. Not that I mind" — she paused and seemed ready for another staring bout, before continuing — "but you must have work to do, questions to ask me. Fire away."

"What's behind your husband's mania for privacy?"

"Did I say mania? Perhaps that's too strong a word. And it comes from a place of sweetness; he's trying to protect me and the children. You see, and I'm sure that he didn't tell you this, but I'm not his first wife. He was married before to a woman called Belinda."

"You're right. He didn't tell me that."

"It's not something that we ever talk about because we're a happy family and that conversation has nowhere to go but become something that leaves us all in tears — and so, it's not something we discuss with the children. They, of course, know about Belinda, but what they know less about is that before I married Trent, I was the au pair. You can see the situation: a professional man suddenly finds himself alone with two toddlers, he hires a young woman to come and be a live-in maid to help bring the children up. You can think what you may, but it was quite innocent: we ate meals together, we did family things together, we went to church on Sundays, and over time a certain fondness grew between us. And I have to say I'm eternally grateful to Trent for recognizing the situation and proposing. There are plenty of other scenarios that don't end as well for the nanny. This is a stuffy town, and it isn't the done thing, but Trent did it. And we've lived happily ever after."

"Until now."

She made a face at me but didn't dispute. "Until now, as you say." She leaned forward to place her glass on a coaster on the low table and then leaned back into a great yawning stretch.

I felt the awkwardness of the voyeur in her home.

"You will have noticed I'm not as concerned as you are about Abbie, and that's because I have some inside information. But now I'm going to be the one with a mania for privacy — as it's a young woman's secret I'm holding on to."

There was another of those pauses. This time I looked out the window, into the backyard, where the intruder had stood with shaded eyes against the glass, rather than try my luck in locking my gaze with her again.

"It seems that I have no choice but to tell you, but I have to ask that this not get back to Trent — it would hurt him terribly, and I fear it would damage his relationship with Abbie irreparably, and a father's love for his daughter is the most important thing a girl can have. Abbie ... how should I put this? She's gone and gotten herself in the family way. And she came to me about it, and, to put it bluntly, how she might have an abortion. I think it might have helped that she doesn't fully identify me as her mother. She leaned on that 'step' so she could think it was more of a woman-to-woman conversation without being fraught with the tenuous strings that tie mother and daughter and make every communication a minefield of emotion."

"And so, you helped her?" At last, we were getting somewhere.

"Yes and no. I mean, regardless of what I think from a moral standpoint, I could hardly counsel my daughter to break the law. And I have my relationship with Trent to consider; it put me in a difficult position — if it came out at a later date, it wouldn't go well. But yes, I gave her a name or two where she might look for help."

"When did this conversation take place?"

"On Sunday morning."

The doorbell rang.

"Who can it be?" she said out loud to herself as she jumped up off the couch and hurried to the entrance. I had the same question on my mind and trailed behind, looking at a translucent spot on her back where her white shirt stuck to the sweat. I peered over her shoulder as she swung the door wide: there was a small woman with sharp eyes in a face the same colour and texture as a dried apple standing on the porch.

"But, Eileen, what are you doing here?" she said.

"I work here. You know that."

"I do," laughed Jane. "Don't be silly. But why are you at the front door?"

"I lost my key, didn't I?"

Jane didn't laugh at this news. "But where? Where did you lose it?"

"Now who's being silly?" asked Eileen. "If I knew where I dropped it, it wouldn't be lost, would it?"

Jane conceded this was true.

Without waiting to be asked, Eileen bustled into the house, pushing past us. "Excuse me, but there's work to be done."

"This is Mr. Bird," said Jane. "He's here to help us find Abbie."

"Find Abbie?" exclaimed Eileen. "You don't need a fancy bird to find Abbie. I saw her, just now, standing at the bus stop on the corner."

V

I STEPPED INTO the fray: "Which corner?"

"At the end of the street, on Roncesvalles. She's waiting for the streetcar."

"Southbound?"

"That's right."

"Heading toward the lake?"

"I know my north from my south, Bird Boy." I ignored the insult — I'd asked for it.

"Just now?"

"Just as I came here."

There was no time for waiting. I left without ceremony and raced down the road. The sun was climbing, the air had warmed, and the humidity clung to the clammy places where my limbs met my body. My shoes pinched my toes, my tie flew into my face and over my shoulder, and the beer still slopped around my stomach. The only saving grace was I hadn't taken Mrs. Linklater up on her offer of a coffee. For all my internal whinging, and feeling every ache and pain, it wasn't far to the brick posts — the gates had disappeared long ago — that guarded the entrance at the top of the street. As I approached the intersection, the metallic screech of the streetcar pulling to a stop sounded and, as in a dream, where I could near the goal but never reach it, the front doors opened and the girl from the photograph in my pocket stepped up into the trolley; a boy, with sandy hair and an earnest profile, in a bright white cardigan, a possessive hand on her elbow, assisted Abbie into the vehicle. He stepped in behind her, and as I turned onto Roncesvalles, the double doors of the Red Rocket closed with a pneumatic wheeze; there was a clang and the streetcar pulled away. Through the moving window, the portions of their bodies moved in isolation, like the magician's assistant in her zigzag box. Three more steps brought me to a standstill, where I stood, hunched and gasping on the sidewalk.

But the streetcar wouldn't wait. A steady jog took me back to the Linklater house, where the company car was parked on the side of the road. The front door was closed now, but I could catch up with Jane later — and Eileen didn't look like she missed much either. I threw my hat on the passenger seat, slid my keys in the ignition, put the car in gear, and gave it some gas. Chasing from behind a steering wheel was more my speed.

Of all the streets in the city, Roncesvalles is the most lopsided; the businesses, the fruit markets and Polish delis, the German bakeries and schnitzel houses, line one side, and the other side is residential. There are two churches on the quiet west side, yes, and the library Abbie frequented, but no businesses unless you go way up to the top where they have the show, and a restaurant or two, or down at the bottom where it gets seedy at the bus terminal and the Edgewater Hotel. Someone had been sleeping in the zoning division when they planned this one, or maybe it was intentional, and the tony west side wanted to keep the taint of money from its delicate nostrils. Churches and libraries only, please — just the collection plate and overdue fines.

Like Eileen said, I turned south. The streetcar wasn't in sight at this stage, but the best thing about the trolleys is they stay on the tracks; there are no surprise turns, no jogging onto side streets or doubling back. Just simple and straightforward. The light turned red in my face at Queen and, as I was cursing my luck, sweating and swearing, the Queen car, on the east–west cross street, trundled through the intersection — and looking up through its windows, I saw the midsections of my couple on the lam — his white cardigan and her sleeveless blouse moving down the car to find seats near the back. They'd transferred from the King car, going south down Roncesvalles, onto the Queen car, moving east into the heart of the city and it was just my dumb luck, being behind them by the right margin that allowed me to see the switch. Now I wasn't chasing a streetcar I couldn't see; I was right behind the one I needed. I set the car's indicator and waited for the light.

When it turned green, I let the through traffic pass before swinging onto Queen Street and through the heart of Parkdale. Traffic, as always, was bad on this stretch, and we crawled across the clogged artery filled with the clots and clumps of double-parked cars, vehicles waiting to make a left turn, and red lights, before ducking under the train tracks at Dufferin; coming up out of the underpass into the sunshine at the Gladstone Hotel was like coming up for air after being submerged in a murky lagoon. I'd caught up to the streetcar by this stage and rode its bumper, waiting for my couple to emerge. Just past Trinity Bellwoods Park, a sketchy patch of green in the middle of the city, the two alighted. They turned back and walked along the sidewalk straight toward me; I was at a disadvantage, being in the car, and made a quick decision to sit tight, rather than call Abbie's name, potentially alarming her.

She crossed in front of me, less intense than in the photo, which emphasized the stark contrast between her black hair and blue eyes. Seeing her in the flesh, even from a distance, what struck me was the delicateness and vulnerability of her figure. Notwithstanding what had been said about her athleticism and training regime by Thad at the club, she didn't ripple with muscles or exude strength. She had the same black hair as her brother, but hers was long and straight, and instead of his sullen expression, she had an air of determination about her. Cardigan Boy, who stood at least six inches taller, gestured up the street, and they turned north on Bellwoods Avenue, disappearing from my line of sight.

I breathed a sigh of relief that they weren't going to go for a walk in the park. I couldn't hack another jaunt through the foliage; I'd tried it once today and it'd almost killed me. Communing with nature — the mania the flower children were so wild about — was not for me. Abbie and her friend, from their look and actions, didn't appear to be this stereotype of the new teenager, the blissed-out, free-loving bohemian.

The groan of the streetcar wheels announced it was back in motion. In the block following the transit stop, there wasn't a parking space, so I turned up the next side street and took the first spot available. There was a little connecting road that cut back to Bellwoods and I hustled across it to get a line on my couple. It was a quiet leafy neighbourhood full of two-storey semi-detached houses with laneways running behind them. As I rounded the corner, the pair came into sight a half block up; not wanting to create panic, I maintained my pace, strolling up the street the way any pedestrian on a Tuesday morning might. Abbie and her friend disappeared up a walkway on the east side of the street, and I was forced to use my running shoes again, or lose my second mark of the morning. The sign on the lawn read St. Matthias Anglican Church. Not what I was expecting — not sure what I was expecting, but it wasn't this: a squat, barn-like church, set back from the road, sinking into the grass.

I pulled the heavy wooden door and entered the building. As soon as it was open a crack I could hear the yelling, a terrible barrage of voice upon voice; the loudest cried unknown syllables, one after the other in a stream of gibberish that swirled around me: "An-an-an-ab! Yo tori say so? Blockus mia mook onin mac; fent duct lettum seggum. Heams si a shid steb versed ta a bleat rof neo." And it wasn't just the meaningless words that were disorienting; it was the way they were said, shouted in a plaintive voice, gasping in desperation as if every sound were wrung from an empty vessel. The voice rose in pitch: "Meg uto bug pia anemanohen meh; meg uto. Wa yell trah tashi." After the haze of humidity and the luminous glow of the outside, my eyes couldn't adjust quickly enough to the light. As I progressed up the aisle, I made out a figure thrashing on the floor at the front of the church, shouting these unknown words, while a group hovered over him.

Quite apart from the horror of the cluster under the altar, this space had that clean, culty feeling that all Protestant Churches have for the Catholic. It was a big, open room with pews on either side of a central aisle. Outside, the rooflines had met in a single peak; inside, the arch of the open ceiling was jointed in a gambrel roof that gave the whole place the feeling of a barn. There was the faint whiff of what the priest might call incense, but to me smelled like the kind of stuff stoners hide their habit beneath — maybe I'd been too quick to dismiss the hippie element in this case. I stood, my eyes adjusting to the darkness, still unable to see Abbie and her beau; the couple had disappeared into the open space of the room. A second voice, steady and steely, rose above the disordered yelling, to create a braid of sound at the front: "I have sinned. I have led a dissolute life; I have fornicated like a dog in the streets of the city. I have stolen from my neighbour and my brother; I have not only coveted his wife, but taken her, and from forth of her loins came the fruit of our lust. And that child ..."

He was interrupted by a scream, keening, high in pitch, as if someone was being tortured; it cut through and silenced all other voices. The screech was held indefinitely — until the air was fully out of the tire. And then silence. The figure on the floor had stopped moving. He might have been dead. My eyes were still adjusting to the dim interior, but I wasn't waiting for an invitation; I moved forward up the central aisle. A man, dressed in a priest's backward collar and white surplice looked at me. He resembled Linklater: they had the same slender frame, similar oversize glasses and thinning hair combed across the forehead, and the same level of unquestioned authority in their gaze.

"Who are you? And what are you doing here?" said the voice I'd already heard rising above the desperate shouting.

"I might ask you the same thing. What the hell was that? I'm a private detective, Patrick Bird. I was following a young couple — she's a sixteen-year-old runaway — and they came into your church." The body on the ground groaned and twitched. It was hard to ignore the twisted thing beneath us, but I could hold my tongue until I had answers about the girl's whereabouts.

"I am Minister Ayscough and this is St. Matthias Anglican Church, my domain. Presently, I am tending to the spiritual needs of one of my congregation, and if you can't see it, we have reached a critical point in time, and I don't mind telling you that you have barged in on a spiritual service."

I wasn't about to apologize.

"I am providing to one in need; and in breaking the circle of faith you have placed a soul in jeopardy." The figure lying on the ground resurrected itself and fell to sobbing and groaning on the flagstones beneath Ayscough. "Detective Bird, I don't care if you are looking for the mayor himself, I cannot allow you to interrupt our work. A soul hangs in the balance. The only thing that you could say that would interest me in the least is if you were to tell me that you were on a quest for your salvation. Now get out of my church. I have work to do here."

"You keep your next world, but I need to know about this one. I'm looking for an runaway teen, and I saw her come into this church. Her name is Abbie Linklater. Do you know her?"

"Young man, your impertinence is unparalleled. You can see for yourself that there's no one in the church but the six of us in this ceremony and you; there is nowhere your mystery girl might have gone. You have been stupid enough to make a mistake, there is no need for you to compound it by being so rude as to interrupt our work." He turned his back on me.

He was right: the church was one big open room — there was nowhere to hide.

The figure on the floor rolled over onto its back and began to mumble more meaningless syllables: "Asus naturs nevus sram yoni nana lutop penute." He was a thin man with long hair and a ragged brown beard that spread down his neck like a rash; his eyes were ravaged by mania, his clothes matted with dirt.

Still, I wasn't convinced that Ayscough didn't know more; I took a step forward and reached for his shoulder to spin him back toward me. Two of the participants in the ceremony, looking like pysch-ward orderlies on their day off, left their positions on the points of a star inlaid into the wooden floor, and intercepted me with professional diligence.

Ayscough turned back to face me when he reached his place on the pentagram. "And now I'll ask you to leave because my services are needed here by a congregant. I fear your interruption has already tainted the ceremony beyond repair."

On either side, the church bouncers squeezed my biceps with their oversize paws as they frogmarched me back to the door.

"Abbie — your father is looking for you." If she was out there, she needed to know that help was close by. "Abbie — my name is Bird — call me at 383-0467."

"Out. Get out. Before I call the police. This is a place of worship, not a cattle auction."

I wasn't about to give these bastards any help; I let my legs drop from under me. My flop didn't deter them in the least; they dragged me up the aisle as roughly as they could.

While the stooges fumbled with the door, I had one last chance to turn and see Ayscough. His eyes met mine through the half-light, his face relaxed, confident he'd won the first round and I'd be moving on. I was tempted to put aside the passive resistance and give them something they'd really remember; one last push to fight one against five, to take a swipe at that smug face and wipe the calm superiority off it, if only for a second. The impulse throbbed; I resisted and let the off-duty orderlies guide me through the door. They stood on the threshold, their eyes fixed on me, watching my slow retreat. I wasn't so happy to be shown off the premises, but walking was better than running away — and better still than crawling.

VI

"EGGS?"

"Over."

"Two or three?"

"Three."

"Bacon, sausage, or ham?"

"Bacon. Can I have a sausage as well?"

"No. It's one or the other. No substitutions."

"Uh. Bacon then. No, make it sausage."

"You sure?"

"No. But put down sausage for now."

"White or whole wheat?"

"White."

"Coffee or tea?"

"Coffee. Black."

"Uh-oh. Serious stuff today. All business; not asking after me? No, 'How are you today?' or 'Nice to see you.'" Rosie, the waitress, ripped a piece of paper from her pad and dropped the remaining fan of sheets into her apron. She was petite, with eyes younger than her face; loose curls spilled from under a paper cap, rolled down her shoulders and onto her back.

"Serious stuff is right. I'm on the tail of a sixteen-year-old runaway."

"Look at you: the knight in shining armour running around saving little princesses. Sure is an upgrade from busting down hotel doors and getting pictures of married women in their skivvies."

"Don't kid yourself, Rosie, they aren't wearing their skivvies when I take the pictures. And I'm moving up in the world. The Royal York last night. Only the best for me."

"Beautiful. Is that supposed to sell me on what a hero you are — catching them in their birthday suits."

"It's how we all come into this world."

A hand came up to cover her yawn. "Spare me the philosophy. Not interested."

"Love to chat," I said, "but let's get that order in. I'm starving." I pointed to the phone booth in the corner as Rosie turned back to the kitchen.

"Yeah, I hear you, Mr. Big Shot: you got an important call to make. Go to it. Don't let me bother you none."

I sat on the stool, slid the track door closed, and dropped my dime in the machine. The phone rang three times on the other end before the click of the receiver being lifted sounded. "Sidney, here."

"Hullo, Sid. Patrick checking in." It was just my third job where we weren't joined at the hip, with his brain doing all the thinking and him doing all the directing, so I was on a short leash. He wanted to know what was happening, but he'd let me know he didn't think a sixteen-year-old runaway would cause too many complications.

"Everything run smooth last night?"

"Smooth as butter. Beautiful pictures. Can't wait to see them developed. The expression on his face."

"Don't love your job too much."

"No?"

"No. It's not the best part of the job to fall in love with." He paused. "Vickie said you were late."

"No more than two minutes."

"Just passing on the news."

"She told me the same last night."

"Okay. You find little, lost Linklater yet?"

"Not yet, but I'm getting close." I told him about my encounter at St. Matthias Anglican Church.

"Beautiful. Disrupting religious services. Just what we need at the agency, to have the Anglican diocese busting our chops for interrupting the worship of our Lord, Jesus Christ."

"Yeah, I'd hate to be the one who brought your empire crumbling down around you."

"Ha ha. Listen, you know who St. Matthias is?" Sid had the curse of a bear-trap memory: nothing went in that didn't stick; he was forever full of useless information. I don't know how he negotiated the clutter to find the simple facts, like where he'd left the car keys — and sometimes he couldn't — but most times it worked for him. His question was rhetorical, and I held my tongue before he continued. "He's the guy who came in and pinch-hit for Judas after he hung himself from the tree. I mean, couldn't they continue with only eleven? So they went and recruited a new guy and that's Matthias. Imagine showing up for your first day of work: 'Hi, I'm the new Judas? What's your name?'"

"At least the bar's set pretty low — I mean, as long as you don't kill God, you've done better than the last guy."

"Look at you? Theological student before noon. What d'you have for breakfast?"

"I just ordered now."

"Hey, you're on my dime. Find the girl first, eat later."

I ignored him. "Listen, we know Abbie went into the church. Linklater's a big shot. Why don't we just call in the police and let them take a look around and find her."

"There's something to that. But the problem is you never saw her in the church. You can see how raiding a religious establishment doesn't look good when it's splashed on the cover of the *Telegram*."

"We're calling it a church, but it's more like a loony bin than anything else. It was like they were torturing some poor guy when I was there."

"I know. I know. The minister ... what's his name?"

"Ayscough."

"That's right, Ayscough. He's taken a left turn away from the Anglican hymn book and has brought in these Pentecostal ideas. I saw something about that: adult baptism, speaking in tongues, I don't know what all."

"How do you know this stuff?"

"It's in the paper. It's no secret. Don't you read? He's unorthodox, but the ministry is reluctant to move him because his church is growing, which is not something many can say these days. And that church, where it's located, they're doing plenty of good works that are getting good press. He's like the real Jesus — taking in the lovers, muggers, and thieves. They're coming in off the streets, just out from the hospital across the way on their day passes." He meant the institution on Queen Street, which had recently been renamed from Hospital for the Insane to the Ontario Hospital as if changing the name could chase the demons from the minds of its patients. "He's a real modern-day miracle worker, healing the lame. You can't get better PR than that. I don't know the details —"

"That's a first."

He ignored my interruption and continued. "He's got the local do-gooders singing his praises, how he heals souls and makes the world a better place."

"Well, I don't like him," I said.

"And he always spoke so highly of you. But, yeah, I've heard not everyone is in support of that brand of Bible-thumping. You know what else? St. Matthias is the patron saint of alcoholics. That's pretty funny, eh? With the clientele that he's bringing in off the streets? But he's making it work: he's recruited some congregants with cash from midtown and managed to mix and mingle them with the bums sleeping in the park. It's like the lambs lying down with the lions. It was all in the paper."

I adjusted the phone receiver against my ear. "Have you ever met Ayscough? He looks a little like our man Linklater. I'm not suggesting they're long-lost brothers or anything, but it's strange that they have something about them that's the same. Maybe it's the same kind of clean-shaven, short-sighted singleness of purpose."

"Everyone's a philosopher."

"I get that quite a bit."

"Tell me about it."

"Second time this breakfast."

Rosie appeared with a cascade of plates running down her arm; my stomach growled a plaintive rumble, but she passed by and on to a booth in the front half of the restaurant where three old ladies sat.

"What about this church? You want to just give up on St. Matthias?" I asked.

"What do you think?"

"I told you already. I want you to get in touch with the police and make a friendly visit down there to inquire about girls taking shelter in their building."

"Yeah? No. You've already been down there and put Minister Ayscough's nose out of joint and got the brush-off. He has a lot of friends in the city between his good works and soul-saving. I think we wait until we have a little more before breaking down the door."

"But waiting in a missing persons case is the worst thing we can do. In an hour she'll be gone."

"I know. I know. But the problem is you didn't actually see her go through the door. And you didn't see her in the building, and so our case is weak."

"I saw her turn down the path — and when I got there: nothing."

"Hmm. Any other doors?"

"I don't know. I mean, I was in such a rush to catch up with her that I went right through the front door —"

"Fair enough."

"And when I got into the church, suddenly I was in the middle of that screaming and speaking in tongues and 'Sinner, thou shalt repent.'" Across the restaurant, my breakfast still hadn't materialized. "And afterward I was pretty much seen off the premises. I wasn't so sure they weren't going to throw me in a straitjacket until I'd confessed all I'd done wrong in my life."

"Had we world enough and time …"

"What?"

"Well, you'll need to circle back and take a look and see if there are any other doors that could be used. Maybe there's a hall or a rectory. But hold off for now while I make a few calls and let me think about how we want to approach Minister Ayscough. A little diplomacy will be needed. Wait until our next check-in. It sounds like when you enter the church you're in the main room: there's no balcony; there's no basement; there's no cloakroom or anything like that. Just one big open space?"

"That's right."

"You got anything else for me?"

I told him about Shoeless Joe and my jaunt in the park. "Busy morning," he said. "Lots going on. Good to know you're getting a workout. How do you figure the runner?"

"I don't know. He tried to go in the front door, and when it wasn't answered he went around back looking to see if there was anyone in the house. I don't figure it exactly, but he wasn't your typical break-and-enter man. Not in daylight like that. I mean, ringing the front bell makes it look like he knows someone in the house." I remembered the package I'd lifted from the runner's jacket and patted it in my pocket. I was curious, but wanted the moment to myself when I opened it up.

"Sometimes they ring the bell first, to see if anyone's home before breaching the fortress."

"Yeah, but this guy didn't have any tools. He was on foot. I just don't like the coincidence. The daughter's missing and there's some stranger lurking around the premises. And more than lurking, I felt like he was looking for someone, the way he was peering through the patio doors."

"I hear you. Nobody hates coincidence more than the detective agencies. Keep plugging away."

Rosie came out of the double-hinged door to the kitchen.

"Breakfast beckons," I said.

"I won't stand between a man and his food."

We said our goodbyes and I hung the receiver back in the cradle, slid the folding door, and stepped into the noise of the diner: the radio playing a pop song from across the ocean, the subdued splatter of grease coming through the cut-out into the kitchen, the gurgle of the coffee machine on the counter, and the low hum of voices.

"There you are," said Rosie.

"Here I am."

"Like a bad penny."

"What's up? Food with an insult today?" She placed the plate on the table and slapped my hand away before sliding the coffee cup into place and taking a quick step out of range.

"Keep your hands to yourself, loverboy."

"That's not what you said last time we met."

"It's what I'm telling you now." She pulled the scratch pad from her apron pocket, found a pencil behind her ear, and moved to a new table. My knife cut into the first of the three eggs and the yolk bled yellow onto the plate; I adjusted a piece of toast to higher ground and discovered a single rasher of bacon hiding underneath it, in perfect complement to the sausages. I grinned through a mouthful of breakfast; the empty leatherette seat across the booth didn't return the smile.

I pulled the crumpled envelope out of my pocket and placed it on the tabletop, beside my half-finished breakfast.

There was an unpleasant lump in its midsection, like an anaconda that had swallowed something too big. On the outside, a pencil had written the single word SMART in shaky capitals. Judges always get a little sticky when you open someone else's mail, but maybe I could claim I thought it was addressed to me. I ripped the envelope along the short end and shook it. The lump fell first, and I caught it in a cupped hand above my half-finished breakfast: a single bullet, looking a little scuffed and dull, like it had been lying in the shed a few winters too many. Still, it raised the stakes. I returned the bullet to my pocket and shook the envelope again. Nothing budged, so I squeezed the edges and got a finger and thumb inside and tugged out a sheet of unlined paper. The same pencil had written something as cryptic as a poem — although I didn't think it was one:

> I THOUGHT YOU WERE SMART.
> YOU THOUGHT YOU WERE SMART.
> BUT IT DOESN'T SEEM LIKE THAT'S
> THE WAY IT IS ANYMORE.
> I'VE ONLY COME FOR WHAT'S MINE.

There was, unfortunately, no signature at the bottom of the page.

I signalled to Rosie that I was ready for a refill. She came slowly, making sure to check in with every other customer before getting to me with the pot in her hand and a blank expression on her face. "More coffee?" she said from a distance.

"Please."

She poured with her left hand, the right free for running interference. "You finished?" she asked, motioning to the plate.

"Not yet. You know me better than that."

"I don't know you." She took a step back, her knuckles white on the plastic handle of the coffee pot.

"Thanks for the bacon."

"Thanks for nothing." She turned back up the aisle and I turned back to the note.

If, as I supposed, the fleet-footed drifter's appearance at the Linklater house was no coincidence, then the next logical step was that this note, and the threat of the bullet, was intended for someone in the house. Abbie had been sticking her nose into other people's business all summer long; Linklater was obviously a pretty smart guy; Jane had the type of quick confidence that I'd call street smarts if she wasn't living in such a big house; Nelson didn't seem to fit the bill; Eileen didn't miss too much; and I hadn't met the gardener. And that cryptic last line: "I've only come for what's mine." Of all the unlikely words in a threatening note, "only" seemed to hit a human note, almost balancing the menace of the scuffed-up bullet.

VII

THINKING ALWAYS GAVE me an appetite, and I attacked what was left with renewed vigour. The last triangle of toast cleaned the plate, scraping against the half-dried yolk clinging to the china, and the dregs of the third cup of coffee gave me the lift to return to the phone booth for one more call.

I opened my book to find the number for the best friend that Linklater had given me first thing that morning, dropped the dime, waited for the tone, wedged the book onto the short shelf beneath the phone, and dialed. Three rings and a female voice answered. "Hello, Moore residence. Bridget Moore speaking."

"Hello, Mrs. Moore. Can I please speak with Lena?"

"May I ask who's calling?"

"My name is Patrick Bird and I'm a private investigator hired by Trent Linklater. Not to beat around the bush, but his daughter, Abbie, has gone missing —"

"Oh, my goodness. That's terrible news."

"Mr. Linklater told me Lena and Abbie were close and provided me with this number. I'm following up on leads — and I think the assumption that teenage girls might share secrets with their close friends is a good one — so I'm hoping to talk to Lena."

"Yes, of course. How long has Abbie been gone?"

"Two nights at this stage. Please keep this quiet. Mr. Linklater's concerned about it getting out into the community. He wants this whole investigation done as privately as possible."

"Of course. Oh, dear. Poor Trent. How's he coping?"

"I'm sure he'll feel better when Abbie is home."

"I'm sorry, I wish I could help more, but Lena just left for work, about twenty minutes ago now."

"Do you think you could give me the name of Lena's workplace and maybe I can catch up with her there sometime this afternoon?"

"Of course. She buses tables at the Bohemian Embassy. Do you know where that is?"

"I do."

"On St. Nicholas Street, off Wellesley, just west of Yonge. I can't remember the number, but it's a short street — more of an alley, really. Maybe if you go after lunch; I think she gets a break sometime in the middle of the afternoon."

The timetables of the young: my investigation was destined to be bound by the schedules of minimum-wage work. "Thank you for your help, Mrs. Moore. And can I ask you: Have you seen Abbie this summer?"

"Not too much. Not as much as we used to."

"Have you noticed anything different with her?"

She paused. "As I said, we've seen less of her this year than in the past, but it seems that as the girls get older, things change in their friend group and in themselves, a natural progression as one grows up. But maybe it's something different — but I don't know. Try Lena."

I told her I would, thanked her for her time, and rang off.

Having been warned off seeing Lena until later in the afternoon, I headed to the library where Nelson had told me his sister was spending most of her time. The High Park branch was just south of the streetcar stop where Abbie and her friend in the cardigan had boarded the tram. There was a lobby with a checkout desk on the first floor, a raucous children's section through an archway, and a semi-open staircase that started on the back wall and turned a couple of corners to get to the second floor. Mounting the stairs, I came out in a well-lit open space with high ceilings, rows of stacks, and the aggressive sound of loud whispering. There was a help desk straight across from the top of the stairs, staffed by a woman my age in a striped shirt. I made a beeline to the table and waited while she did whatever it is that librarians do with cards and date stamps and pockets over a hardcovered tome called *Remembrance of Things Past,* so thick its shape was more brick than book. Who could have so many memories? She fiddled with the flyleaf, her focus on the binding, her brown hair pulled back off her forehead and criss-crossed by a web of barrettes, clips, and pins. I stifled a throat clear, which would have belied my impatience as she moved from the card to the tape dispenser and went to work reinforcing the endpaper's attachment to the board of the cover. Sensing my presence, her small eyes, under brows that had been plucked into an arch, looked up to meet my gaze. "Yes, may I help you?" She smiled the smile of service, displaying a mouthful of crowded teeth, all fighting to get into the front row.

"I'm Patrick Bird, an investigator looking into the disappearance of a sixteen-year-old girl." I handed her one of Sid's business cards.

She passed a cursory glance across the type and placed it face up on a spare piece of real estate on the desk. "Pleased to meet you, Mr. Bird. Janice Webster: How can I help?"

"So far this morning I've interviewed a few people, and they've let me know this girl has spent a fair amount of time here at the library. Her name is Abbie Linklater — and she lives just down High Park Boulevard." I gestured vaguely toward a window. "Here's her picture. Do you recognize her?"

A smile spread across Miss Webster's face, this one not her work smile for the library-going public, but genuine and inward, in response to the image of Abbie with her serious look and straight black hair. "Of course, we know Abbie. She's one of our best customers. She spends a lot of time here. It's good to know we can still pull in some teenagers. Sometimes I worry that we're losing the battle to television." Her voice held a trace of prim disappointment at a world gone so wrong.

"How much is she here?"

"Oh, Abbie. Some days she'll be here for a stretch of three hours at a time, sometimes less. She's not here every day, but we see her on average about four or five times a week."

"When did you last see her?"

"Just this morning."

That was bold: our girl had run away from home only to show up in the neighbourhood library, just two blocks away. "What time was that?"

She continued to smile, but a twitch in her right eye hinted at anxiety creeping into her public face. She reached up and worried at one of her hair clips. "I think it would have been from when we opened at ten for a little more than half an hour. She came with a boy today."

She made this last pronouncement without the prudery and reluctance I'd met from Thad and Trent. Was I getting closer to the heart of the mystery, closing in on the father of the unborn child? And like so many mysteries, it seemed like it would turn out to be a simple slice of everyday life made sordid only by the intrusive eyes of others. "They left together at about ten forty-five." That lined up with the timing of when they boarded the streetcar out front.

"Was he a clean-cut boy in a white cardigan and fair hair parted on the side?"

She nodded a clear-headed, straightforward affirmation.

"And this boy in the cardigan — how were he and Abbie together? Did they seem close? Did they look like a couple to you?" I remembered his hand on her elbow as she mounted the trolley car's steps.

"They were a teenage boy and girl, if that's what you're asking. So, one jumps to conclusions of course. But did they appear as a couple? I don't know. I mean, she went through her usual routine, reading newspapers" — she indicated a pile behind her — "and he wandered around looking bored."

"Getting ready for married life, eh?"

She ignored my attempt at humour. "Is she in trouble? I wouldn't want our Abbie to be in any sort of danger."

"None of us do; that's why I'm trying to find her. If she was here this morning, under her own will, living her normal routine, it doesn't appear that anything too serious can be going on; but you never can tell."

"Hmm." She made a quiet vocalization that sounded like it had been refined through hours of workplace practice.

"Maybe you could help me understand what it is that Abbie does while she's here? Her behaviour, as you noted, isn't exactly typical, at least not in its intensity for a sixteen-year-old."

"Yes." She nodded. "She's been conducting research."

"Uh-huh?" I prompted, waiting for news of a study into the human reproductive system and ways of getting rid of the unwanted things that grew inside.

But Miss Webster surprised me: "She's been combing through old newspapers. She looks at the *Globe and Mail*, the *Daily Star*, and the *Telegram*; she tries to do about a week at a stretch, and she just reads them. We have to order them from central storage, but that's a service that we offer. She's been working her way through old issues. A week at a time."

This was a surprise, but to be fair, it shouldn't take four months of study to tell the birds from the bees. "What year?"

"Starting in 1951: January and working her way all through the year."

"And has she told you what she's looking for?"

"No. I've encouraged her; I mean she's a serious girl and so we want to help as much as possible. Us librarians know a few tricks of the trade — how to find information — and we might be able to expedite the process. But Abbie has not been amenable to help. She's polite; she's friendly, but terribly reserved. Again, not exactly what one would expect from a girl her age."

I looked again at the pile of old papers lying on the counter behind her and gestured toward them. "Is that to-day's pile?"

"Yes. She asked me to hold them. Being with the boy today, I don't think she was able to spend as much time as she would've liked on her research." She smiled an indulgent grin, warming to the idea of Abbie's blossoming love interest. "Would you like to take a look?"

"Please."

She swivelled in her seat and, still sitting, moved her legs from the knees down, to walk herself back to the pile of print on the sorting shelf. She pulled the old newspapers onto her lap and, using her feet, propelled herself back to the desk in the same fashion. "Here you are."

"Thank you again. Abbie hasn't been home in two nights; close to three days. I'd appreciate it if you gave me a call if you were to see her again. The office number is on the card. I'm not around much, but it goes to an answering service. Her parents are really feeling the strain of this. You could call them, also, if she were to show up — they just live down the street. Do you have their number on file?"

"Not up here but down at the main desk: yes."

I picked up my week's worth of papers and headed to a big table beneath a picture window overlooking a square of grass. I put the pile on my left and picked up the Monday paper to begin my search: "Baby and Blind Sister Die in House Fire"; "Royal Tour Ends: Queen Elizabeth says Not Goodbye but Au Revoir"; "City in the Grip of Fear as the Boyd Gang Still at Large"; "Anglican Women's League Producing Welcome Kits for Italian Refugees"; "Record Tobacco Crop in South-Western Ontario"; "Plans for Lakeshore Expressway Revealed"; "Leafs Shellacked in

Beantown"; "Don Mills, the Model Community: Planning for the City of the Future"; "St. Joseph's Hospital to Expand with New Wing"; and "Strike at the Clarke Tannery Enters Third Week."

After ten minutes, I felt numb at the mass of useless information on the front pages alone. I was looking for a needle in a haystack — except maybe it wasn't even a needle — it could be a pin or an awl or toothpick for all I knew. What was Abbie looking for? Was I on the edge of seeing some pattern in the miasma of shifting and contradictory information that had splattered on the windshield since eight thirty this morning? The wipers made a desultory swipe across the glass at the smear of a few dead bugs, their gossamer wings hanging loosely in the breeze, but none of it made me any the wiser. I flipped a few more pages of the paper idly, waiting for some random facts to jump from the print. Nothing did. A bored hand scratched my midsection, a yawn escaped as the lunchtime breakfast settled in the basement of my stomach; early afternoon fatigue threatened to take over. The case had enough life to keep me awake, but not this part of it. Ten minutes of reading headlines, and I was done: I folded and stacked the remaining papers and returned them to Miss Webster. Her wordless smile at their homecoming suggested she hadn't had much faith in my long-term commitment to the project. "And you'll call if Abbie shows again?" I asked.

"Yes. Absolutely. We need to get her home."

I came out into the light of the street, blinking in the fierce sun, sweating instantly in the humidity. A neighbourhood babushka waited at the streetcar stop, but neither Abbie nor her friend in the cardigan — lightning wouldn't strike twice. But Eileen, her shopping basket in hand, appeared, turning the corner onto Roncesvalles. She stopped at the light, and I was glad I didn't have to run to catch up to her.

"Hello, there."

"Bird Boy appears again. You're still pecking around? Did you find Abbie yet?"

"Yes and no. Still pecking, but I haven't found her."

"She's found the sense to go a little farther away than just down the block if she's run away."

"She's a smart girl?"

"What do I know about that?" Eileen had the habit of turning my questions back on me with a friendly unhelpfulness. And I wondered who, as the note had said, had thought themselves so smart.

"I'm asking you."

Her face broke into a broad smile and her eyes almost disappeared into the creases. The light turned green and she started across the street to the commercial side of Roncesvalles.

"Are you coming to market with me then?" she asked as I trailed along in her wake. She didn't wait for an answer. "Here, make yourself useful." I caught up to her and found her basket in my arms.

We passed into a fruit market, me falling behind, as we entered through the narrow doorway. "Listen, Eileen," I said, feeling at a disadvantage carrying the basket. "Let me ask you a couple of questions about the family." She was looking hard at the fruit and her sharp eyes threatened to ripen an unexpecting quart of strawberries. I ploughed on. "Were you at the house on Sunday — the day Abbie left?"

She put about a dozen apples into the basket, one by one, giving them the once-over to make sure they passed quality control. "I was there. Sunday's a workday for me. I start later, after church."

"Did anything happen on that day? When was the last time you saw Abbie? Were the parents —"

"Slow down. You're rushing around like a dodo. I'll tell you." She placed a bunch of bananas in the basket and led me to the back of the little store where there were a variety of greens lying in an open fridge. "The mister and missus were out playing golf. That'd be their usual on Sundays after church. The little mister, Nelson, was out at his job; I've never seen anyone for work like that boy. He loves his money, almost as much as his da does. So, it was just the two of us at the house, Abbie and me." She added a ball of iceberg lettuce, tight and crisp to the basket; I shifted it from one hand to the other as it grew heavier.

"She was up in her room and I was in the kitchen cleaning the breakfast dishes when the doorbell rang. I dried my hands and answered and here's a ragman on the stoop in a dirty old suit that hasn't been cleaned since the begining of time. I told him, we didn't have anything for him, and I'm trying to close the door and he stuck his foot in, familiar, like he has some business in the house and he said, 'I've come to see Mr. Linklater. Tell Trent Mickey's here and I want to talk to him now.' He's a bold one, like he can tell me what to do in his dirty clothes, when he doesn't even have shoes on his feet, but loose boots like he works the fields." She passed me a green cabbage and a bunch of carrots.

"So, I said to him, 'Mr. Linklater's not home.' That surprised him fine, and he took a second and said, 'He's not home?' like he didn't believe me, and I had to tell him again because he's so thick he won't hear the first time. 'Do you want me to tell him Mickey called?' I asked. And he was slow, like he's thinking about something and couldn't make sense of it, and he said, 'No. No. Don't say anything. I'll call again.' But he wasn't so sure of himself now."

We were at the cash, and Eileen unloaded the produce onto the counter, and the greengrocer worked the register. Eileen produced some bills from a change purse and passed the money across the divide.

"It was like he couldn't imagine the family not home waiting for him that very Sunday. So, he took his foot out of the door, and said, 'I'll call again. No need to say anything right now.' Goodbye and good riddance, except when I turned around to go back to the kitchen, Abbie was sitting on the stairs behind me looking at the closed door."

Eileen and I came back out on the street, walked two doors down, and entered the butcher. "And Abbie said, 'Who was that?' and I said, 'I'm sure I don't know.' But she's like you, she keeps asking questions. 'What does he want? Have you ever seen him before?' And quick quick, faster than I can snap my fingers, she's got a pair of shoes on and runs out the door and she's away, gone down the street."

Eileen turned to the butcher and said, "Five pork chops." And looking back at me, "Well, it's none of my business."

"And that was the last time you saw her?"

"It was. Until this morning."

"And did you say anything to the family?"

"I didn't. Not Sunday, the day Abbie went out. She missed dinner, but maybe she called to say she was at a friend's house or something. It didn't seem to bother the family. And if they're not fussed, I'm not fussed. And then Monday's my day off. When I arrived today, I found you and Mrs. Jane busy with your heads together and then you ran out the door doing your best dodo." She laughed, looking at me as the man behind the counter passed her a parcel wrapped in pink grease paper. "Nobody's asking Eileen anything. There's no need for me to get involved in the muckety-muck's business."

"No, I suppose not."

"I'll let her mother start worrying about her before I get myself worrying too."

We were back out on the sidewalk. The basket had grown heavy, the sun was melting into the haze of the sky.

"What time was it on Sunday that Abbie left?"

"Just about three o'clock."

"We might find her yet." I tried to pass the basket back to Eileen.

"What? You're not carrying the shopping home for me? What kind of a man are you?" Her eyes disappeared when she laughed.

I was thinking about my trip to the Bohemian Embassy, but Eileen put me in mind of the chance to have a second conversation with Jane Linklater. "I guess I could — and maybe have a chat with Mrs. Linklater."

"Mrs. Jane? But she's out again. That woman is busy. No wonder they need me to cook dinner. But you can carry the basket."

VIII

AFTER EILEEN TOLD me bye-bye Birdie at the door, I was back in the car, crossing town to the Bohemian Embassy. It was on a quiet side street off Wellesley, a little south of the main mess of weekend frolics in Yorkville. I'd been there once before, to humour the girl of the moment who thought herself cultured; what little I remembered of the evening came through a haze of alcohol — which I'd consumed before arrival. The Embassy itself served only interminable cups of muddy coffee. All that remained of the evening were the flitting images: the raised platform at the end of the big room, women in black and hirsute men, the haze of cigarette smoke, rhymeless words of anger, and unwanted feedback from the dubious sound system.

I climbed the banister-less stairs two at a time until I got to the midway landing, thought the better of it and went step by step. At the top, I turned the corner and, seeing the big room, open the length of the building, had the flicker of the memory of the church. Here, of course, no pews, no God, and no writhing sinners speaking in tongues on the dais at the front. At least not in the daytime — some of the nighttime poetry readings might reach that level, but not now. In the afternoon there was no gatekeeper seated on a stool, doing her best to smooth the pleats of her miniskirt on her awkward perch where she'd greet you at the top of the stairs, without any greeting whatsoever, take your money, and put a smudge of a rubber stamp on the back of your hand.

I passed into the cavernous room, the small tables, covered by red checked cloths, an empty wine bottle on each holding a candle stub, unlit in the daylight hours. A spattering of customers, either in pairs, or alone, sat spaced throughout the room. I paused, unsure whether to wait to be seated; the place seemed devoid of staff, and so I pushed through to find an isolated table. There was some tinny folk music coming from a speaker somewhere above me, the voice clear and cloying: Someone wasn't marching anymore.

After hustling all morning and not having a second to spare as the case opened before me, I might have been glad for a moment to myself, to sit and collect my thoughts, but I was impatient to keep the ball rolling, and the wait for service grated. At last, a bearded man in a pair of jeans and sneakers appeared from somewhere. He wandered aimlessly through the checkerboard of tables, and I was about to give up on my initial thought — that he worked in the establishment — when he drifted in my direction. "Did you want anything?" he asked, managing to leave me guessing as to whether he was an employee or some casual customer pedalling reefer. Perhaps both. "The menu is on the wall," he said, raising an arm to about four o'clock to indicate a scrawl of chalk on a black surface. "The kitchen isn't open until five," he continued, negating most of what was written on the board, "but we have coffee."

"I'll have a coffee. And I'm looking for a girl who works here, Lena." I wondered if her mother, the frosty-voiced Mrs. Moore, knew her daughter worked in an establishment as questionable as this one. The whole case seemed to be about absent parents waking up to discover their children were no longer the kids they'd once known.

"Lena, huh?" he said. "I'll see what I can do." The answer didn't inspire confidence. He drifted away and passed behind a screen on the far wall, leaving me to wonder when I might see him again.

A sulky girl in a skirt cut above the knees with some sort of piping hemming the bottom, a cream turtleneck, and a looping string of fake pearls running down to her belly appeared from behind the screen. She had the requisite beret on her head and a maroon velour jacket to complete the outfit. The bearded man came behind her, and when she paused in indecision, he cut in front of her, coffee held in two hands like some steaming benediction, and led the way to my table.

"Here." He gestured at me.

She had a bored expression on her face; and although she looked like what she was, a little girl playing at being grown-up, she was doing a pretty good job of it. She would fool some and plenty of others would allow themselves to turn a blind eye to the deception and see where it led.

"You're supposed to get your own coffee," she said. "There's no table service here until five."

"Hi, Lena. My name's Patrick Bird and —"

"Did my mother send you?" She had a mouth designed for chewing gum, big white teeth, straight and in line. There was a certain force to her personality, though, and she stared the waiter down until he took his patchy beard and frustrated curiosity and made a retreat.

"She's the one who provided me with the name and address of this place, if that's your question. But I'm not working for her. I've come to ask you about your friend Abbie Linklater. She's gone missing and her father's hired me."

"Oh, Abbie," she said, and her shoulders slumped forward as some of the fight deflated from her chest.

"Can you sit down to talk to me about Abbie for a couple of minutes?"

"Sure." She sat, but didn't offer any information. Rather, she asked me a question: "How long has she been gone?"

"Since Sunday afternoon. Two nights and I guess two days now. When did you see her last?"

"We haven't been such good friends lately. As recently as Christmas, we were, but Abbie's changed. We're not interested in the same stuff anymore."

"No big fight or reason for the break?"

She looked me over carefully and I could see the calculations in her head: should she disclose what she knew to me — older, squarer, the establishment? Again, I felt the distance between our generations; although only eight years separated us, the shadow of the war had darkened my world, but not hers.

She sucked in a breath. "No big fight, but I think it hurt both of us. We used to depend on each other — we were always there — but that's changed, so I'm angry at her — she's gone and gotten herself interested in things that don't mean anything to me." She crossed one knee over the other and leaned back in her chair.

"When did you see her last?" I asked, conscious she hadn't answered my initial question.

"She came over to my place on Sunday afternoon. The day she went missing. It was the first time I'd seen her in a while. My parents were out."

"Did you know she was planning to run away?"

"Who knows? I don't know what I knew and what I didn't. I haven't been much good at guessing what's going on in Abbie's head recently. When we were kids, for a long time it was like we shared a brain, like we knew each other's thoughts, but not anymore. When she does tell me what she's thinking, it doesn't make a lot of sense. I guess she'd say that I'm not trying to understand where she's at and what she cares about. She'd think it was my fault."

I waited her out and she continued, "She told me she wasn't going home that night, that she had to follow up on something; but she's said things like that before. You know, it was getting a little, like, exhausting. The friend with the constant crisis. Crying me, me, me. She came to me because she needed help, but I don't think she cared much about me anymore. It was always what she needed."

"Was she having boy trouble?" I asked, trying to steer the conversation toward the tangible explanation Jane had provided.

"Oh, no!" Her surprise was genuine.

"You're sure?"

"Nothing I knew about her troubles involved a boy; that's not where Abbie's head is."

"Her mother told me that she's pregnant; she led me to believe that she's off somewhere getting an abortion."

Lena laughed outright, her white teeth a crescent of light in the dusk of the interior.

"No?"

"That's what her mother told you?"

"Stepmother was what I was told."

"Yes, stepmother." She laughed again. "Well, someone's lying. My guess is that's the kind of thing that Abbie'd say to end a conversation with her stepmom. It's something that would make sense to Mrs. Linklater — that she could understand; that she would keep quiet, and Abbie'd have a little time to do whatever it is she wants to do. But, no, Abbie's not pregnant, she hasn't changed that much."

"So, no abortion. No boys in her life."

"Not boys who are getting her pregnant, if that's the question."

"I saw her today with a young man in a white cardigan with sandy hair combed off the side of his head."

"Good for Abbie. So, is she lost — or did you find her?"

"I saw her, coming out of the library on Roncesvalles with the boy in the cardigan and tailed her to a church the other side of Trinity Bellwoods Park, St. Matthias Anglican Church. When I got into the church, the two had disappeared."

Lena rolled her eyes at the idea. "Yeah." She looked like she needed a piece of gum. "That's great. She's got a boy in tow. I'm happy for her, but I'm not convinced it means anything. Abbie's got a project these days and she's a bit obsessive about it. If you can help her move it forward, she's your best friend; if you want to do anything else, like going to Yorkville on the weekend, swimming at

Sunnyside, crashing a party, or seeing a movie, she's not too interested."

"So, the boy doesn't mean anything to you?"

"Nothing."

"His description — you've seen him before?"

She smirked. "I feel like I've seen a hundred of him before. He sounds like just the perfect square boy for Abbie. I wish her well. I really do. Did she meet him in church?"

"Maybe. Did you ever go to that church at Trinity Bellwoods?"

"No."

"Do you know where Abbie's family goes to church?"

"Roncesvalles United, right next to the library. Same as my family."

"Okay. Let's go back to Sunday. She came over to your place sometime in the afternoon. Do you know what time?"

"Maybe three or a little after."

"And did she have a purpose?"

"You're catching on now: everything she does has a purpose. She came to return a book." Again, I paused, as there had to be more to it than just the book. "She'd borrowed a book from my mom earlier. Or she didn't borrow it from her; she just took it. They have a fairly easy relationship like that. They talk books. Dull, old books."

"What was the book, and why did Abbie have to return it then? There's got to be more to it than this." Lena's drawl and constant eye-rolling was making me impatient.

She covered up a big yawn, but not before I got another look at her straight white teeth, the big molars and the sharp canines. "The book was *Wuthering Heights* — and I can't tell you anything about it, because I haven't read it." She could sneer pretty well for a sixteen-year-old. "But the big deal is there was a picture of my mum and Abbie's dad folded inside the book and there was an inscription on the back of the photo that was a little suggestive. I guess Abbie understood from what was written there that our parents have been playing musical partners, and that upset her puritanical little mind."

"And it doesn't bother you."

"Whatever. I'm not sure it's happening. Not like Abbie. And if it is — it is. These things happen. Let's not pretend they don't."

"But Abbie was upset by that information?"

"Yes. She returned the book, but kept the picture. The photo, the idea that there was some sort of sordid romance, the evidence of her father's unfaithfulness, it all feeds into Abbie's obsession — that there's something wrong with her mother's death. Her real mother, the one who died when she was a baby. That's her project. That's why she's spending literally all her time at the library, searching through old obituaries and newspapers, trying to find the missing pieces of information that'll tell her something about how her mother died."

"She could ask her —"

"She doesn't want to ask anyone in her family. They don't talk about Abbie's mom. They never have. It's understood that you just don't. And Abbie doesn't trust them. She doesn't even want them to know what she's thinking. Right now she doesn't trust her father; and I don't think she's ever trusted her stepmom."

"But she talks to you about her thoughts."

"She did before; but there's only so much space in me to listen to her wild talk day in and day out. I have a life as well." I looked around the dim café, the checkerboard tables, the molten wax of the candles frozen hard on the empty wine bottles. "I think that's why we're not such good friends anymore. She wants to live in like 1951 and I want to live in the present. The world is exciting; the most exciting time ever. Don't you think?" She leaned forward, her boredom momentarily on hold, her beret childishly askew. "I'm living it and Abbie's stuck in the past."

"Do you know how her mother died?"

"No. She started to tell me on Sunday; she got as far as telling me the date she'd died. She'd just discovered it and was all excited. I remember it — because it's the same day as my mother's birthday. December fourth. But I'd just heard too many of her crazy theories of the past and told her so."

"And the year was 1951?" We were getting somewhere now.

"Yes. I think so. Abbie was two at the time. But I'd had enough by then — and told her so. I tried to explain about the give and take of being friends. You try to care ... maybe I've let her down, but honestly the number of hours I've heard her talk without ever getting anything; it's too much. If you're wondering why she ran away — that's why. She's obsessed with the past. Totally obsessed with 1951. If you want to know where she is now — that's the answer: 1951. I can't help you. That's how our Sunday ended. She was upset; started crying and talking about how a friend helps a friend and all this stuff, like I'm the one to blame. And then she was gone and that's the last I've seen of her."

I thanked Lena for her help and handed her a card with the company number on it, in case Abbie reappeared; although I wasn't kidding myself as to where her allegiance lay, given the sisterhood of teenage girls. I spared my stomach the last half inch of coffee lurking in the bottom of my cup and headed back down the narrow staircase with a date, fourteen years earlier, burning in my mind.

IX

IT WAS ABOUT three o'clock when I came out of the Bohemian Embassy and into the little alley that was sheltered against the blaze of July. Even in the shade with my jacket slung over my back and hanging loose from the hook of a finger, the humidity crawled inside my shirt and cozied up to me. Its warmth caressed my chest and ran its soft hand across my shoulders, but I didn't have time for a tryst with the tropical weather; I was heading back for a return engagement with Miss Webster, the librarian, and the stack of newspapers piled behind her desk.

I cut across Dundas, north of Trinity Bellwoods Park, and resisted the siren call of St. Matthias, knowing that Sid had asked me to wait on him; it would have been too true to type for me to knock on the door and pick a fight with the man of God. There was a parking spot right out front of the library on Roncesvalles and I fed some loose change that hadn't found its way into Rosie's tip jar into the meter. I cranked the dial of the mechanism, felt the resistance against my turn, heard the clicks, and saw the flag pop up for two hours.

Business had picked up at the library. At the top of the stairs, I found myself in a line, behind a middle-aged man with two lifeless strands of pale hair combed over a bald head in an unsuccessful attempt to dull the gleam. He was insistent that the library should already have an advance copy of something called *In Cold Blood* despite Miss Webster's calm retort that this was not the case. My patience was wearing thin when Comb-Over gave up and shuffled off in a huff.

"Back so soon, Mr. Bird?" asked Miss Webster.

"I've come to have another look at those newspapers." I gestured toward the stack of broadsheets folded behind her.

"Of course." She passed the pile over the counter and I took a look at the top *Telegram* for the date — and there it was: December 11, 1951 — a week out from the day Lena had mentioned. I flipped the pile over, wondering about the lag from the time of death to the first reporting, but my error became clear to me; the papers were upside down — in reverse chronological order — and here was the one I was looking for, now on top, December 5, the headline in two-inch block capitals: "YOUNG MOTHER KILLED IN BOTCHED BANK HOLDUP."

"Mr. Bird," Miss Webster interrupted my epiphany, "I'll have to ask you to move on — we have other patrons who require assistance."

I lowered the papers, putting my reading on pause, pushed away from the desk, annoyed at her self-importance, at the loud whispering that filled the space, at the crowded tables, and the oppressive hush that underpinned it all. Needing a moment alone with this revelation, I found an upholstered chair with an unfortunate stain that was tucked into a corner of the building and dropped the pile of print onto the carpeted floor.

I picked up the *Telegram* and began to read:

> The spate of bank robberies that have plagued the city reached a new crisis point yesterday when at approximately 10:45, a young man with dark hair entered the Roncesvalles branch of the Bank of Toronto with the intent of taking what was not lawfully his.
>
> Contrary to many of the brazen attacks of recent months, including the one that happened at this same branch just two weeks earlier, this robber did not immediately proclaim his intentions. He lined up in the queue with the other customers, directly behind Belinda Linklater, with devastating consequences for the mother of two.
>
> When she was called to the counter, the gunman made his move and accompanied her to the till. It was at this time, eyewitnesses confirm, that he covered his face with a balaclava-type mask and produced a handgun from inside his clothing.
>
> This heartless criminal took the young mother as a shield and

demanded money from the teller. Other patrons were ordered to place themselves face down on the ground. They lowered themselves to the floor. All the while the cowardly thief held Mrs. Linklater prisoner, keeping her positioned in front of his body.

As bank staff complied with the robber's demands, teller Stanley Johnson made a fatal decision: taking matters into his own hands he availed himself of the branch revolver. Schooled in the Bank of Toronto's Robbery Prevention Training, Johnson, a veteran of the war, reached for the bank's security Smith & Wesson.

While the cash was being handed across the counter, in a cloth bag the robber had provided, Mr. Johnson used the cover of activity to take aim and fire.

Tragedy ensued.

With a criminal's cunning, the robber sensed the movement, and jerked in Johnson's direction, pulling the young mother with him. The bullet struck Mrs. Linklater in the chest and she collapsed to the floor, a crimson pool forming beneath her. In the chaos that followed, the robber fled the building on foot with approximately $2,500.

An ambulance was called for Mrs. Linklater, 27, of High Park Boulevard. She was pronounced dead on arrival at St. Joseph's Hospital later that morning.

She is survived by two-year-old
twins, Nelson and Abigail, and
her husband, architectural engineer Trent Linklater.

The suspect was not found,
despite his midday crime witnessed by more than a dozen bank
patrons and employees. He is described as having a medium build
with dark hair worn slightly
longer than average. He is clean-
shaven with blue eyes. He was
last seen in a blue pinstriped
jacket and pants and a white
shirt open at the collar.

Any witnesses with infor-
mation on the crime or the
whereabouts of the fugitive are
asked to call the Toronto Police
Department immediately. He should
not be approached in person
as he is considered armed and
dangerous.

So, there it was. And, of course, there was more once you
moved back from the front page. On page three: "Eyewitness
Identifies Bank Robber as Escaped Criminal, Edwin Boyd."

Manny Zacharakis, 47, a pipe-
fitter and patron of the Bank
of Toronto on Roncesvalles,
has provided the *Telegram* with
an exclusive eyewitness account of yesterday's tragic
robbery.

Mr. Zacharakis, who was working on a nearby building project,
entered the bank at approximately
10:45 to withdraw money. Waiting
in the queue, he noticed that the
man in front of him was fumbling

in his jacket as he reached the front of the line.

In the words of our eye-witness: "It happened so fast. One minute there was your average citizen waiting his turn in line in front of me. The next second, there was this masked robber, holding the woman in front of him and waving a gun. She was so scared. It was awful."

The masked criminal is reported to have shouted. "This is a holdup. Everyone down." Mr. Zacharakis says that he lowered himself to the floor. The gunman passed a cloth bag that our witness identifies as a dirty pillowcase across the counter. "Heads down. Heads down!" Mr. Zacharakis heard the gunman yell multiple times.

Mr. Zacharakis complied with the demand and put his face to the ground so that he was not able to see what followed.

He did, however, hear the explosion of a gunshot. "I was terrified at that moment," reports Mr. Zacharakis. "I didn't know what had happened, but I was worried that the robber had lost his cool and that we'd all be dead. Of course, once I heard the shot, I couldn't help but take a look.

"That's when I saw the woman slumping. She was very beautiful and so young. I was scared for my life. It was terrible to see her fall to the ground."

Mr. Zacharakis was unaware at this time that the shot had come

from behind the counter, from the
gun of Junior Accounts Manager
Stanley Johnson, an employee of
the bank.

"I couldn't believe it," said
Zacharakis. "After the shot,
the gunman took off right away.
I thought we were all going
to be dead, like in a hostage
situation."

He was unaware of any at-
tempt to chase the criminal. "We
were all in shock, especially
since a woman lay dying right
beside us. Our focus was on her
and not the bank robber. As soon
as he was out the door, people
started to move to see if they
could provide any first aid to
her. And the manager called for
an ambulance."

As to a description, in this
year that has already seen a record number of bank robberies in
our city, Zacharakis said: "When
my head was down, I thought
about what I had seen of the man
in front of me, and I am quite
convinced that he is the notorious Edwin Boyd that has been in
all the newspapers."

Also on page three — the whole broadsheet was garishly
devoted to coverage of the crime — was a statement from the
police, under the headline of: "Toronto Police Department
Comments on Rash of Recent Bank Robberies."

Late yesterday afternoon, the
Toronto Police Department held
a press conference to discuss
the Roncesvalles bank robbery.

Detective Edward Tong led the proceedings and assured reporters that the city remains safe in the face of mounting violence.

Detective Tong expressed his condolences, on behalf of the entire force, to the family of Mrs. Belinda Linklater, who was shot dead at the scene.

He refused to comment on the Bank of Toronto's policy of having tellers use guns, saying that he understood that businesses were intent on protecting their property, but he warned against any form of vigilante justice: "Leave the shooting to us. We're the professionals here."

When asked about whether this robbery was linked to the numerous other robberies that have happened this year in the city and surrounding environs, Tong said, "Obviously that's something that we're considering. We're looking at the evidence and will come to a conclusion. I'll keep you posted."

There have now been three high-profile bank robberies in the past two weeks. On November 20, the Boyd Gang hit this same Bank of Toronto at Roncesvalles and Dundas. Less than ten days later the escaped convicts, under the command of Edwin Boyd, knocked off a Royal Bank on Laird Avenue to the tune of $46,000, the biggest heist in Canadian history. And now, on December 4, we have our first fatality in these lawless times.

When Tong was asked direct-
ly about whether this could be
the work of the notorious Boyd
Gang, currently terrorizing the
city, he was unequivocal: "I
don't think so. This was the work
of a lone gunman, not a gang.
And Boyd and his cronies tend
to take charge. Boyd likes to
vault the counter like a gymnast.
He's a showman. He stands on the
counter and makes his appeal to
the people. This has a different
feel about it."

An unnamed source within
the department told this report-
er that the police do not consider the robbery to be linked
to others. In the words of the
source: "This was done by an
amateur. Not putting on a mask
until he approached the counter,
not taking control of the situation, not having a getaway car:
all point to a poorly planned
attempt."

Below the police update was a further article, entitled,
"The Forgotten Man: Stanley Johnson, Bank Teller."

When Stanley Johnson went to work
yesterday, he could hardly have
imagined the events that would
come to dominate the day, and
the fatal role he would play in
them.

Johnson is the junior clerk
at the Bank of Toronto on
Roncesvalles who fired the bullet that struck an innocent

bystander, Belinda Linklater, in the upper chest, killing her upon impact. This was the second robbery at this branch in two weeks and it is easy to speculate that the repeated attacks might have affected staff's composure and judgment.

Johnson, 28, of Concord Avenue, has been taken into police custody for further questioning. At this stage, no charges have been laid.

Prior to working for the bank, Johnson served in the Canadian Armed Forces where he acquitted himself honourably in the Dieppe Raid, avoiding both death and capture. Later, he returned to France's coastline, this time to the triumph of the battle of Juno Beach on D-Day. His war record is spotless, and he was awarded the Atlantic Star upon discharge.

Johnson lives with his wife, Marya, and their two young children. The family had no comment for this article. A neighbour, David Welland, said of Johnson: "He's the nicest guy you could ever meet. You see him every weekend, tending to his garden and playing with his boys. This is an unreal story. I can't believe it. It's a tragedy."

There will undoubtedly be repeated calls to de-arm bank employees after this incident. The Bank of Toronto has not responded to questions about its employee safety training program.

It did release the following statement: "Our heartfelt condolences go out to the Linklater family for their tragic loss. We will continue to work to make our banks safe and welcoming environments for our customers through enhanced security. We are co-operating fully with the Toronto Police Department to ensure that a tragedy such as this never happens again."

Page three also had a picture of the outside of the bank in happier times. There was a further photo, perhaps in poor taste, showing two ambulance technicians loading a stretcher into the back of the vehicle. Neither the body nor the face could be seen — it could have been any old photo, and not specific to this story. There was one last article on the page, and it was about the victim: "Tragedy Strikes Engineer's Family."

Belinda Linklater was struck down in the prime of her life in a bank robbery gone horribly wrong. The young mother leaves behind her two-year-old twins, Nelson and Abigail, as well as her grieving husband, Trent Linklater.

Trent Linklater's name may be familiar to those in the city as one of the leading engineers working on Toronto's proposed lakeshore highway. Before moving to the city, the young engineer and his family lived in his hometown of Belleville.

He and Belinda, née Greene, were married on January 22, 1946, in Newcastle-on-Tyne, England, where the couple met while Trent was serving with the 2nd Canadian Infantry Division. The birth of the twins completed what to many appeared to be the perfect family.

Belinda Linklater leaves behind a mother in her hometown of Newcastle. As of press time the *Telegram* has been unable to contact her for a statement.

Trent Linklater did not comment on the events of the day.

Mrs. Linklater is remembered by friends as a loving wife and doting mother to her young family. She was a member of the St. Vincent de Paul's chapter of the Catholic Women's League and was known as a steadfast friend who was always willing to donate her time to support a good cause.

Her friend and neighbour Alice Crowe said what so many are feeling. "How could this happen to Bea? She was the kindest soul; she would never hurt anyone. I can't imagine the world without her. It breaks my heart to think of those two children growing up without their mother."

There it was, the mystery of the past, now clear; the hours in a study carrel, pouring over old papers on loan from the central depository explained. Now I knew what Abbie had been doing with her time, away from her friends, shunning boys, giving up swimming, lying about abortions; now I knew the obsession that held her in its tight grip.

X

BELINDA'S DEATH MEANDERED in my mind like a circle in a spiral as I walked south on Roncesvalles and tried to digest this new information. Abbie's mother hadn't just died; she'd been killed. Things were coming together, falling into place to complete the picture, but crawling around behind the couch, I still hadn't found the missing puzzle piece that completed the sky. Rather, I had a whole cache of fragments, some cerulean blue, others cloudy white, or cut by a rainbow, or full of a flock of birds flying southward — and look, here was a bolt of lightning knifing through the centre of the puzzle — and all these images overwhelmed and complicated the picture, rather than complementing and completing it. The mass swirled in my brain as I walked, sifting it, waiting, trying to have it settle in the kaleidoscope of my mind.

I was tempted to phone Sid with my latest find. He might temper my mania and provide a solid background of fact from his encyclopedic brain. Just having a sounding board was useful. But it was a little too early to call the boss with my end-of-day report; he didn't like to hear from me before 4:30. Usually by that time, he was prepared to give me some sort of a conditional pardon for the rest of the day. But I'd learned that on the early calls, he liked to send me home and dock an hour or two from my pay. Fine: I could dog it and walk beneath the big blue sky while I tried to figure this out and he could pay me for doing so.

My wander took me through the intersection where earlier that day Abbie and the boy in the cardigan had transferred streetcars, and this time I passed through the traffic lights and swung left along the strip of parkette that runs on the verge above the train tracks. Across the rail line, and the Gardiner Expressway, three lanes of fast traffic each way, and the old road, Lake Shore Boulevard, choppy glints sparkled on the lake. There were sailboats bobbing on the water and waiting, like me, for a bit of breeze to push them in one direction or another, a puff of wind that might get us closer to where we were trying to go. In the near distance, perched on the shoreline, like a mausoleum to old Toronto, the Boulevard Club sat, severed from the city by the traffic that roared east and west along the new expressway. I stood at the fence, staring south, feeling my body relax as I wondered what the hell was going on in this case.

Finding the girl didn't feel that complicated; I'd already spotted her once and she continued to circle around her neighbourhood. It seemed that if I kept trolling up and down Roncesvalles and Queen, I'd bump into her soon enough. It wasn't a detective that was needed to find her — a beagle, a leash, and the excuse of walking the dog would be enough. But something was off; I wasn't sure a single person I'd talked to had been straight with me. Everyone said they wanted Abbie found, but then left me floundering without the information I needed: sleek Trent with his need for discretion; sullen Nelson with the reticence of teenage years and a brother's unerring ability to miss everything; Jane, sweaty in her tennis clothes, busy repeating lies told to her by Abbie; Ayscough barring the doorway to his church; Elleen with her mocking glance, treating me as if I was a game for her entertainment; Miss Webster handing me a mountain of newsprint rather than telling me what was in it; and Lena, rolling her eyes until they got stuck in the back of her head. The problem wasn't just the blur and jumble of what I'd been told, it was the conflicting information, the truth and the lies, that I needed to wade through. It wasn't the simple divorce case, like last night, where Victoria, the wife, and I conspired to reach a single focal point. It was disparate, shattered; not a prism, but a clutter of broken shards. And now, here was the decade-old death of Belinda Linklater, shot in the chaos of a bank robbery gone wrong.

I stared across the arteries stretched below me as a commuter train pulled into Sunnyside Station, and began to wonder about other pieces, further complications, that didn't fit the puzzle: the shoeless man who'd been sniffing around the backyard, and the boy in the white cardigan who accompanied Abbie to St. Matthias, the bank teller held in custody and his young family, the possibility that this had been a set-up of some sort and it wasn't a tragic accident — but actually murder. It seemed like that's the direction Abbie was headed. But at the same time, it seemed impossible to plan a botched bank robbery that involved both someone on the inside and the outside.

Gazing out across the ribbons of traffic, I saw, in the parking lot of the Boulevard Club, where I had started the search earlier that morning, two of those loose threads — the shoeless man and the boy in the cardigan — in conversation with a short-haired woman wearing tennis whites, with a racquet resting on her shoulder. The sight jolted me: it was as if I'd conjured these figures from my mind and made them whole. I exhaled, looked away, and looked back across the traffic at the parking lot, distrustful of eyesight that had manufactured exactly what I was looking for. It was a fair distance to the Boulevard Club; I couldn't see their faces, but what was visible was the shoeless state of the scrappy man in baggy pants and the blazing white cardigan of the boy. I was pretty sure it was them, but couldn't be certain until I was closer. I looked back up King Street toward the pedestrian overpass at the bottom of Roncesvalles — it was a bridge too far.

It was decision time, and I took the shortest path between the two points, jumping over the wrought-iron railing and starting down the weedy embankment toward the train tracks. The pitch was steep, covered in loose pink shale, dry dirt, and scrubby vegetation. Half sliding, half skipping, I arrived at the bottom of the slope, looked up the tracks, and saw the train pulling out of Sunnyside Station and rushed to beat it, crossing the four sets of rails and pulling up before a drainage ditch. From this lower vantage point it was impossible to see the trio in the parking lot. The train roared behind me, rumbling the ground and creating a whoosh of air as it passed. In front of me, rush hour had started; the traffic was fast and relentless and I began to regret taking the shortcut, but there was only one way forward at this stage. I hopped the scrubby ditch separating the train tracks from the highway and stepped over the next guardrail, watching for a break in the westbound traffic. If I could traverse the three lanes heading out of town, there was a concrete median, wide on the bottom and tapering to a plateau, like a stylized *A*, where I might rest and catch my breath before completing the crossing.

I waited and watched and waited more, thinking I would never find a safe passage. After a minute of standing, wasting time, I said, "Go, go, go," to myself in a final attempt to screw my courage to any sticking point, no matter how feeble it might prove to be. The cars rushed past. Talking to myself did nothing to slow the flow of traffic, to stop the rush of happy commuters whose workday had ended, and were now free to drive to their suburban homes where wives in pastel sundresses, cut above dimpled knees, awaited them on the backyard patio with a Black Label chilling in the fridge, as a toddler crawled around their new lawn. "Go, go, go," I said again and propelled myself into the road, and there opened before me a space to dodge into, a second pocket, so I could scoot across the middle lane, the blare of a horn, the blur of a transport truck, the great suck of air as its slipstream passed, the flicker of a fast-moving shadow, a second to pause as vehicles sped on either side of the tight-rope of the dotted line and then I scrambled onto the inner shoulder and found myself panting on the concrete divider between eastbound and westbound traffic.

In the pause, as I caught my breath, I looked up, and there they were, closer now, clear in my sight: Shoeless Joe, who I'd lost in High Park; the boy in the cardigan, who

I'd lost at the church; and a woman I'd never seen before, tall and thin in her whites, the racquet now held across her body like a shield. Her brown hair, in a pixie cut, made her look both boyish and severe, depending on the expression on her face. In my excitement I yelled at the group; my voice was swallowed by the din of the highway — and thankfully so — a warning would only scatter the threesome and lead to another failure of a foot race.

I turned my attention back to the highway; I was through the worst of it, the next three lanes, while moving fast, were heading into the city and against the afternoon rush. Sticking to what had worked before, I sucked in a lungful of air mixed with exhaust fumes and said, "Go, go, go," and watched as a solid mass of steel, chrome, and glass sped by. When my incantation failed, my confidence faltered and I feared I'd be stuck on the median until after the commute had calmed. I put a toe onto the gravel of the shoulder, spotted the speeding gaps, lengthening and narrowing in a metallic dance, breathed deeply, and plunged into the roadway. There were horns, the Doppler of an expletive from a joker in a convertible, the explosion of noise from the unmuffled exhaust of a motorbike, and then it was over and I hopped a steel guardrail bolted to short wooden posts, and landed in another scrubby stretch of grass and weeds that separated the expressway from the parallel Lake Shore Boulevard.

This road, older, smaller, and slower, would not pose the challenges that the highway had. There was no central median; what I was doing here was jaywalking compared with the gauntlet of crossing the highway. I looked both ways, just as they teach in kindergarten, and started across the open lanes toward the parking lot of the Boulevard Club.

There was the jab of a horn and the screech of brakes. The crunch of the bumper knocked my knees out from under me. I popped up into the air for a split second and then landed on the still moving car. Half skidding, half rolling across the flat plain of its hood, my momentum was finally stopped by the glass of the windshield. The startled face of some old biddy in the passenger seat stared back. I groaned, rolled once more, and dismounted gracelessly from my perch and collapsed on the pavement. There was pain: the clipped kneecaps, the crunched nose, the sore shoulder, the battered torso, the bruised ego. I closed my eyes, hoping the world might go away.

"Young man. What were you thinking? Where on earth did you come from? Are you okay? Goodness. I think he's dead, Phyllis."

"I'm not a good driver to jump in front of," a second voice said. "Honestly. I'm fine when there's some road in front of me. But not this."

"Phyllis. Go back to the club and call an ambulance."

"You're faster than me, Myrtle. Help. Help. Call that boy; he works here."

I opened my eyes.

"He's alive," said Myrtle. She had a thin crown of white hair that formed an angelic halo with the sun behind her. Was this what heaven looked like?

"Someone's coming to help us," said Phyllis.

"Where on earth did you come from?" said Myrtle. I had the same question myself. "We were just turning out of the club and there you were."

I tried to sit up and felt a little dizzy, and decided lying down was the better option. It was clear now: I'd been looking up and down Lake Shore and had managed to miss the car coming out of the club's parking lot; Phyllis and Myrtle — whichever one was behind the wheel — had been busy looking westbound at the oncoming traffic, and had missed seeing me coming straight across the road. The good news was that they weren't moving at speed; the bad news: they hit me. Phyllis moved around to the front of the Lincoln Continental. "I don't think there's any damage to the car."

"Hello, ladies. What's going on here?" It was a familiar voice. I squinted against the sunlight and saw Thad from the bowling alley. "Hello, Mr. Bird; we meet again."

"Hi, Thad. Help me sit up."

He stood in front of me, his face showing concern. "You look a little rough. Are you sure you want up?"

"Let's give it a try." I lifted both my palms up to Thad's outstretched arms, and he gave a firm and steady pull; there was a searing sensation across the shoulder that had borne the impact of the car's hood and then I was sitting. I found a soiled handkerchief in a jacket pocket and wiped it across my face. It came back with a smear of blood. One of the old biddies found my hat, rolling on its brim, and returned it. Thad played traffic cop and coaxed Phyllis, now behind the wheel of her big boat of a car, back off the road and into the parking lot. I cursed under my breath and Myrtle said, "I never was so surprised as to see your face suddenly appear, pressed against the glass of the windshield, staring at me like that. It was quite the strangest experience of my week."

XI

PHYLLIS AND THAD returned from the big Lincoln, which was now docked safely in the parking lot, away from the traffic on Lake Shore. The two of them and Myrtle stood over me as I sat on the sidewalk. "Should I call an ambulance?" asked Thad.

"No need. I'm okay. I was trying an experimental crossing. Apologies, ladies. Came from up there." I pointed to the ridge that ran above the train tracks.

They stared without saying anything.

"I came down in a rush, trying to catch up with some people I saw here in the parking lot." I made a motion with my arm to point across the asphalt and it made me feel a little unsteady and nauseous. I was wobbling, but on my feet. The mystery trio had disappeared in the moments while

I had been coming out on the wrong side of the wrestling match with the Continental. I reached for Thad's elbow to steady myself.

"Young man," began Phyllis, "I really think we should call an ambulance. I worry — what if something in your insides got knocked sideways — and if you don't find out until you get home. Don't you think that —"

"Insurance companies," said Myrtle, "were built for this kind of situation. You need to register the accident. It's no use to remember next year, when your kidney fails, that you were hit by a car sometime in the past."

It wasn't my kidney that was going to fail. I shook my head. "I'm okay enough. It was nice to have met you two; I only wish it could have been under better circumstances."

"Well, if you insist." Phyllis looked relieved. The mention of insurance companies had dragged a cloud across her sunny brow; it lightened as the worry of claims adjusters and premium increases dissipated. "We'll be off then. And thank you, Mr. Jankowicz." She pressed a bill into Thad's hand and the two shuffled back to their tank.

Thad made the bill disappear. In his street clothes he looked a little older and sharper than the young man I'd met in the bowling alley. He took a drifting step back into the lot. "Hold up, Thad. I have some questions."

He paused, looking back at me.

"You may wonder what the hell I was doing" — Thad's face was incurious — "coming down the hill like that and crossing the highway —"

"I didn't see —"

"— and getting hit by those two in their boat. I was trying to get to this group I saw talking in the parking lot. A woman — maybe fortyish, maybe a little younger, in tennis whites with dark hair cut short; a scruffy guy without shoes or a jacket in his shirt sleeves; and a young guy, maybe about your age, in a bright white cardigan. They were standing just over there, having a conversation. I've never seen the woman before; she looked like a club member. But the boy in the cardigan was seen with Abbie earlier today, and the scrub has been skulking around the edges of this case since the very beginning. You see them?"

His Adam's apple bobbed in his long neck and his eyes narrowed. "Yeah. Over this way. I was just off my shift, heading home. When I came out the door, I could see them. She's a member, but I don't know her name. I don't spend much time on the courts. But the guy in the dirty shirt looked like trouble. I was walking over to see if help was needed, and I was just there when we heard the screech of brakes, and the horn, and there you were, rolling over the hood of the car. Your situation looked more urgent, so I came to help you, and I guess their meeting broke up about the same time. The last I saw, the shoeless guy was pulling the boy in the cardigan with him off that way." Thad pointed west.

"On foot?"

"On foot."

"And the woman?"

"She got into a car and was off."

"You see what make?"

He frowned. "It was red. Maybe an Impala."

"And it's gone now?"

"Gone before you got up off the ground."

"Okay. Did you hear anything that was said when the party was breaking up?"

"Yeah, the rough-looking guy, as he walked away, said back to the woman getting into her car: 'Remember: the Edgewater, room three oh seven.' She was trying to end the conversation and get in her car and he kept repeating it. Shouting it."

"You're sure?"

"I wouldn't tell you if I wasn't."

"And the woman, how did she respond to that?"

"She didn't say anything. Like I said, I think she was trying to end the conversation. She just got into her car and that was it. And the barefoot guy pulled the boy out of the lot and onto the path."

The sidewalk led along the lake to the pedestrian bridge I'd shunned for my highway crossing. Over the bridge was the intersection of Queen and Roncesvalles, where I'd seen Abbie and her mystery boy switch streetcars, and on the northwest corner was the Edgewater, a fleabag hotel, no longer on the edge of the water, but farther back now, behind the train tracks, across Queen Street, and beside the bus terminal.

"You going that way?"

"Uh-huh."

"Let's go." I don't know if Thad was interested in my company, but it didn't seem like he had much choice. Off work, he wore a short-sleeve shirt with a light green checkerboard pattern; it looked like the latest style but was missing the bottom button and the corner flapped with each step. I'd started the day by losing a foot race and was only getting slower as it went on and the blisters and bumps caught up. My sports jacket had a rip running from the right pocket and my forehead was still leaking red into the handkerchief. Thad looked at his watch and I asked, "Am I slowing you down?"

He shook his head. "It's okay. I have to be somewhere by seven. I need to get home and have dinner first. But I'm okay."

"Date with the girlfriend?"

"No girl. I have a date with the chessboard. Tournament tonight."

"You play chess?"

"Yes. And you?"

"No. I'm not even sure which way the pieces move. Are you good?"

"For this city, maybe; but in the bigger world, no. I dream" — he paused and looked at me, unsure if he should confess his aspirations to one who so clearly couldn't understand — "of becoming a grandmaster. All my thoughts are consumed by the sixty-four squares of the board, the world, where everything is contained, and known, not like this." His gesture included the highway, the ramp of the pedestrian bridge, and the facade of the Palais Royale, an aging dance hall, one of the few remnants of the now long-gone amusement park, its lustre faded by the grime of exhaust fumes and the drone of the highway.

The boy came to life as he talked about the game.

It had been a long day and as our walk continued, I grew slower. My knees remembered their kiss with Phyllis's Lincoln too well and creaked with each step up the ramp onto the bridge; the overpass itself was uphill onto the embankment where the city proper started. I felt like an old man before thirty. I spun my crumpled hat in my hand and tried to punch it back into shape.

"One of the old women down there called you Jankowicz? That's your last name?"

"That's right," he said. "It's a common Polish name." He looked at me and I felt his defensiveness.

"Plenty of Poles in this neighbourhood. You live off Roncesvalles?"

"I do now," he said without elucidating.

Talk with Thad was drying up, either because of something I'd said, or because he was too busy dreaming of chess. His next comment appeared to suggest it was the latter: "There was a chess player called Bird in the last century."

"Really? Was he any good?"

"No. Not really. He was famous for his strange openings and his unconventional beliefs. He succeeded in putting others in awkward positions. He has some famous games, but not too many wins. He played the King's Gambit. I'll give him that; he was a fighter."

I tried to steer the conversation back to this world. "You ever see that boy in the cardigan before?"

"Not that I remember. Not at the club at least."

"Fair enough."

We lapsed back into silence for a second before he asked, "And you? Are you getting closer to finding Abbie?"

The pain in my knee flared and I grunted. "Two steps forward and three steps back. I'm meeting lots of people, but every time I feel like it's breaking I run up against a wall. The good news is I saw Abbie today — from a distance — so we know she's still out there. But something isn't right. I'll feel happier when we have her back safe at home." And even as I said the words, I felt the crumpled note and bullet in my jacket's inside pocket. Its weight swayed forward and, with each step, came back and bounced on my chest, right where the GPs put their stethoscopes when they want to see if you have a heart.

"That's good," said Thad.

We came off the bridge at Roncesvalles and passed by the bus station on the corner. The next door up was the Edgewater; Thad and I stopped for our goodbyes and I thanked him for his help. He continued into little Poland, home for dinner before the big tournament, and I passed through the plate-glass doors and climbed three steps into the dingy lobby of the hotel.

The inside was dark after the glare of the late afternoon; if anything, the humidity was increasing as the day progressed. There was a threadbare carpet that had once held some maroon arabesques, now barely visible in the gloom. A thin man smoking a cigarette sat on a stool behind a glass-topped counter. There was a bar off to the left and the noise of drinkers who'd gotten an early start on the night spilled into the lobby. I shut the slurs and swears of their banter out as I approached the counter. The clerk put down the paperback he was reading, looked up lazily, and scratched a boil on the back of his neck. Behind him was a handwritten sign tacked to a corkboard that read, "We rent rooms by the week." It didn't say that they rented them by the hour, but that was true too. There was another sign with a long and familiar story about giving credit and how that ended badly for everyone.

"I'm looking for the guy in three oh seven."

Without a word, the thin figure turned on his stool and looked at the pegboard behind the counter. His finger flicked a key hooked onto a ring and it rattled. "Not in," he said, his back still to me.

"You know when you last saw him?"

Now he swivelled on the stool and put his cigarette in a half-full ashtray. The smoke rose in a column between us.

"Who wants to know?" His words didn't bend the vertical plume rising to the ceiling, but a few ripples appeared in the line.

I dug around in my pocket, found a card, and passed it over to him.

"Patrick Bird, private investigator, huh?" he read.

I nodded my head.

"We run a clean ship here," he said, contrary to the evidence of the grimy lobby. "And I have to say that private dicks aren't great for business — kicking down doors, rousing up the guests, getting people divorced. No one likes that. I wouldn't be too surprised if you and I haven't met before now."

"It's possible," I conceded, trying to place his wraithlike face in my tired mind.

"You been in here before, then?" He took a long pull from his cigarette and the tip glowed red in the lightless vestibule.

"Once or twice."

"Business or pleasure?"

"Both." My allegiance to truth only went so far.

"So it goes: lots of pleasure here and lots of business." He nodded silently, waiting. He didn't like me, but there must have been so many people who passed his desk every day that he didn't like.

A couple came down the stairs, laughing and goofing, bringing some life into the lobby. She was a loud blond; he was a round man with a thick thatch of waving hair on the top of his round head. She released his hand and stepped toward the desk; closer, she looked more like a girl than a woman, as she stepped between the clerk and me, the fob of a key chain between her finger and thumb at the end of a thick arm. "Here, Dexter, for you."

There was a cloud of something sweet and sickly around her.

He held his palm out, she dropped the key, and his fist closed on it.

The man stepped forward and put a hairy paw on her back at the pinch of her waist and guided her to the aura of light made by the door to the outside. "Let's go, baby," he said, and she squealed with delight at the idea of getting out of the hotel.

I looked at the fob lying in Dexter's open palm: 305 — neighbour to my party.

I took my wallet out of my pocket and thumbed through to find a five-dollar bill. I folded it a few times until it was a square about the size of a matchbook and held it between my knuckles. "You tell me when three oh seven checked in and what his name is?"

Dexter took another pull on the cigarette and stared at a water stain on the ceiling for a minute. He mashed the butt into the ashtray, and with his hand free, reached for the bill and plucked it from my grasp; he unfolded it and laid it flat on the counter, before turning back to where the keys hung. This time, he reached through the fobs into the small grid of mailboxes, to find a card that was stamped with the Edgewater's name on the top, and had a host of letters and numbers in tiny writing in a configuration, that, from where I stood, looking at it upside down, was unintelligible.

He tapped it twice on the counter. "Name is Mickey Doyle, no fixed address. No ID presented, so who knows if that's his name. Checked in on Saturday, July tenth, at two p.m. Room didn't open until three. He took a week to start and paid cash up front. That's what I got for you."

"And what about the room upstairs? Any chance I get a peek into that?"

"No can do. We run a business here. I already helped you more than I should. People got a right to their privacy."

"Fair enough."

I pulled my wallet back out of my pocket and was looking for the right denomination when he spoke up: "Put your money away. I meant what I said about people's privacy. That's why they come here, so they don't have to deal with this bullshit — it's the least we can do for them."

"I hear you." I'd pushed too far, but there was one more thing I was looking for. "You know what time Mickey is coming back this evening?"

"No idea."

"Or what time he went out this afternoon?"

"Listen, buddy," he said, "you spent your money, you got what you paid for, now fuck off."

XII

BUT I WASN'T quite gone yet; I needed a phone. There was one in the lobby, but I didn't fancy airing everything I knew in front of Dexter, who seemed like he was as sharp as he was thin. I drifted toward the opening to the bar and poked my head in; through the haze of smoke a second phone was visible, mounted on the back wall by the loudmouths. No booth: it wouldn't do either. I turned to leave and bumped right into the clerk who had migrated from his perch behind the counter to crowd me.

"I said to get out."

That hadn't been exactly how he'd phrased it the first time, but Dexter wouldn't get an argument from me. I turned to the door and he added, "I don't want to see your face in here again." The five-dollar bill lay face down on the

counter; it was the problem. No one liked to be bought —
and once they'd accepted the payment, the anger followed
fast. Stepping into the sunlight, I flipped the battered hat
onto my head. The Gray Coach terminal was just south of
the hotel. It had a bank of pay phones in an anonymous setting and a public washroom that was cleaner than anything
the Edgewater could offer. Its waiting room had plenty of
windows — the light penetrated through the grime — and
played host to the bustle of commuter traffic; it was a boost
of life after the gloom of the hotel lobby.

The men's room mirror didn't do me any favours; my face
dirty, my head scraped, some dried blood smudged below
my temple. No wonder Dexter had given me the bum's rush.
Even by the Edgewater's standards, I looked rough. I took
the already stained handkerchief out of my pocket, soaked
it in cold water, cleaned the smear off my face, had a go at
tidying up the scrape that was the source, and winced at the
cold water's sharp sting. A bruise emerged from under the
dried blood on my cheekbone. There was nothing I could
do to improve the rip in my jacket, but I brushed off the
dust on my pant leg. Things were improving, but the result
still wasn't pretty. I pulled on the roll of cloth on the hand-
drying machine, looking for a patch of towel that wasn't
too wet or too dirty, but didn't find what I was looking
for. I settled for the best of a bad situation, took a deep
breath, closed my eyes, and dove headfirst into the damp
towel.

Back out in the terminal, I headed to the bank of pay
phones side by side on the far wall, dropped a dime in, and
dialed Sid's number. "Where the hell have you been?" he
asked. "Me and the missus are trying to get out tonight. I
thought you'd never call."

"I had an accident." It was fresh on my mind, having seen what I looked like in the mirror. The smell of institutional soap and mildew from the communal towel stuck in my nostrils.

"Not the company car?"

"I'm alive. No broken bones or anything like that, since you're asking."

"And the car?" I could tell by the way he said it, that he believed the update on my health was a stall before I broke the news to him that the Ford was a writeoff. There was the temptation to string him along.

"Is parked. I was hit while I was crossing Lake Shore."

"On foot?"

"Yeah."

"What were you doing that for?"

"Just trying to catch up with the shoeless guy."

"Did you catch him?"

"Well, no: a car caught me."

"Are you okay?"

I thought he'd never ask. "Yeah. Some bumps and bruises, rips and tears, but I'll make it."

"That's my boy." Always someone's boy; Dexter's angry scowl flashed in my memory.

I provided him with an update of the case, including my trip to the library and the newspaper stories about Belinda's death in the 1951 bank robbery.

"Linklater. Linklater: I knew that name from somewhere. I remember it now. Detective Tong was on the case."

"That's right."

"Well, he was on the case, until Steve Suchan shot him on the Dundas overpass."

"That would have been …"

"Just months later. Tong was shot in early fifty-two."

"Ending the investigation into the bank job on Roncesvalles."

"Maybe. The investigation would go on, but a lot ended when Tong died. He was a good detective."

"So, you know anything else about this?"

"Not off the top of my head — but I'll take a look into it. But listen, I need you to go over to the Linklater house. He's home from work and he wants an update on the case from you."

"Are you serious? Can't you do that?"

"Yeah. He's looking for you to be there around six. Can you make it?"

"Jesus, Sid. I've been going since first thing this morning. My best suit just got ironed by a Lincoln."

"He wants it, and wants to hear it from the investigator on the case. He's paying for it." I didn't say anything. He broke the pause and added, "And so am I. Listen, Linklater is top shelf; it's not one of those divorce jobs, like what you and Vickie got up to last night. Nothing like that. This is the golden goose — we've got to milk it while we can."

"He hasn't even told us everything he knows." Milking a goose didn't sound so fun to me either.

"We don't get to choose our clients. We just get paid by them. Get up there and make nice."

"All right."

"Good man." In the space of the conversation I'd been promoted from his boy to a good man. That's the way it is when you do what others want. "And one other thing. Remember Linklater is paying our bills for some time to come. He wasn't too happy with your performance this morning. Play nice. I know it doesn't come natural to you, but just pretend — see if you can fool someone."

"That arrogant ass —"

"That's exactly the kind of attitude I'm talking about. It gets you in trouble."

"I'm not in any trouble, Sid. This case is breaking. I've been chasing it all day and good things are happening, but if Linklater thinks he bought me when he cut you a cheque, he doesn't understand how it works."

"Well, one of you doesn't."

There was a pause while I stewed.

"Just don't mess this up. You have to know you have a knack for that, to take what's going right and screw it up. I don't know how you do it, but it happens. I'm saying this now, so you can hear it and there's no misunderstanding."

"You don't own me either."

"No, but I sign the cheques." It's never pretty to be reminded of the truth; I remembered Dexter's sudden hostility at the unfolded bill lying blue on the hotel desk between us. And he wasn't so different from me: his lot could be mine, sitting behind a desk in the perpetual dusk, watching the drifters and grifters slow parade to their empty rooms, listening to the guffaws from the bar, and having gumshoes and shakedown artists act all superior as they terrorized the guests. Everybody had a boss: a grindstone, a treadmill.

I sucked in a breath. "I hear you."

"That's all I'm asking. You do what he wants. We'll settle the score at the end of this. Keep track of your hours and expenses. I'll take care of you. Overtime as needed."

"Okay. I'll head up there."

"Good man." But all judgment stung, even the positive.

"I didn't say I'd like it." I knew he didn't like my tone, and that was the small victory I used to justify the retreat to myself.

We said our goodbyes and I dropped the receiver into the cradle of the pay phone and detached myself from the wall I'd been propping up. Ignoring Sid's pleas for urgency, I grabbed a hamburger and a cup of coffee at the counter. The sandwich disappeared fast; the black coffee was too hot to bolt. I stood waiting for it to cool, got impatient, and dropped a creamer in. Blowing a long breath out through pursed lips, the grey masses churned into a mushroom cloud in the paper cup. I slid a dollar bill onto the counter, weighed it down with a quarter, and stepped out into the daylight.

North on Roncesvalles: past the delis and fruit stands; past the Polish church; past the library, dark now, with the newspapers, holding their forgotten secrets, sitting in a pile, the patrons gone home, and Miss Webster riding the streetcar on her solitary commute. I turned onto High Park Boulevard, slowing at the approach of my destination. From across the street the massive stone house stood immobile, its grey slates on the roof, the shutters closed behind the windows, reflecting black nothingness back at me. It was hard to believe any life existed inside that building. But my thoughts were disproven before they could settle; the door opened and Nelson emerged onto the porch. He pulled it shut behind him and started down the steps. I moved forward to meet him as he came through the wrought iron gate to the sidewalk.

"Nelson," I said.

"Mr. Archer?" He'd remembered our conversation from earlier this morning.

"Bird."

"Yeah, I know." He smirked at his joke.

"Out for dinner?"

"I ate mine already. Just now. My dad and stepmom are still at the table if you're wanting to talk to them. Or maybe you're just running some surveillance on the house."

"No. I was invited to provide an update."

"It doesn't look like you found Abbie."

"Not yet. But I have a few leads." I took a shot: "Do you know how your mother died?"

A flicker of emotion crossed his face. I had his attention now. "No, it's not something we talk about."

"Well, that's what your sister's been working on all summer long at the library and out around the city."

"Really? Why wouldn't she tell me?"

"You really don't know."

"I just told you, I didn't." He wasn't happy squeezed between the unknown memories of the past and my questions in the present.

He looked younger than his sister, and younger than he had at his workplace, with the full spotlight of a summer evening shining on him. Gone was the banter about *The Maltese Falcon* and hard-boiled movies. His mouth fought between opening to ask what she'd found, and clamping shut in the face of questions that hurt; he wasn't sure that he wanted to know.

"She was shot in a bank robbery that went wrong up the street here — at the old Bank of Toronto. A man came in for a holdup, and the teller wanted to be a hero and pulled a revolver out of a drawer and tried to shoot the robber and missed. The shot hit your mother. She was dead before she reached the hospital."

"What the — Bank tellers don't have guns. That's bull-shit." He was at that age where anything that didn't fit was bullshit.

He could bluster all he wanted. But they still had guns. Just a year ago in North York there'd been a case where a robber had a shootout that killed a customer trying to be a hero. But it was hard to argue with someone who cared so much that facts didn't matter. "I'm sorry I'm the one that's telling you; that there isn't a better way to hear it."

"No," he said. "I don't believe you. What are you trying to do coming in telling me this crap? I don't believe you."

"Belief isn't the issue. It happened. The truth isn't nego-tiable. I'm about to go into the house and tell your parents what I've discovered. Do you want to come and hear? They know how your mother died. It won't be a surprise to them."

"No. I don't want to know. I don't want to hear." He was working himself up. His voice was wavering and his eyes blinking. He pulled the tail of his shirt up and rubbed them.

"I know it's not easy." Perhaps I'd forced the issue, but he needed to grow up; he needed to know who he was and where he came from. Talking to him was like trying to make an omelette without breaking any eggs.

"Leave me alone." And he was gone, running down the street, and I was back to standing alone across from the great stone house.

Except my nerves were a little rattled now. The conver-sation — it wasn't an interview — hadn't gone down how I'd anticipated. The boy was younger than I'd thought. The way he'd shot off, I wondered if we'd have two runaways and not one. Sid'd like that — he'd double the fee.

XIII

I FACED THE house again, as grey and lifeless as ever, climbed the porch steps, and rang the bell. Footsteps sounded in the hallway and Eileen's wrinkled face appeared in the wedge of light as the door swung open. The half uniform of a frilled apron was too big for her small frame.

"Mr. Bird," she said, very professional and polite, but I could see the twinkle in her eye that laughed at me and united us in the class of those who worked for the Linklaters. I could hear her mocking voice in my head, the unspoken words carried in her expression even before she said, "You've come to help me wash the dishes?"

"Bird here?" came the unseen baritone from down the hall. "Bring him in, Eileen. Bring him in."

"Mr. Linklater's eager to see you, Mr. Bird." She made every comment a light jab. "Come this way, won't you?"

I followed her down the hall, through a plaster archway, and into the dining room, dominated by a huge table of dark wood. The couple sat at the far end. There was a lamp on a sideboard, and some beams of light struggled through thin curtains on the far wall, but a muted shroud hung over the scene. It was hard for me to see the expressions on their faces as my eyes adjusted to the darkness. It had been this way the whole day: running around outside, hustling and cursing in the sun, meeting shadows in the dusk of indoors, and fighting to know what was happening. Jane had her back to me as she faced her husband in conversation; she turned as I entered and I saw a faint spark in her eyes in the half-light.

Linklater stood up and pulled out a chair. "I don't think you've met my wife," he said.

"Yes. I was here this morning and had an opportunity to talk to her then." Jane looked older in the context of dinner with her husband; she aged beside his stiff maturity, holding herself as lady of the table, her tennis whites traded for capris and a floral print.

"Good. Then we can dispense with the introductions and get straight to the update. I spoke to Mr. Cowan at the agency, and he told me you would make time to give us an update. Come and sit down and let us know: Are you any closer to finding Abbie?"

"Would you like some pie, Mr. Bird? Well, not pie, but we have an apple crumble that we are just about to enjoy with coffee. You didn't have an opportunity for coffee when you were here in the morning."

Eileen appeared through a swing door from the butler's pantry, pushing it open with her back, carrying two full plates, with forks lying beside the dessert. The crumble, a mess on bone china, smothered with thick cream, smelled of cinnamon and baked apples, as steam curled up through the darkness. I couldn't remember the last fruit or vegetable I'd eaten; I didn't count the soggy lettuce and mushy tomato that had clung to the greasy burger I'd shot at the bus terminal.

Jane laughed. "I don't hear your voice, but judging from your eyes, I'll take that as a yes. Let me help." She stood and followed Eileen back into the kitchen.

"Jane must like you," said Linklater. "You're getting the royal treatment. I don't know when I last had the same." He looked more relaxed than when I'd met him in the morning. "But enough interruptions. Let's get down to what you've found out about Abbie."

I started a chronological retelling and was just coming to the part where I came back to the house and had my first unsuccessful sighting of Shoeless Joe — although he'd had his boots on at that time — when the saloon door swung again, and Linklater interrupted, "Yes, but your man Cowan told me you'd located Abbie. That you'd laid eyes on her."

"That's right." And to give credit where it was due, I said, "It was Eileen who tipped us off. When she arrived at work this morning, she told us she'd just seen Abbie at the bus stop."

"Is that so?" He turned and looked at the cook, standing silent in the half-light. "You saw Abbie today, Eileen — and you didn't speak to her?"

Eileen looked at the curtained window and said, "I saw her, but she didn't see me. So I just went about my business and didn't bother her."

"She was with a boy wasn't she, Eileen?" asked Jane.

"But, Eileen — Abbie is missing. She's run away."

"Trent," Jane interjected once more, "I don't think Eileen knew at the time. It was when she got to the house and spoke with Mr. Bird and me that she first heard Abbie had disappeared."

Linklater shifted to his thinking face; a vein popped and created a fork in relief on his forehead. His brows knit. "And what did you do, Bird?"

Eileen put a cup of coffee in front of Linklater and another at Jane's empty spot and withdrew wordlessly. Jane placed a mug and a mountain of messy cobbler topped with cream in front of me.

"I was in pursuit. I got to the corner in time to see them — Abbie and the boy she was with — board the King car south. It pulled away before I could catch it —"

"Before you could catch it? You were right there. Were you even running?"

"I told you. I wasn't at the corner. I was approaching from a distance. I saw it, but I didn't catch it. I came back and got my car."

"Let him tell his story," said Jane.

"But who's this boy?" asked Linklater. In the world in which he moved, he probably appeared decisive, a leader who wasn't afraid to demand answers, make tough choices, and take charge, but to me he just seemed impatient.

"I caught up to them at the intersection at Queen in time to see them transfer onto that streetcar and I tailed them to Bellwoods where they got off. While I was parking" — I took a sip of the black coffee and burned my tongue — "they started north up Bellwoods Avenue —"

"Yes, we're getting somewhere now," said Linklater.

"I was on foot, following them up the street and they turned into a property on the right-hand side of the road and just disappeared. When I got there, I followed and discovered it was a church. I went in, but they weren't there. There was some sort of an exorcism or something happening."

"An exorcism? They're Catholic?" exclaimed Linklater, a piece of oatmeal from the crumble clinging to his upper lip. Jane leaned across and wiped his face with her napkin. He frowned at her.

"Well, maybe not an exorcism; but someone was writhing on the ground, speaking a language that didn't sound like any language I'd ever heard, and the priest was standing over him going on about sin."

"What is this, Bird? What are you telling me? Where was Abbie?"

"That's the thing, there was only the one big room in the church, just full of empty pews — and she wasn't there."

His head came up and his glasses caught the light, giving him a strange sightless look. Above the twin reflections that hid his eyes, the telltale vein popped out on his forehead again. "And you left it at that? What did you do, man? This is my daughter we're talking about."

"Trent …" Jane took his hand in hers.

I took advantage of the impasse to shovel a forkful of crumble into my mouth.

His hand had come free from Jane's hold. "I mean, you were there — and you'd seen her go in. And you just turned around and left?" The coffee wasn't the only thing that was hot.

"I spoke with the minister. His name's Ayscough. I explained —"

"Ayscough? I know that name. Does he have a brother called William?"

I took a sip of coffee to wash down the cobbler. "I have no idea. That wasn't what our conversation was about. But I can tell you he had two guys who looked like psych ward orderlies see me off the premises."

"That's the thing about you, Bird, you have a way of rubbing people the wrong way. What's the expression, 'You catch more flies with honey than with vinegar'?"

Jane smirked behind her coffee cup, her eyes finding mine across the table. Sid's plea to be on my best behaviour flickered, and I tamped my worst impulses back down. I didn't know anything about honey or vinegar, but something about Linklater stank enough to attract a swarm of insects. "I'm telling you what I discovered. I found Abbie: at some point in time between ten thirty and eleven this morning she was at St. Matthias Anglican Church on Bellwoods. I was unable to search the building; I was asked to leave, really, shown off the premises. I couldn't follow up further, short of calling the police and after checking with Sid, Mr. Cowan, we determined that you might not want so public an approach."

There was a pause as Linklater formed a steeple with his hands under his chin. "I think we need to go back to this church. If she was there this morning, I'm not willing to give up on that opportunity. I want you to go there with me now, Bird. I know an Ayscough in the city and he's a good man, even if he is a banker. How many Ayscoughs can there be in this town? I think we shouldn't lose time. Let's confront these people immediately. I don't want Abbie out on her own for another night. I think if we go together, and I do the talking this time, then we might make some progress." He rose from the table, and his chair made a screech against the hardwood. Jane also stood.

I shovelled another piece of the crumble, now at a manageable temperature, into my mouth. It was good; there was something beyond just sugar and cinnamon. "What's in the pie that gives it that nutty flavour?" I asked.

"You'd have to ask Eileen," said Jane. "She does the cooking. I'm not sure I could boil an egg these days."

"We're going, man. Come on. Time is of the essence," said Linklater, looking down on me, as I dabbed at my lips with a napkin. "It's probably allspice; she puts it in damn near everything."

"Darling," said Jane, "don't. She's a treasure."

Linklater was trying to lift me from my chair with his glare; I took a last mouthful of the cobbler, savouring the soft mush of cooked apple swimming in its juices. "Delicious," I said, standing up and rubbing my stomach.

"What happened to you?" Jane stepped toward me and raised her hand to the side of my head where the scrape was still raw.

My arm went up defensively and I took a step back.

"You've been hit."

"I had a little run-in with a Lincoln Continental. You should see what it looks like. I didn't get to that part of my story; for another day."

"Let's cut the chatter and get going," said Linklater. He was in the hallway, pushing an arm into a jacket sleeve and picking up an eyeglass case from the side table.

"Are you sure you're okay?" she asked me.

"Jane," Linklater interrupted, again demonstrating the decisiveness that got results, "we don't have time for this.

Bird and I need to get to the church and find out what's happening. Bird, come on. We'll take my car and we can talk on the way." He pushed the front door open and light flooded into the hallway, throwing shadows onto the vestibule tiles.

"It was very nice to see you again, Mrs. Linklater. I hope next time we meet it's under better circumstances." The slipstream of Linklater's exit dragged me through the doorway and onto the path that ringed the house and led to the driveway.

He'd already opened the door on his side of the car. While Jane had a Coupe de Ville, Linklater drove the family vehicle, a sprawling Rambler wagon. I walked to the far door and he leaned across the bench and popped the lock. I opened it and slid inside as he said, "Have to keep the doors locked. This neighbourhood isn't what it once was."

"You get people rummaging around inside here?"

"Overnight, yes. It happened last week." He looked at me as he backed into the street. "Probably kids playing games, but I don't like it. It never feels good to have someone going through your stuff. Leaves you feeling violated."

"Not a good feeling." I was going slowly, letting him take the lead. He'd promised that we would continue my update on the ride to the church, but I wasn't so sure he wanted to know more.

After a long silence, he spoke to my thoughts, saying, "Do you think Abbie is going to be there? I want this whole thing to be solved. I want her home. You may not have noticed it, but I can be impatient. Jane is always telling me that I need to slow down, that sometimes I just need to wait. But not now. Not for Abbie. Not in this situation."

"When we get where we're going, then we'll know."

He scowled at my non-answer and swung the station wagon onto Queen Street. "Come on; help me out. Try a little harder."

Like many people who liked to lead, Linklater needed a follower or two, seconding his thoughts and emotions, a Robin to his Batman, hyping his caped exploits, letting him know they were with him. He'd bought my services — and I would play nice if that was what the job demanded — but he could hire a team of cheerleaders if that's what he wanted.

"What the hell is she doing at this church anyway? It doesn't make any sense to me."

"I never had the opportunity to finish the update. But some of her activities since leaving home indicate what she might have been up to."

"Such as?"

"Such as she's been investigating the death of the first Mrs. Linklater. Belinda." I'd said it now. It hung in the air between us, under the rear-view mirror, above the vinyl-covered bench of the Rambler. He braked for a red light at Dufferin and pursed his lips like he was going to whistle, but he didn't make a sound as he pushed a thin stream of air out.

"That's what this is about?"

"That's what it looks like."

"And what do you know about it?"

"I can tell you what I know, but I think I should be asking that question of you. You could have saved me a lot of time, by levelling from the get-go about some of this history. I spent the day running around the city, finding out about Belinda and a bank robbery that happened over a decade ago and left her dead. You could have saved me that. And it isn't just that you could have saved me the time — it isn't about me — but time is of the essence in these runaway cases. The hours you saved might have gotten me to Abbie sooner."

"Pshaw," he spat. We were gliding smoothly past the asylum on the south side of the street; its outpatients milling on the sidewalk. A man stepped onto the road without looking, and Linklater was forced to break and weave into the centre of the road. He cursed under his breath. "Nothing would've helped you move faster; you've already found my girl. It wasn't even you who found her; it was Eileen, and then you went and let her slip through your fingers. Bird, don't deflect the blame here. Men accept responsibility. We learned that in the war. But you were too young for that."

If this was his idea of honey, the vinegar would be pretty sour, but I remembered what Sid had said and kept my mouth shut, even as my hand clenched on my knee.

"I told your man Sid how rude and impertinent you'd been this morning; I see we're here again. You've made a mess of this job and you're looking to blame someone — and you think that someone is me. There's something you need to understand about our relationship: I'm paying to have Abbie found — and I'll set the tone of this investigation."

"That's fine," I managed. "I can do what I'm told." If he was paying me to tell him what he wanted to hear, I could oblige. A little lie never hurt anyone; except this one seemed to be causing some pain.

"Any more impertinence and I'll be letting Mr. Cowan know, pronto."

"Yes, sir." He had to stop this nonsense; one more jibe would put me over the top. He swung the car onto Bellwoods, and we crept up the side street, looking for a parking spot for his Rambler.

"Good. I'm glad that's clear. Don't worry about Belinda. That's ancient history; we're here to collect Abbie. That's all. Once she's safe and sound with us, none of these old stories will mean much. We'll be bringing her home soon. I'm feeling optimistic." He passed the church and backed into a spot a little farther up the street. "Just let me do the talking. I understand men like Ayscough — at least I understand his brother — and we may need to smooth things over a little — spread some honey on the situation — to get what we need. Especially after you rubbed him the wrong way this morning."

I let it go.

"And if honey doesn't work, I'm not above threats."

XIV

LINKLATER POPPED OUT of the car and stood on the street, surveying the scene; I joined him on the sidewalk.

"Did you lock your door?" he asked.

"No. You're afraid the person who's been breaking into it at your house has followed us down here?"

"Lock it, will you?"

"You want me to lock it?" Fifteen minutes in a car with him had destroyed all my good intentions. He pushed past me to do it himself, and in the process gave me a shove that, had it been any harder, would have demanded a response. I smiled broadly. "No need to get tough — it was locked already — I was just having a little fun."

He yanked on the door handle to make sure. "In case you haven't noticed, Bird, I'm not in the mood for your fun.

Stick to doing what you're told to do and we'll get along better." The sun had dipped and its rays shone straight at the facade of the church, lighting it in a gaudy glow. Without the two Baptist bouncers manhandling me, and the rush of chasing and losing Abbie, I now saw the hall, attached to the building and running perpendicular to the back end. There was a patch of scrappy grass where it ended, and then the rectory, a rambling house faced with brick painted white, shimmering in dusk's horizontal rays. It was like Sid had guessed: there was more than one building the runaways could have disappeared into. "Let's go. And remember, let me do the talking here. You've done your job to trace Abbie, but I'm taking over now. No freelancing. And especially, none of your jokes."

"You're the boss. You lead." But before Linklater could move, the door to the hall opened and a man stepped out into the light. At first, I thought it might be Jesus himself; he had a ginger beard, eyes that glowed in the twilight, and when he saw us, he produced a beatific smile. As he came closer it was clear that his face was rounder, his forehead higher, and his mouth too broad; the lesions on his upper lip made him look more like the leper and less like the Lord. Although he wasn't wearing flowing robes, he did have an ill-fitting poncho draped over his shoulders. He approached, and asked, "Hey, want to hear a joke?"

"Sure," I said. "But first tell us what's going on in there?"

"Did you hear the one about the blind carpenter?" he questioned.

"I told you to let me do the talking," said Linklater. The door opened again, and two old women in clothes that had seen better days stepped into the sunlight. They moved in silence across the grass. "Let's go so we can talk to Ayscough."

The bearded man said, "Wait — you haven't heard the punchline."

"What's happening in there?" I persisted.

The women had approached by now. "Dinner," one of them spat. "And now that dinner is over, the evening service begins."

"Whoa," said the bearded man. "Pushers for Jesus. Too crazy for me." The door was open now and the soup kitchen's patrons filed out.

"The food's good," said the other woman, "but you won't catch me staying for that Jesus junk they get going after the meal. I prefer my God a little quieter."

"Eat and run," said the bearded man. And then: "He picked up his hammer and saw."

I was slow on the uptake, but when I got there, I laughed.

"What's it worth to you?" asked the joker with his hand out. Linklater had already shot me a look of disgust and moved with purpose over to the church's closed door.

I dug in my pocket and gave my new friend a quarter — I'd charge it to the expense account. "Thanks for the joke."

The line of people exiting the hall went their separate ways into the falling dusk now the meal was over. I joined Linklater and he glared at me to let me know he hadn't appreciated my information-gathering mission with the after-dinner crowd. He pulled the door back and the light behind us streamed into the church. Although many of the mission's diners had escaped the service by leaving straight from the hall, it appeared that an even greater number had moved through an interior door into the church. The pews were almost full; the burning incense didn't stop Linklater from wrinkling his nose as he looked for his daughter amongst the urban paupers. Ayscough was up front and the light coming through the stained-glass window danced on his surplice as he spoke: "… the parable of the tax collector from the book of Luke:

"What woman having ten pieces of silver, if she lose one piece, doth not light a candle, and sweep the house, and seek diligently till she find it?

"And when she hath found it, she calleth her friends and her neighbours together, saying, Rejoice with me; for I have found the piece which I had lost.

"Likewise, I say unto you, there is joy in the presence of the angels of God over one sinner that repenteth."

Ayscough looked up from his Bible, squinting at us through the rays of light that flooded the front of the church. "Please, if you have just arrived, come and be seated and join our humble congregation. All are welcome." And returning his gaze to the audience, he continued, "And I am like that woman, sweeping her house, searching for that piece of silver, rummaging through the dust and chaff in the dustpan, so that I too might rejoice when what was lost is found."

"I lost a quarter," screamed a woman sitting near the front. She had a battered velour hat on her head.

"Yes, Marcella," responded Ayscough from his pulpit, "we have all lost something in our lives, and have known the tragedy of that loss. Hold that feeling. Cherish it. Let it bring you closer to God, for that is how the Lord feels when one of us sins; but He feels it in his heart and the pain is a hundredfold. He has lost the love of a child. And when He feels this way, He thinks —"

"Will you give me the quarter I've lost?" shouted Marcella, rising from her seat with one hand holding her flat-topped hat on her head, the other outstretched in supplication.

"— think on the joy that our Lord feels when one of his wandering sheep, lost in the valley, alone on the slopes of the mountain, across the river, and far, far from the comfort of the hearth, comes home again. A storm is approaching; won't you come home again to the hands of the Lord? God loves a repentant sinner; and although it's hard to understand, it's our sins that have given us the key to the kingdom of heaven."

"A quarter, Reverend! Only a quarter!" wailed Marcella. The two bouncers who had given me the quick goodbye earlier in the day approached, and immediately Marcella stood, subservient, and walked with them to disappear behind a screen at the back of the church, to what I assumed must be the hidden door to the adjoining hall.

"The Lord loves a sinner; no matter your crime; no matter what you have done, if you take his name in your mouth and call for help, if you use your voice to ask for support, if you take Jesus as your saviour in your heart and open it for Him, if you confess your sins aloud for the community to hear without shame and in the true spirit of repentance, if you mend your ways, if you walk on the straight and narrow: He will embrace you. He will take you in his arms and lift you through the sky, and lead you to the gates of his kingdom where you may live your everlasting life among the believers. You need not be damned by your sins; you can be saved by them."

Linklater looked at his watch. Patience is a virtue, but it wasn't one of his.

"The road to heaven is paved with bad intentions, with sin, with slips and trips, with evil thoughts, with mistakes. It's not an easy road, but if you are willing to take that first step and confess your crime, to share your sin publicly with the community, and to renounce it, you have begun on that long road, then you have started that arduous journey that will end in everlasting life under the light of the love of our Lord Jesus Christ, in the bosom of the Blessed Virgin Mary, and infused with the Holy Spirit.

"Who among us has not sinned? Who among us has not felt the slow burn of shame at what they have done? Who among us has —"

A man about three pews up from us jumped to his feet. "I'm a sinner. I've shirked and stolen. When the draft came to my door in forty-three, I ran and hid and my brother was taken in my place. He died in Normandy. Since that day I've lived buried beneath my shame."

"And what's your name, sinner?" asked Ayscough.

"I'm Arthur. Arthur the sinner."

"Arthur. Slow down. Come and join us at the front here. Come and join us in the sanctuary. Make way, allow Arthur to pass. Come: you can feel safe here, amongst the flock; the Lord will judge with mercy. Can you feel his grace swirling in our humble temple?" Arthur made the awkward passage across the sharp knees of others in his row, his hands bracing his weight against the seatback of the next pew, before moving down the left side of the church, passing through the shadows that clung to the wall, and emerging beside Ayscough at the altar.

"Arthur, have you sinned?"

"Yes, I have."

"Kneel, Arthur."

Arthur knelt.

"What have you done?"

"I told you. I lied. I denied my name when I was called to serve my country and fight in the war overseas. I ran away —"

"The coward!" whispered Linklater.

"— my little brother was drafted instead of me and was killed on the beaches of Normandy. Since his life ended, I've been tortured by his death, and the only way I can banish the thought of it is to run from it; the only way I've escaped that gnawing beast is to drink. I've been lost in my drunkenness since the day of his death, and who knows what sins I've committed, because all that mattered was to stop the pain tearing at my insides. I've stolen from the pockets of the innocent to feed my thirst; just last week I took fifteen dollars out of the pocket of a man sleeping in the drunk tank. I've lied. I've cheated. I've taken what isn't mine. Just to quell the pain I feel inside."

"But that's no excuse, Arthur."

"No." Tears streamed down his face.

Linklater readjusted his posture.

"But what if I were to provide you with a solution; with the answer to these problems? What if I was able to chase this terror away for good and forever. Few know it, but the Lord Jesus Christ came with a sword in his hand for these purposes. He came as a warrior to split us asunder from our sins with one quick cut of his blade. If you can accept Him into your heart, if you can walk in faith with Him, if you can welcome the balm of his grace as it washes over you, then you can save your soul and take the first steps on the journey to everlasting love."

But before Arthur could throw his soul on the grace of Jesus, a second head popped up out of the congregation. "My name is Stan, and I have sinned."

Ayscough held up a big palm like a cop directing traffic, but Stan blew the light and kept going right through. "I killed a woman. A woman I didn't even know. I shot her down. Right through the heart. I never meant to kill her. It was never my intention. But I did." Stan was a short, round man in an oversized shirt and a pair of baggy pants that hung on an angle, cutting under his paunch. His protuberant eyes bulged further with each new statement. He played to the crowd, turning as he spoke to include the whole congregation. "My father came to this country from Poland. He tried to fit in as best he could. He raised us right. He changed his name from Jankowicz to Johnson; he called me Stanley, not Stanislav, and we thought we fit in and belonged to the city. And that was a dream I had too, but no ..."

Linklater stiffened in the pew beside me.

"Stanley," interrupted Ayscough.

"I did what I could. I met a girl I loved, we married, and she had my son, a beautiful boy, born when I was overseas fighting. And when I came home, our second son was born. I had a job; we had a house. I was so happy until that fateful day. So happy. I've barely seen my family since. Not my beautiful wife, not my boys. I'm sliding —"

"Stanley, we've heard your trials and tribulations many times. The Lord and the congregation have heard your sins and your confessions. You have welcomed the Lord into your soul and accepted His grace and bathed in the power and the glory of His love."

"But the nightmares still —"

"Stanley!" thundered Ayscough. "Do not lose your faith. Consider: we must not doubt the ways of the Lord. We are flesh; we are weak; we have our failings, our sins great and small, but surely the greatest sins are doubt and despair. Find your faith, Stanley. The Lord may test you, the devil may tempt you, but these are not reasons to lose faith. Come to the front. Join Arthur and me here at the altar and welcome

Jesus again. Have faith: the Lord moves in mysterious ways. It is not ours to question; it is for us to believe."

Stanley, chastened, tears rolling from his glassy eyes, pushed his way to the front and threw himself on his knees beside the upstaged Arthur. "I'm a sinner. Worse than a sinner — a doubter. The worst of the worst. Heaven won't have a seat for me. What will I do? What can I do? I've failed my whole life and now I have failed to accept the Lord's grace. I'll never —"

"Stanley," admonished Ayscough in a booming voice that at last silenced the sinner. "Quiet. Bow your head and prepare to pray with me." Ayscough dropped to his knees, creating the tableau of the man of God between the two criminals — some stigmata and a few centurions and everything would be complete. He began to pray: "Hear us o' Lord from heaven, your dwelling place, and bend your ears to our pleas. We are sinners. We are men who have transgressed your sacred laws. We are those who have done wrong in the eyes of heaven; we are those who have killed and robbed. And dear Lord, we are those who have lost hope and succumbed to doubt. But today, on this day, as we kneel before you and confess our sins to you and the congregation gathered before you, we submit to your judgment and your grace; we beseech you to look down upon us and to share your love, your wisdom and omniscience, your beneficence and care. We put our lives in your hands and await your grace. Amen."

The three men remained motionless at the front of the church; the dipping sun had dropped and the light from the stained-glass windows had risen to plaster its psychedelia above them on the back wall. A moan came from one of the three shrouded figures. There was a movement and Arthur tumbled from his knees and rolled onto the floor where he lay still. The moan came again.

Ayscough rose and looked out at the congregation. "Thank you for joining us today, and thank you for witnessing our confessions. Through faith in the Lord and the strength of the community, we will save souls one at a time, to fill the Kingdom of Heaven with the lost and forgotten of this world. Amen."

The echo of an "Amen" was murmured back, and then the house lights went up and the motley crowd began to shuffle past Linklater and me to the door.

"Jesus Christ," he whispered. "What the hell was that?"

XV

THE CHURCHGOERS WERE up from their pews and moving past us, out the door into the golden dusk. Linklater and I, rather than fighting the stream of people, waited for the crowd to pass, and then rose to approach the altar. As we stood, Linklater gave me the reminder: "Let me handle this." He led the way to where the preacher stood talking to his two attendants. "Minister Ayscough?"

Now that we were closer, and Ayscough and Linklater stood together in the glow of the church, I saw my earlier impression had been correct — the men looked remarkably similar. They both wore square-framed eyeglasses; they both parted hair of a mousy colour on the right side and had a tidy sweep of it come across their brows. Ayscough's nose was longer and thinner; Linklater's face was fuller, better fed. They faced one another across the altar, each believing in their own internal power, poised to have some sort of mental — or in Ayscough's case, perhaps spiritual — arm wrestle. Linklater didn't need to tell me he'd take the lead; I was only too happy to sit back and watch the sparring.

The minister stood motionless, looking at Linklater, waiting for a further question, but offering nothing at the calling of his name. My client was forced to continue; it was good to see unease cloud his brow. "My name's Trent Linklater, and this is a private investigator whom I've hired, Patrick Bird. My daughter, a sixteen-year-old girl, has run away from home and we're trying to locate her. Bird here" — he made a vague gesture in my direction as if he were reluctant to acknowledge me — "let me know that he followed her to this church earlier in the day ..." He trailed off weakly without managing to punch a question into his opening statement; he was an engineer, not a courtroom lawyer.

Ayscough relented and deigned to help him out. "Yes, I met Mr. Bird earlier today."

"I have to ask you, Minister Ayscough, have you seen my daughter? Her name is Abigail — Abbie. You must be able, as a man of God, to understand a father's concern."

"I hear your concern, Mr. Linklater, and appreciate your distress, my challenge, earlier today when I first met Mr. Bird" — he didn't bother to look in my direction — "and again now, is that I run a church — I minister to the souls of my flock — and while I appreciate that you're having a family crisis, your crisis is worldly. My work transcends that — and when it's interrupted, when I have people barging in the door and making demands, it breaks my communion with the grace of the Holy Spirit; it puts the souls of these poor sinners at risk. To paraphrase: 'What would it profit me if I were to find your daughter and lose a soul from my flock?'"

The vein on Linklater's forehead made an appearance and throbbed for a second before he said, "I appreciate that. And that, I may say, is why we waited until your ..." he fumbled for a word, before giving up and saying, "service was finished before approaching you with our request for help. Have you seen my daughter?" He put a hand in his pocket, came up empty, and turned to look at me. "Bird, do you have the picture of Abbie?"

I produced the photo and handed it to Linklater as if I needed a go-between for my interactions with Ayscough.

"Here she is," said Linklater, passing the photo on. "Have you seen her?"

The minister held the picture up before his face, his eyes magnified behind his thick glasses. He held his gaze steady on the photo, making us wait, before pronouncing, "Abbie. Is that her name? Yes, I know Abbie." He turned to one of his lackeys and said, "Can you please go and get Paul and tell him he's needed in the church." The lackey left and Ayscough turned back to us. "Paul's my son. I believe your daughter, Abbie, is a friend of his. I've seen the two together this past week. I trust he'll be able to answer your questions and help you with your inquiry."

I was burning with humiliation as these two conspired to find an easy solution where I had failed. A better man might have been satisfied that Abbie was safe and the mystery was being resolved. But not me. There was the temptation to interject, to derail the conversation, to lay the crowbar across the tracks and watch the train come a cropper, but I held my tongue and let them proceed with their solution-making.

Ayscough turned to Linklater. "Paul'll be here in a minute and I'm sure he can solve your problems. I have further work to do tonight, so if you'll please excuse me." And without waiting for our answer, he swept his surplice around him and sailed through the doorway to the hall.

Linklater looked over at me with a sneer, showing me the ease with which he had solved the problem. He was as childish as me; busy scoring points off his daughter's disappearance — the thought boosted my motivation to restrain my self-destructive forces. The remaining orderly detached himself from our group, wandering the church, tidying up from the service.

"We're almost there," said Linklater, cowed into a whisper by the surroundings. "Abbie will be with us in a second."

I'd been down this road a couple of times already — so close and yet not close enough.

Paul, still in his bright white cardigan, appeared in the doorway to the multipurpose room where dinner had been served. He stepped through, appearing nervous and agitated as he came forward, his eyes searching our faces. He made the right decision and addressed himself to Linklater. "Good evening. My father said you wanted to talk to me."

"That's right," said Linklater, in his element as he prepared to bully the boy. "My name's Linklater, and this is Bird." He said my name like he was scraping something off his shoe. "We understand that you've seen my daughter, Abbie. She's been missing from home for the past — well we're getting on three days now."

"You're Abbie's dad, then?" the boy said, mixing respect with caution.

"I am. And I'm asking the questions. Bird" — he indicated me with a nod of his head — "trailed you from

Roncesvalles to this church earlier today. He saw you with Abbie — so don't bother to deny it. Just tell us where to find her now."

"She's in Belleville, sir. I put her on the train this afternoon — she took the three o'clock milk run."

There it was. Linklater had gotten what he wanted, and it threw him a little off balance. "Belleville? What's she doing there? I don't understand?"

"She said she needed to see her grandmother."

"Yes. That's my mother," muttered Linklater, trying to catch up with the turns that the conversation had taken. "But why would she …?" he made the mistake of thinking out loud.

"She said she —" began Paul.

"It's fine. We know where she is; that should be enough for now. You say you put her on the train?"

"I took her to the station."

"Did her grandmother know she was coming?"

"Abbie phoned ahead if that's what you're asking. I wasn't part of that call, but that's what I understood."

"And what did her grandmother say?" Ayscough was veering into uncharted territory here.

"Abbie used the phone in the office and the door was shut. I knew she wanted privacy. From what she told me, her nanna was happy to have a visit."

Linklater's face did not share the joy. "Has Abbie stayed here, at the rectory, the last two nights?" I glanced at Linklater, surprised at the question, and took the full glare of his gaze, magnified through the thick lenses of his glasses, for having the gall to look.

The young boy in the cardigan said, "The rectory's pretty large, and we have always taken in those in need. There's a women's dormitory — just a room with two sets of bunk beds — and so, with my father's permission, a space was found for Abbie. There was nothing …" his voice trailed off as he too felt Linklater's glare. Luckily for him, it was directed at me. No one wanted to know too many details about young couple's sleeping arrangements.

"Earlier today —" I began, wanting to get around to the sightings I'd had of him and Mickey Doyle and the mystery woman with the pixie cut.

"Enough." Linklater cut me off. "We know where Abbie is, and everything else, frankly, is a waste of time. 'Vanity,' as the Bible has it. 'All is vanity,' isn't that what it says about the trifles of this world?" He fumbled in his bluster, and I didn't fight it. There was enough vanity to go around.

He turned to Paul. "Thank you for your time, young man. We won't bother you further. We know where Abbie is now — and can follow up on that. I'll call Mother and make sure she has arrived safely and then we'll have to arrange for her return home." He raised his eyes to the roof as if looking for answers there. "Come, Bird, our work is done." If he had a surplice to swirl, he would have swirled it too; as it was, he turned sharply and strode back down the centre aisle, leaving me to follow.

Paul stood beside me; I had a couple of questions I wanted to get in before Linklater dragged me in his wake. "I take it from what you said about the room at the rectory that you're not involved with the girl — fair enough — but then tell me what she's doing here?" I knew — we'd seen Stanley's confession — but I wanted him to say it.

Linklater turned and shouted down the length of the church, "Bird!"

The violence of his voice caught Paul by surprise, and he was silenced before the first word could escape his open mouth.

"We're going now, and unless you plan on walking back, you should come. Now."

I looked at Paul, questions still in my mind, angry at being publicly chastened again. But what did I care? She wasn't my daughter, and it wasn't my closet that had the skeletons dangling from the hangers. Linklater could do what he wanted: he could bring her home and see if she stayed; he could lock her in her room like you might a little child and see how that went. It was his family.

"Thanks for your help," I said to the boy, and turned and trailed Linklater out of the church.

He held the door for me to make sure I crossed the threshold without another question. He, too, was glowering with anger; we weren't much company for one another, both harbouring our resentment. He was mad enough to be polite and opened the passenger door for me before his own. Once in the car, he revved the engine with adolescent petulance before putting the Rambler into gear. We drove north on Bellwoods. He couldn't maintain the silence and came out with: "Which part of 'Let me do the talking,' don't you understand?"

The gloves were off now. "Call me crazy, but I'm trying to solve the problem that we've got here: Where is your daughter? And more importantly, what's going on in her world that would cause her to want to run away?"

"That's what you don't understand, Bird: We know where Abbie is. She's at my mother's house in Belleville. The job is done. Everything else is window dressing. It's just a question of making a call and checking in with Mother, and once we've confirmed that Abbie's there, I'll send you to drive her back. You can leave tonight, pick her up first thing tomorrow morning, and we'll have her home in time for a late breakfast. I'd say that counts as success."

I stifled my challenge; so many "but"s and "if"s and "why"s. Was Abbie in Belleville? Had Paul been telling the truth? Had Abbie been telling him the truth about where she was going? All day I'd been chasing this girl and she'd been just out of reach; Linklater had asked one question and now assumed he'd solved the whole puzzle. We were near the goal, but it didn't mean we had the prize yet. I thought I'd checked my soul at the door a long time ago — playing peekaboo with a camera in hotel rooms for six months could do that to you. But something beyond my dislike of Linklater had shifted and made me buckle at the idea of taking this long ride to Belleville and playing the chauffeur on the way home. This case had pushed me up the mountain to the moral high ground and suddenly truth and understanding seemed important. Or maybe it was just my reaction to Linklater. Maybe he was right and the rest, the details, the history, the first wife dead in the bank robbery gone wrong, Stanley in Ayscough's church, and Mickey Doyle lurking in the background were all just window dressing.

I was working hard to talk myself out of any emotional involvement in the case as we travelled west across Dundas, but was having a tough time of it. Hadn't we just witnessed Stanley Johnson, the bank teller who'd shot Belinda, confessing his sins? And if we'd heard it, and Abbie had been there for three days, she'd heard it too. The church was the living library for the research she'd been doing all summer, and it was in these last days that the narrative had coalesced and the revelation had thrust her from her family home. I'd planned to use the homeward journey to ask Linklater about Stanley and get his thoughts on the penitent sinner, but our current impasse made conversation impossible. This was the cold fish I was dealing with, who could sit in his pew and listen to the story of his first wife's death and not shift an inch.

He stopped at a red light and decided to give me a little advice: "You see how I was patient with Ayscough, let him think he was the one who was running that show, that's the kind of thing you can learn from, Bird. As I said earlier: you can catch more flies with honey than vinegar. You're young: you have time. I'll be sure to tell Sid that you're proving to be an apt pupil."

Maybe I did care after all, because I let this go without comment, without telling him to go fuck himself and get his daughter himself; because as long as I stayed silent, as long as I didn't fall for the bait being dangled in front of me, as long as I waited until this car ride was over, I'd have a 150-mile trip with Abbie tomorrow morning — and I might get a chance to ask her some questions on that journey and find out a thing or two yet about what had been happening in her messed-up family for the last sixteen years. I nodded my head at the idea, and Linklater, seeing the movement in his peripheral vision, assumed I was signalling my agreement.

"That's right, Bird," he said. "I knew we could get along."

XVI

WE DROVE BACK to the big grey house without further conversation. I locked the door of the Rambler without being asked — no more fun and games. Darkness had fallen, and in a reversal of the day, the light from the house escaped through the transom above the front door and remained crowded in a soft glow on the porch. Linklater walked through it and used his key to let himself into the house. On hearing our entrance, Mrs. Linklater came down the stairs. She'd changed into some sort of a lounging robe cinched at the waist with a belt.

She asked, "Did you find her? Is Abbie home?" And sensing our mood, her face fell. "No luck?"

"No," said Linklater, "we got good information. Abbie took the train to Belleville to go and see Mabel this afternoon."

"But why?" Jane asked from the bottom step of the stairs, flushed and querulous. It was good to hear her ask the questions in my mind.

"I am going to call Mother now, before it gets too late, and send Mr. Bird to pick Abbie up. He can drive to Belleville tonight, find somewhere to stay, and bring her home in the morning."

"Do you really think she's there?" asked Mrs. Linklater, continuing as my proxy.

He squinted at his wife through his glasses, pushing them up his nose to the top of the bridge, and said stiffly, "I have no reason to disbelieve the boy who told me this information. A simple phone call to Mother will answer these questions; just give me a minute to make it."

"Yes, I suppose so." She sounded as unconvinced as I was.

"I'll call now."

Linklater climbed the stairs — the same stairs he'd led me up twelve hours earlier, to see the empty and impersonal bedroom belonging to his daughter. Left with me, Jane said, "It's been a long day. You must be tired, Mr. Bird. Unfortunately, Eileen's gone for the night — or I'd ask her to fix you something with your drive ahead of you. Still, I used to be pretty handy in the kitchen; can I offer you anything before your drive?"

"I'm fine," I said, curtly, still smarting from the conflict with her husband.

"Won't you sit down?" She gestured at the L-shaped couch. I was conscious of my ripped jacket and a day's worth of dirt and grime dusting it and the seat of my pants, but before I could answer that I was fine standing, she came closer and lowered her voice. "But what do you think? Do you think Abbie really went to her grandmother's?"

She was in my space, but I resisted the impulse to step back. I was tired of being pushed around by this family. I could feel the heat from her and smell a not unpleasant sweetness on her breath. "That's what the boy she was with today told us."

"A boyfriend?"

"I don't think so — but we were in such a rush we didn't get the chance to ask him too many questions."

"And the abortion?" It startled me to remember that was what Mrs. Linklater had told me in the morning; I'd long since discarded the idea, as Lena had suggested, as the outlandish lie of a teenager to back her mother off.

"That's what she told you?" I looked into Jane's pale grey eyes, more luminous than the heavy stones of the house; there was a dangerous gleam that shone in them. As she leaned toward me, I saw my parabolic reflection in the sheen; I was attracted even as a tremor of fear warned me away.

"Yes," she said very low.

I pulled my gaze away and looked at the surface of the dining-room table in the dark of the next room; a safe shimmer of light smeared its surface. "I talked to her friend, Lena, and she doesn't believe Abbie's pregnant."

Jane pulled her brows together and the lids slipped down over the luminous eyes. "And you believe Lena over what I told you."

"I think both might be true. Abbie could have been setting you up — to try to explain her disappearance before it happened."

She paused to consider, her face very still. Linklater's muffled voice drifted down the stairs from the floor above.

"Did she specifically tell you that she was pregnant?" I asked.

"Not in so many words. You know the way teenagers talk. It was all very obscure. A friend of hers was in trouble. Her friend needed help. She had to do something that might seem wrong, but it had to be done — there was no choice — she wanted to do it safely. There was a break between the letter of the law and the moral path and she was looking for some way to negotiate that. How to reconcile. Oh — I don't know. It was vague — something like that and I understood it to mean something very specific. Maybe I was wrong. It seemed clear to me that the friend was her; it seemed that the moral problem she was describing ... well, I was a sixteen-year-old girl once, and that's the biggest moral problem you could have." She paused. "Not that I had that problem."

"So, she never said 'abortion.'"

"Goodness, no. Now you're going to put it on me: like it's where my mind is, not Abbie's. Mr. Bird, you do have a way of tying one in knots. No wonder Trent gets frustrated with you." She tempered her insult with a smile from her bright eyes. Although she was the stepmother of sixteen-year-old twins and the mistress of this mansion, directing cooks and gardeners — even private investigators — her smile shifted the timelines and she aged backward, projecting a sense of youth and innocence.

Somehow in telling me I'd tied her in knots, I'd been manoeuvred back a step and was playing defence, like I'd been bullying her and pushed too hard and now it was my turn to apologize. It was a relief to have retreated out of her aura. "I have to say, Mrs. Linklater, with respect, that this case has been a little confusing; I'm not sure people are telling me the truth. I get a different story from every person I talk to." I could put up defensive barricades too.

"I haven't lied to you yet," she said deliberately, putting her hand out. I felt the heat jump from her to me before her fingers wrapped around the inside of my elbow.

"That's good," I said as she led me to the wine-coloured couch, "but there's a hole in this case; it's the death of the first Mrs. Linklater. No one talks about it; no one seems to know about it, and that's where the answer to this mystery lies."

She released my hand at those words, shook her head twice, turned to look at me, and lowered herself to the couch. I felt obliged to join her, even though I wasn't sure I wanted to.

"Belinda? But that was so long ago. Ages now."

"It is. But sometimes the wounds fester and time doesn't heal and it —"

"So, you think this trouble Abbie's in — if she's in any trouble — has to do with Belinda?"

"I do. What can you tell me about her?"

"I'm pretty sure her maiden name was Greene. She was a war bride. Trent met her when he was overseas and she came back with him after the war. I worked for them. I've told you that already. But that —"

Jane was interrupted by the sound of Trent clumping down the stairs. She jumped up from the couch and smoothed her lounging robe. I stood also and we turned to meet her husband as he appeared in the open archway.

"I spoke to Mother, and Abbie arrived safely. They're doing well. Everything's good. Everyone's safe."

"Thank God for that," said Jane. She went and stood with her husband and, paired with him in the matrimonial pose, she regained some of his years and manner.

"So, Bird, I've arranged with Mother that you'll pick up Abbie in the morning as early as possible. I said you'd be there around seven and then you're back here in the city close after nine. I'd like to get this tidied up as soon as we can. I don't believe in letting the grass grow."

"Did you talk to Abbie?" I asked.

He hesitated. "Yes. I did speak to her. She is —"

"Where I'm going with my question" — I cut him off — "is that I'd like to know that she's going to be a willing passenger in the car. I can't drive for two and a half hours on a highway with someone who wants to jump. It isn't safe, and it isn't doable in a one-man operation."

"Yes, Bird. Abbie's ready to come home. She apologized for the trouble she's caused; she understands that this is her home and where she should be. She won't cause you any grief. I told her about the seven o'clock start time and she'll be ready to go."

"Okay."

"This has been a long day for you, Mr. Bird," said Mrs. Linklater. "We appreciate what you're doing to bring our girl home." She put her arm around her husband's shoulders and the two stood together united against the trials of parenthood.

I picked up my hat and Linklater stepped forward. "What with gas and lodgings and a meal on the way, I'll provide you some more expense money." He peeled some bills from his wallet and put them into my hand. They found a home in my pocket and it reminded me of my interaction with Dexter at the Edgewater earlier that evening; the power of money, the subservience of the underling, the incoherent shame of taking payment: the food chain of life.

I took some steps toward the door and said, "I expect we'll be meeting up at about nine tomorrow morning ..."

"With Abbie — Abbie's homecoming!" sparkled Mrs. Linklater.

"Expect?" said Linklater. "We will."

"Bye, then." My hand was on the doorknob.

"Good luck," said Jane as I passed across the threshold. I didn't hear if Linklater added anything more because I was a little stuck on her parting words wishing me luck in an assignment that seemed so straightforward that none would be needed. The door closed behind me and I stood on the porch in the fresh air and exhaled a long breath, glad to be free of the claustrophobia of the house.

The car was where I'd left it, parked out front of the library from my second trip there. The meter had run out hours ago, but the city didn't ticket after rush hour. I popped the trunk and looked for the small grip with my morning freshen-up kit: a spare shirt and underpants, a toothbrush, comb, and socks, for days like today, when I didn't make it home. The street light caught the boots and jacket I'd inherited from Mickey Doyle that I'd forgotten all about.

I pulled them out from under the shadow of the lid and took another look at their greasy tongue under the street lamp and there it was, the same as it'd been before, the faded and smudged cobbler's stamp. But this time, with a little more information, the store name didn't look like ELEGANT or MELVILLES; now I could read it: BELLEVILLE SHOE AND BOOTS. The roads were converging.

I drove south on Roncesvalles, planning to swing onto King and catch the expressway from Jameson. But as I approached the corner, I gave in to my craving for one more cup of coffee for the road. Just before the streetcar depot, I pulled over and parked the car; I walked the last few steps, past the Edgewater, to the bus terminal, where the take-out counter was laying out slop long after the dinner hour had passed. The menu was written in chalk above the open kitchen, and I was debating whether I wanted fries with the coffee when I heard a familiar voice ordering a club sandwich and a cola. It was Dexter, sitting on a stool at the counter, looking as at home in the bus station as he did on his perch at the Edgewater. I turned away, pulled down my hat, and forgot all about the coffee I thought I'd needed. If Dexter was here, he wasn't next door, and that was my break. I pushed back out onto the street where the hot air of the day lingered, unwilling to call it a night. The same went for me: I hurried up the hotel's front steps and into the empty lobby.

XVII

AS I PASSED through the lobby, I could hear the party in the bar getting started as the night wore on; the drunks were working themselves up to the loud and proud crescendo of inebriation, before the anticlimax of the crash. I took the first steps up the staircase at the back of the lobby, and a screech from a streetcar shuttling in the yard behind the hotel came through the open window as it searched for a resting spot for the night. The tram's overhead arms jostled on the wires and a spark lit an empty patch of darkness. I turned the corner to the next flight of stairs, spinning around the short runs of five steps, the ninety-degree turns, the vacuous landings, the windows out onto the shuttle yard, the cracked linoleum tiles, before emerging on the third floor. I'd been in the Edgewater plenty, but tonight it looked its seediest:

scuff marks on the tired paint job as if the guests had been climbing the walls — maybe they had — the dull shadows surrounding a dead sconce, the faded colours of the once bright runner, the scars of cigarette burns. I counted up the doors, in a low-rent repetition of the night before: 301, 303, 305. And 307.

I rapped on the panel with my fist and strained to hear some sounds: the creak of bedsprings, the thud of footsteps, and the squeak of hinges grinding without oil. But the door didn't move.

"Hi, there." It was the blond I'd seen leaving the Edgewater earlier in the evening with her friend. "I think you got the wrong door. I'm in 305."

My face must have shown my surprise.

"Lots come looking for me." When she smiled, her teeth showed white against the gaudy circle of her lips.

"I'm looking for my friend Mickey, in three oh seven."

"Really?" Her eyes assessed me. "I wouldn't've thought he had too many friends. He was —"

"You've met him?"

"Oh." Her voice sounded distant. "I've met plenty like him."

When it didn't sound like she was going to say anything more, I reached for the handle. "I'd be careful. He's got a gun in there."

And I had a single bullet wrapped in a note in my pocket. My hand hovered over the knob, and I waited, trying to figure out what was going on. "You saw it?"

"Sure, I saw it. You think I'm lying?" She took a step through the doorway and joined me in the hall outside 307. "It was on the dresser when I was in there."

"When was that?"

She thought for a while, her bored eyes looking even more bored when she concentrated.

"Yesterday or the day before. Must have been the day before. Yeah, the day before. But he didn't use it or anything, didn't even seem to know it was there. It was just lying on top of the dresser, like he didn't care who saw it and who didn't. Not that he had too many visitors."

I rapped on the door for a second time.

"I don't think he's in there now," she said and reached for my wrist. "You want a date?"

"I need to talk to him."

"Really? You'd rather talk to him, than me? Have it your way then." She said that, but closed the distance between us all the same. "Someone was in there with him earlier. People are always coming and going in this place. But that was before. It's been pretty quiet since then."

"When was that?"

"Hey, what's your name? Don't you like it quiet?"

"Was it a man or a woman?"

"Before? I don't know. I been busy too. But he's not in. You haven't told me your name yet."

I grabbed the handle and twisted the knob. The mechanism clicked as it turned. The door swung inward; Doyle lay on the bed, fully clothed down to the socks on his feet. There was a pillow over his face. The air was hot and stale and the sharp smell of alcohol welcomed us to the room. Three bottles of rye stood in a tidy row on the dresser, two empty and the third had a couple of inches left, but the gun the girl had told me about was nowhere to be seen. My first thought was Doyle was sleeping off a drunk. But no — the utter stillness of death was in the air. I swore, a short sharp syllable into the hush, and it was swallowed by the silence.

Doyle's unmoving rest, undisturbed by the drinker's raspy breathing, was the kind of peace only death can bring.

I crossed through the door frame and the girl, staying where she was, said, "Drunks," with as much scorn as she could muster. The knot holding her plaid shirt in place had come undone — by design or accident, I didn't know — and it hung open.

"He's more than drunk," I said, approaching the body. "You should be glad you don't know my name. Go back to your room and shut the door and make like you never met me." I took two steps across the room to the bed. I lifted the pillow off the head. It was the same face I'd already seen a couple of times that day. The same but different. Shoeless Joe, Mickey Doyle — call him what you want — still hadn't moved. The expression wasn't pretty: the good looks and charm were gone, replaced by an explosion of blood marring the open right eye and the wide gaping mouth stretching for a last breath that wasn't coming. I put a hand on his chest and felt the absence of life. I put a finger in the mouth and swept the inside of the throat, but there wasn't any obstruction there. The only thing between Doyle and his next breath had been the pillow I'd cast aside. And when I looked at it now, I saw the soft, fading outlines of handprints on the rectangular bolster.

"You got a mirror in that bag of yours?" I already knew what it would tell me.

She nodded, her face slackening to its natural state of exhaustion now that the need to impress had passed; the muscles that had held her smile in place gave up and the frown of her resting face prevailed. I put out a hand and she dropped a round compact into it. I flipped it open and held the mirror against Doyle's mouth. Nothing. Nor the nose — not the faintest mist to darken the glass. I tossed it back to the girl, put a hand on his chest, and felt again where life was not. The body wasn't as cold or stiff as it would become, but the night was warm, and I wasn't a coroner. I wished I'd never opened that closed door, that I'd never seen Dexter in the bus station, that I had never stopped for a coffee on the way out of town. But I had.

It sounded like a sigh going backwards as I sucked in some air in Doyle's stuffy room. I took a look around, wondering what I might find; but it was as devoid of life as the body on the bed. The liquor bottles on the dresser seemed to be the sum total of what he'd brought with him when he'd moved into the Edgewater. I had almost as many of his possessions in the trunk of the car as he had here. There were some stubs in the ashtray and a crushed package of Export A in the wastepaper bin; a grease-stained paper bag suggested he'd wolfed some takeout fries from the bus station for dinner. Three rumpled shirts hung in the closet, a second grimy sports jacket lay folded over the back of the room's only chair. I frisked the pockets — nothing but the room key — and then tried the pants the dead man wore.

"Gross." She'd put her compact away, but ignored my advice to get to her room.

I extracted a wallet out of Doyle's back pocket. There were two two-dollar and three one-dollar bills, a driver's licence in the name of Michael Doyle, and then, in a hidden pocket, between where the bills lay lengthwise and the slot for the ID cards, my fingers found an old black-and-white photo. It was a snapshot of a teenage girl leaning back against a split-rail fence, a galvanized pail in her hand, a plaid shirt on her back, a pair of jean cut-offs above dirty knees, and her hair blowing in the wind. It was Jane Linklater, younger, but just as pretty. Everybody knew everybody in this little tangle.

"What are you doing?" I ignored the girl at the door and transferred the picture to my inside pocket. Leaning over the bed, the smell of death cut through the haze of alcohol fumes and I saw myself through the dead man's eyes: picking through the corpse's pockets while his neighbour looked on disgusted.

Conscious of her eyes on me, I turned back to her. She had reknotted her shirt across her chest. "Get to your room." My mind raced with the different ways this case was running sideways.

This time she moved two steps back into the hallway, before pausing and saying, "Aren't you coming to see me, then?" She was as afraid as I was.

"I'm finishing up here and clearing out. Are you sure you saw a gun?" I was pulling out the empty drawers of the dresser. The top one held some socks and underwear. The second, some undershirts, but no matter how hard I fumbled in the clothing, I couldn't conjure up the hard steel. "Any minute now, I'm going to make myself scarce. I'll call this in" — my eyes flicked at the body on the bed — "to the police from the bus terminal. If you don't want to be here when they get here, get out now; it won't take them long."

"Take me with you?"

Nothing in this world was clean. I stooped to scan the linoleum under the bed. "No, I can't. I have things I need to do."

"I can help." All her poses, the leer of love, the easy laugh, the cynical banter, and the bored look, faded as something real pooled in her eyes. I kept moving, standing on my tip-toes to scan the top shelf in the closet; someone could show up in the hall at any moment.

"Just disappear for a bit and this'll blow over fast enough. No one's going to care too much about another dead grifter in this place."

"You seem to." I don't know if my crack about the hotel had touched a nerve; it was her home, after all. Something shifted; her posture changed and she grew taller in the door frame as if the damsel in distress and the tear in the eye that had seemed so real just a second before had been an act in the name of self-protection, and once that failed she was moving on to the next pose until she found one that worked.

She ran the back of her wrist across her face and smeared her eyeliner. "Have it that way then, you louse." She turned and stalked the few steps to her room. The door slammed behind her.

I put the pillow back over Mickey's face, the way it had been when I found him. I wiped the wallet clean of my prints, and then the doorknob, and the handles on the dresser. The Gideons Bible on the bed table was as void of meaning as everything else in the room. Using my shirttail as a mitten, I pulled the door shut behind me and stepped into the hall. I hit the fire exit at the south end of the building and slipped down the stairs two at a time. I came out in an alley that separated the hotel from the bus station. The air had begun to cool and it felt good against my forehead after the furnace of the third floor.

XVIII

THE FIRE DOOR opened into a pockmarked alley that doubled as a loading bay for the station. Diesel fumes and the sweeping arc of a bus pulling into its spot gave me a rude welcome. I stuck my neck around the corner before sliding through the shadows and onto the sidewalk. A streetcar pulled up, a magical box of colour and light moving through the night streets, and I retreated from its glow. Peering through the glass panel of the terminal doors, I saw Dexter inside, still on his dinner break, sitting at the counter, rolling his empty pop can onto a greasy plate. My eternity up in 307, inexplicably compressed in the springs and coils of time, as I said goodbye to Mickey Doyle and hello to the girl next door, had passed in less than half an hour. As Dexter pulled his wallet out of his back pocket, I'd already changed my plans; there was no way I could call in the body with the clerk standing beside me paying for his dinner.

I came out onto the sidewalk, found the car parked half a block up, and in a rush of actions without thought, I found myself looking at a half moon floating on its back in the night sky as I sped northeast up the banked curves of the Don Valley Parkway. The night air whistled through the open window. The radio played a raucous song full of noise and yelling, something about Matty and Hattie and some nonsense about a thing they saw with two big horns and a woolly jaw. It jangled on my nerves. I didn't want to think about anything I'd seen. My finger jabbed at the console and changed the station as I searched for something more my speed. Next up was one of those pouty British singers telling me that he was coming back next week because he was on loser street, and it cut too close to home; my finger pressed the next button and the music ended abruptly; there was just the hum of the other cars on the road and the high-pitched whine of the wind being sheared by the open window.

The gas meter read low as the lights from the city started to fade. I pulled off the highway where it ended at Lawrence and cruised through the emerging suburbia, a silent construction site of new townhouses half built, piles of dirt and heavy machinery quiet in the silver light, before finding a filling station. The gas jockey appeared out of the night to fill the tank. The numbers rolled by on the pump, counting up and up the way numbers do. I gave the clerk a bill and he went inside the lighted office for change. Doyle was gone: he hadn't answered my questions; all I'd found was a warm body growing colder, a lost life, and a picture of Jane Linklater.

At the pay phone, my finger fed a thin dime into the slot; it clinked as it dropped into the machine and the tone droned in my ear. The clicks of the rotary dial echoed, a bell rang twice somewhere in the ether, and sleepy words crackled along the line: "Toronto Police Department — Eleventh Division."

I was about to say they should check Room 307 at the Edgewater — that there was someone there who wasn't doing too well. And then something tightened inside. There was the picture of Jane. There was the need for discretion. There was Sid, who I hadn't checked in with. Doyle was dead. There was nothing I could do to bring him back. My breath bounced against the handkerchief held over the receiver as I stood, wordless, and I had the unpleasant sensation of smelling my own breath. A dead drifter in a flophouse wouldn't mean much to anyone. He'd be found soon enough.

"Anyone there? Hello? Speak up," the voice came harsh and mechanical through the wires.

A click ended the conversation on his end; I hung the receiver back on the cradle. The dime dropped in the machine and the sound of the fall, and the landing, did nothing to comfort me. The filling-station attendant loomed out of the darkness and held out a palm with some bills and coins. The bills found their way into my pocket, the change stayed with him, and Sid's Ford Falcon pointed itself east along the 401 toward Belleville, pushing through the night as wisps of clouds hung motionless in the sky.

My eyes focused on the road, looking into the blackness, watching the red smear of tail lights as cars passed, and seeing the long pale beams of the traffic across the verge that separated east from west as they headed into the city. In my mind, on the screen that mirrored the movies, the images played and flickered: Doyle's body lying still on the bed, the pillow over his head; Mrs. Linklater sitting back on her couch, the sweat glistening on her tanned skin in the awkwardness of the moment; the girl, Abbie, and the son of the preacher man seen through the moving window of the streetcar as it pulled through the intersection; Linklater's stern face, the lenses of his glasses magnifying his eyes; the checked tables of the Bohemian Embassy and the girl, Lena, posing as a woman as she delivered my muddy coffee; Thad and his excitement over his approaching chess game; the mystery woman with her pixie cut; Ayscough's ministry and the babble pouring from the mouth of the man on the floor; and Doyle's socked feet sticking off the end of the bed in perfect rest.

The night had grown dark as the city lights faded in the background and the line of traffic thinned in the outer suburbs. Now the sides of the road were pasture scrub, cornfields with their straight stalks coming tall in the middle of July, planted in long rows that stretched in the ghostly gloaming off into the perspective point of infinity. Bales of hay lay on other fields, rectangular cubes randomly scattered across the rolling landscape. Towns came and went, brief oases of colour in the night: a motel sign floating in the air, the splash of light of a filling station punching out of the gloom. And then back to the blackness and the stars, numberless and sparkling, high in the sky, so bright and alive but millions of miles away; like you were looking up at an impossible heaven.

The car lurched onto the soft shoulder, my eyes jerked back to the road, I pulled on the steering wheel, and angled the Ford back onto the asphalt. The white dashes, like stitches of thread, rolled by, shiny grey, disappearing under the hood of the speeding vehicle. A train whistled as it rushed past, the boxcars trundling on the rails, so clean and smooth compared to the screech of the city's streetcars, and again my mind went back to the room with the window overlooking the yard where they shunted the trams back and forth and the figure that lay on the bed that might have meant something to someone at one point, but looked so cold and alone, now, with the pillow over its face. And towns passed by: Pickering, Ajax, Whitby, Oshawa, Newcastle. The road rose and fell over the hills as up and down ceased to have meaning and my little steel box on wheels sped through the night, and my thoughts limped backward through the day, trying to make sense of what made none.

Coming down a big hill into Port Hope, a town nestled between the highway and the lake, my eyes began to play tricks on me, seeing things that weren't there, and fighting the lights. It had been a long day after a short night, and my body was giving out. I pulled off, curling around a cloverleaf, squinty and blinking, happy to see the arm on the speedometer slacken. Following the central artery past the odd house and business sprinkled on the edge of town, I found my way onto the main drag, quiet now in the dead of the night.

There was an old inn called the Queen's Hotel that had once had its day — but that was some time ago now. It wasn't the Edgewater — there was history and elegance beneath the grime — but I doubted the clientele was too different. My Ford stumbled behind the building into a parking lot to nest in a spot between two motorbikes and a Chevy. I popped the trunk and hefted my night bag out, seeing again the dark puddle of the jacket and the lonely boots lying on their sides in the gloom. They wouldn't be going out for any more walks in the park now. I slammed the lid and glanced at my watch; it was tomorrow already. The sound of music spilled out of the hotel and shapes emerged from the night: the sharp orange points of cigarettes being smoked and the limbs of a couple writhing against the wall of the building. I took my business inside to a high wooden counter that faced an ornate staircase going straight up before curling at the top. I dinged the bell for service. The door to the bar opened, the jangle of a guitar, guffaws, the clack of a billiard break, and voices tumbled out. A dishevelled clerk, older, white hair combed back from a high forehead, a cigarette defying gravity on his bottom lip, appeared.

"I'm looking for a room."

He looked at me without saying anything and passed a registration card and a Bic ballpoint across the counter.

I started to fill it out. He hummed something tuneless, turned away, and fiddled with some hooks and fobs. He came back around, a key in his fist, watching my upside-down writing on the card. It must have satisfied him because he began to talk in a bored voice. "Sixteen fifty for the room, tax included. Your car parked out back?"

I nodded.

"Checkout eleven sharp. Cash now. Cash only."

We made the exchange; I gave him a twenty, and he gave me three ones and some quarters back. He opened a pale palm to reveal the key and I plucked it from where it lay. "Second floor, turn right; second door on the right."

"Can I get a wake-up call?"

His eyebrows raised.

"Five o'clock?"

He shook his head no but said, "Five o'clock it is then." A stub of a pencil made a note on the card.

Up the stairs, to the right, a short hallway, second door; key, knob, turn. Bag on the bed, brush teeth, strip down to my briefs, prop the window up six inches, kill the light and lie down on top of the sheets. I dropped my head on the pillow and reached for oblivion; the people living on the ceiling sounded like they were having a good time. I rolled over onto my side and the images of the day spilled back onto the screen of my mind, threatening to keep me awake all night, watching them shift and chase each other around and around the corners of my consciousness. It felt like I'd never fall asleep, like I was too tired to ever drop off, but I must have because before I knew it, I could hear a bell ringing off in the distance. I waited for it to go away, but it kept coming closer and closer. It was a persistent beggar that wouldn't for its life let go. I wanted with all my heart for it to stop and go away and leave me alone and never come back. But it didn't. I opened my eyes and found the phone and picked it up and said something that wasn't a word into the receiver. It must have meant something to someone somewhere because the disembodied voice, bored as all hell, said, "It's five o'clock. Time to wake up."

WEDNESDAY, JULY 14, 1965

XIX

AS THE NEW day began, the sun was a feeble glow under the horizon that grew to a burning flare of red at the end of the highway. I flipped the car's visor down and squinted into the inferno. The miles passed under the wheels of the Ford, and the sun bobbed onto the skyline and sat there for a minute. As it lifted itself up off the horizon, its colour mellowed from scarlet to orange, to a washed-out cream that looked less like fire and more like a garden-party cracker waiting for a square of cheese.

The house I pulled up at, on a tree-lined street, a few blocks off the main strip was the perfect setting to serve stuff like that, on afternoons of cucumber sandwiches and chamomile tea. A tidy kitchen garden grew under a stand of gladiolas at the side of the clapboard house. The boards were freshly painted white, and the gingerbread trim was an orange that zinged in the morning sunshine. The porch swing sat at rest with a couple of throw cushions casually scattered to complete the idyllic picture. A bare bulb burned against the day in a fixture set above the front door and there were lights on in the house and the sound of activity as I stepped onto the porch. Everything was on schedule — I was expected and they were up, readying Abbie for her return journey. I gave a restrained rat-a-tat-tat on the frame of the wooden screen, my knuckles still raw from yesterday's dust-up with the Lincoln.

A woman appeared in the hallway, wearing a jumpsuit that was all black and red swirls — something between pyjamas and casual party wear. She had glasses over a pleasant face and smiled a reassuring smile that took some of the edge off my nerves. "You must be the famous Mr. Bird. I don't know how Trent manages to convince others to do his work for him." She frowned at the scrape on my face, but snapped the smile back into place without too much effort. "But he can be very persuasive, can't he? Very determined to get what he wants." She propped the screen open with her elbow and said, "I'm Mabel Linklater, the grandmother. Come in, come in. Don't let me scare you." Her hair was a fallen tower of tangles, her eyes alive and welcoming. "Come in. You have to have some breakfast before heading back to the big city. I won't have it said that I sent someone on a journey with an empty stomach." Her white slip-ons, neither slippers nor sneakers, made soft slaps on the linoleum as she led me into the interior of the house. We passed down a hallway to come out in a bright kitchen with two skillets sizzling and the smell of breakfast hanging in the air. I was starving.

But not so hungry that I failed to notice the girl who stood over the stove, tending to the food: here she was, the famous prodigal, Abigail, who'd led me on a chase for the past twenty-four hours. She looked up from the frying pans and shot me a mistrustful glare.

"You must be Abbie. Hello."

She scrunched up her face and dropped her gaze back to the stovetop.

"Abbie, as you can imagine," said Mrs. Linklater, "isn't so eager to return to Toronto. She came up here for a visit and to learn some family history from me. I'd say that we had a good old talk last night and caught up on all sorts of things, but now the visit must end."

"I don't know why Dad needs me home so fast," the girl said to her grandmother.

"No, nor I. He can be impatient, your father. And when he gets like that, it's best just to step back and let him have his way. I think I might know someone else with a little of that impatience and strength of will." She looked at her granddaughter. "So let's not be too hasty in judgment."

"Or you could have driven me," Abbie continued.

"Yes, I know. But Mr. Bird is here now, and he looks like a fine young gentleman, who has come all the way from Toronto for you — your father has sent him — so let's not argue with a plan that's already made. Sometimes life is about knowing where to spend your energy, to know what can be changed and what can't." It was true: my mother had the AA prayer in a frame over the kitchen table — they were speaking my language.

Abbie wore a pair of red shorts and a blue button-up shirt, either borrowed from her grandmother or from a bag she had packed somewhere. Her hair was wilder and curlier than the photograph her father had provided; her angry face, tight and creased, couldn't fully hide the blue of her eyes.

"Watch the bacon, dear," said her grandmother. "And here, let me get by you and into the oven. We're almost ready."

"Well, which one is it?" said Abbie. "I can't do both at once."

"No dear," said the older woman. "You decide which is more important."

"Decisions," Abbie shouted, emotions bubbling to the surface. There was a terrific crackle and the grease spat. "Ow!" the girl cried, rubbing an exposed arm. She began to cry.

"Go wash it off, dear. Your tears won't stop it from hurting. Try some cold water."

Abbie ran from the room, shouting, "I fucking hate this!" She disappeared into the powder room and slammed the door behind her. Her cries sounded through the wall.

"Mr. Bird, if you're brave enough, can you finish tending to the bacon? You might want to turn the burner down."

I lowered the flame and used a fork to turn the rashers. Mrs. Linklater busied herself, pulling a plate of flapjacks out of the oven, where they'd been warming, uncovering some scrambled eggs in a shallow pan at the back of the stove, and taking the syrup out of the fridge. "Abbie," she called, "come for breakfast." She turned her attention to me. "You've done well with the bacon, but are you sure you're up for the drive back to Toronto. Hell hath no fury like a teenage girl who isn't getting her way."

"I think I'll manage." She passed me a plate covered by two layers of paper towel to soak up the grease, and I forked the strips of bacon onto it.

"Careful of pride before the fall. These teenagers, so hungry to know the truth, have a way of humbling us. Although a good-looking young man like yourself, maybe you already consider yourself an expert in this area."

"Is that what you and Abbie have been doing since she's been here: Searching for the truth?"

We were at the kitchen table now; standing behind chairs at either end, waiting for the girl we were talking about to appear.

"Abbie! Breakfast is ready," Mabel called again, this time putting a little steel into her voice. "Sit down, Mr. Bird. Let's not wait. Eggs don't improve by getting colder." We sat facing one another, the length of the table between us.

"Abbie wants to know about her mother. Her real mother," I said, helping myself to the scrambled eggs.

Mabel Linklater nodded in agreement, her mouth open to respond when the bathroom door flew open and Abbie burst into the kitchen. "Don't say a thing. He's a spy for Dad. It's none of his business. You promised."

"Come and have your breakfast, dear. You'll feel better with a little food in your stomach. I'm not sure why we all need to be awake at this hour. It always makes me cranky." She smiled her warm smile, looking anything but cranky. "It's your father who has set this up — although you'll be quick to notice that he's not here. But Mr. Bird's been good enough to drive through the night, so the least politeness we can show him is to be hospitable and accept his involvement in our lives with an open mind."

"No," said Abbie, while relenting slightly, and moving to pull her chair out from the table.

"Please begin. Eat. I don't stand on ceremony — taking most of my meals as I do, alone. It's lovely to have some company for breakfast. Pass Mr. Bird the syrup, dear."

Abbie wasn't happy about the direction, but she complied.

"Now, Mr. Bird, you're a private investigator. You must have some exciting tales to entertain us with."

I shovelled a forkful of scrambled eggs, slightly sweetened by the pool of syrup on the bottom of my plate, and chewed while I tried to think of the right response. Charmed by Mabel's warmth, I told the truth. "I haven't been a detective for too long and so I don't have a whole bunch of stories. This is just maybe my tenth case and most of the others were divorce proceedings and ... um ..."

"Probably not the best breakfast table conversation. Quite. Not the impression we get from watching Bogart, is it? He's someone who never looked youthful. I was going to say how young you look but then bit my tongue. You can never tell how comments about age are taken; some people want to be as young as possible today — isn't that right, Abbie? — but then others seem to take it as an insult, as if you were implying that they lacked maturity and world-liness." She drifted, nattering, losing the thread and her so-cial skills at the same time. But Abbie's eyes were on me as her grandmother continued, "Now, Abbie, don't take Mr. Bird's youth and inexperience as a glimmer of hope that you can squeeze out of this trip home. You can't."

"But what about the divorce cases?" asked Abbie.

At the other end of the table, Mabel, in her paisley romper and cat-eye glasses, her mop of dyed black hair and easy smile making her appear younger than she must have been, gave an almost imperceptible nod of the head.

I turned to Abbie. "Well, you know how it happens that sometimes a husband and wife don't get along as well as they thought they could. People grow; people change; those who said 'for better and for worse' and ''til death do us part' start to feel differently. I'm no lawyer, but the way it works right now is that you need some proof it isn't working — and one way to get that proof is for the couple to show that one partner is being unfaithful — is involved in a relationship outside the marriage."

"Do you mean like sex?" said Abbie. Her grandmother hid her smirk behind a coffee mug.

"Well, yes and no. The court is usually looking for an indication that one of the parties spent the night with someone outside of the relationship — often this is done through proving, for example, the husband and another woman registered at a hotel and spent the night together in the room."

"Having sex?" persisted Abbie.

"Really, dear," protested Mrs. Linklater.

"Usually in my role, we allow the couple the privacy of the closed door." I was hedging, taking a different tack than what I told Rosie. "Photographs of them entering the hotel, the hotel room, and the hotel register are usually enough to prove the marital breakdown." The image of Victoria and her beau — which was a slightly different situation, more focused on persuasion than proof — flashed in my mind and I needed to fight a smirk off my face at the thought of those glassy eyes bulging in the surprise of the flashbulb.

"So it's not impossible to obtain a divorce if you want one?"

"Again, yes and no. If both parties want a divorce, it's doable. Divorce proceedings need to be brought forward by the injured party. So, for example, if I were married to someone, regardless of how many affairs she might be having, and regardless of her behaviour, I might choose not to institute divorce proceedings against my wife."

"But why not? If it wasn't working, wouldn't you want out?"

Mabel came to the rescue. "You're still young, dear. It is rarely so easy, so cut and dried. The wedding vows have it right: for better or for worse, in sickness and health, through good times and bad …"

I cut a pancake into quarters and folded a piece into my mouth.

Mabel put her mug back down on the table. "And some religions, like the Catholics, for example, view marriage as a sacrament and don't believe in divorce."

"And my mother was a Catholic?" blurted Abbie.

"I believe Belinda was," said Mrs. Linklater slowly. "I never knew her that well. We went over this yesterday. Your father brought her back as his bride when he returned from overseas. I never met her until she arrived here in Belleville, and I must say, to my regret, I didn't get to know her as well as I should have. Looking back at it now, I blame myself, but she was a difficult person to know. Standoffish. That part of your father's life continues to be a bit hazy. The war did strange things to people, and when I think about it now, I wonder just what your father saw in those years. But now, Abbie, run along and use the washroom — you have a long drive ahead of you."

"So she wouldn't have a divorce?"

"I don't know if the question ever came up. Really."

"But were they happy together?"

"It's hard to say. Likely neither more nor less than any other couple. It's not something that you can really ask of someone else's relationship. At least I couldn't. Mother-in-laws are in a strange position. There was restlessness as there always is when two people come together and the joyous whirl of the honeymoon fades and they discover that they need to learn how to live as one; there are the challenges of young children that are always difficult for the mother — and twins, no less. Not that there wasn't joy as well. But children take work. Even ones as angelic as you and Nelson. And it was difficult for Belinda, in a new country so far from her family. But I always had the impression that coming to Canada for her, part of it at least, was to leave her family in Newcastle behind. I think your mom and dad did well together. It's not easy for anyone ..." She sighed and drifted before snapping back to the present. "But didn't I send you to the washroom to get ready for this journey?"

"It's only two hours."

"Run along."

Abbie went down the hallway and I took the opportunity to ask the question I'd been holding. "I need to check something with you. Does the name Mickey Doyle mean anything to you?"

Mabel nodded. "The infamous Doyle brothers: each one worse than the one before — that's what people said about them. Michael was the youngest. His family had a tiny dirt holding up near my parent's farm. They were poor. There's nothing to grow up there except for rocks. That's what the fields are full of. If you farm beef cattle and have a decent-size herd, maybe; if you have a dairy quota, yes; but otherwise it is just hard work with no reward."

"You knew them ..."

"Yes. We knew them. Them and the Smarts and the McKinnons. All the little farms up there. The McKinnons lost two boys —"

"The Smarts?"

"Jane's family. She was Jane Smart before she became Jane Linklater." Mabel frowned at the name, but I was busy remembering the note wrapped around the bullet: she used to be Smart. She still seemed too smart by half with the games she was playing.

Mabel, lost in her memories, missed my interest. "We used to try to salvage things for the Doyle brothers; find them odd jobs here and there, especially Michael, to help him through the leaner years. He was such a nice boy when he was young, but he seemed to turn and get some poison inside him as he grew older. He went to the war, like all the boys at the time. He was in Trent's regiment — and although I don't know the details, I don't know if that went so well either."

"Who?" said Abbie, coming out of the bathroom.

Mabel and I sat in guilty silence.

Abbie gave us a hard stare and said, "Granny, this isn't fair. You aren't treating me like a grown-up."

"You're quite right, dear." Mabel stood and began to usher us toward the front door. "We were talking about Mickey Doyle — the one you asked about last night."

XX

GOODBYES SAID, WAVES out an open window, a loose tear in the melancholy of departure, the sun burning a hole in the rear-view mirror, the open road in the quiet of morning, the long shadows running in front of us, the speed of the highway: we were off.

"I'm not going to talk to you."

"No?"

"No."

"Why not?"

"Because you work for my father."

"And so?"

"And so you're working against me."

"Your dad is the enemy? Is that what you're telling me?"

"I see you. Don't play dumb to try and draw me out. I've told you I'm not talking to you and I mean it."

"Fair enough. You don't need to talk to me if you don't want to. And you're right, your father's paying the bills. I work for him. Or rather, I work for my boss, Sid, who owns the company and tells me what to do. But the customer is always right, so what your father says goes. And your dad's really only interested in getting you home. He's worried about you. You might not want to talk to me, but you're going to need to think about what you're going to say when you get where we're going, because you can be sure once you enter your house you'll be bombarded by questions from your mom and dad."

"She's not my mother."

"Stepmother."

"That doesn't count for much."

"Well, she and your father might think differently." We both stewed for a stretch as the ribbon of the road unfurled beneath the wheels of the Ford. I resisted the urge to fill the silence with some chatter from the radio.

After a while, I tried again: "They're going to ask you where you spent Sunday and Monday night."

"You wouldn't even tell me what you and Nanna were talking about."

"Fair. Your grandmother and I were talking about the past; she told you. I asked her if she knew a man named Mickey Doyle. She did; she called him Michael Doyle. I think he's in the middle of this puzzle — maybe responsible for your disappearance, and maybe holding the key to a lot of the questions that keep coming up."

"And what questions would those be?"

"Questions about your mother: your real mother, Belinda. The one who was shot in the Bank of Toronto in 1951."

"What do you know about that?"

"I'm learning. For the last twenty-four hours, I've been trailing after you, trying to piece things together and figure out what caused you to run away and where you were — but mostly why."

"And what did you find out?"

"Some things. But there are holes. I know you've been putting a lot of energy into trying to figure out what happened to your mother. I know you've been at the library reading old newspapers; I know you've given up swimming and other sports you used to like; I know you've moved on from some of the friendships you once had as these questions took over your life; and I know you've been down at Reverend Ayscough's church, trying to meet some of the people who might have first-hand knowledge of what went on in those distant years: Stanley, maybe Mickey."

She thought about that for a minute, and then came out with: "I told you I'm not talking to you."

There was another long stretch of straight road and sunshine where the silence hung between us. Broken-down barns slid past the car, their weathered boards hanging loose; dusty yellow hayfields, waiting for the reaper, their stalks waving in the wind; a big truck laboured up a hill in low gear; the Ford's speedometer held steady. Time passed slowly and the car moved fast; the city approached.

And then: "You told my father all that?"

"I tried at times, but I never really got a word in edgewise. He wants you home. He doesn't seem interested in the why. He doesn't want to dredge up the past. His solution is to get you through the front door, and, in his mind, everything'll be solved."

"It won't be solved," she blurted.

"You'd run away again?" I asked.

She was slow to answer. "Maybe. I don't know. I don't think so. I have most of the information I need. Or at least I'm close. But … I don't know what I'm going to do with it. Now that I have it, it doesn't seem to help. I mean …"

I let it hang, tried to let her work out some of the things she needed to, but it fizzled and the moment passed. I poked at her again. "Your stepmother thinks you went for an abortion."

She snorted. "I know. It's not nice, but I let her believe that. It was a way to buy some time, so when I disappeared she could stall Dad along for a bit. I didn't think that she'd tell him, and thought she might be able to slow him down for a day or two."

"It's true, they didn't call me in until you'd been gone two nights. So the boy in the bright white cardigan didn't get you pregnant?"

"Paul?" She turned red.

"Yes, the minister's son."

"Paul's not my boyfriend. He's just a friend. He's been a good one too."

"You stayed at the church the first two nights."

"That's right, but it's not like you think."

"Okay. I believe you."

"They have a rectory with a sort of dormitory section. Not for the people who eat at the soup kitchen — but for what they call wayward young women. They provide them a space to stay for as long as needed. There was a spare bunk and Paul got me a spot."

"As you scoped out Stanley Johnson and Mickey Doyle?"

"What do you know about them?"

So much for playing honestly with her. It was a new day and the sun was shining, and I hadn't thought a whole bunch about it, but here came my memory again, and with it, images of that small room on the third floor of the Edgewater with the empty bottles, the motionless pillow, and the open eyes not seeing the ceiling. "Not much: unlike you, I haven't had the chance to talk to either one." That much was true. "That's where you can help — by pooling what we know, maybe we can come out ahead in the long run."

She thought about that for a while, staring out the passenger-side window. "So, tell me what you know and then I'll think about whether I have anything worth sharing."

"Sounds like a bit of a one-sided partnership."

"Yes, it's one-sided. My terms. It's up to you if you want to accept it."

"All right. I'll trust you. I'll tell you what I know — or what I'm guessing at this stage. You have a stepmother whose name is Jane. She's been around for as long as you can remember; and no one in your family ever talks about your real mother and what happened to her. As you get older, you start to wonder about your mother and who she is and where she is now. You start snooping around. I don't know the background of how you got your leads or where you found your information, but I do know that at a certain point, sometime fairly recently, you found out that your mother had been shot in a bank robbery gone wrong, not far from your house, in 1951, when you and your brother would have been about two years old. Have I got that right?"

"Keep going."

"There was a holdup at the bank — your garden-variety stickup — but the teller, a guy called Stanley Johnson, had a gun — which is the way some of the banks do it — and he jumped up and decided to be a hero and took a shot at the robber, who was using your mother as a shield. Nobody loves a hero. The bullet hit your mother instead of the bank robber and she was dead before she got to the hospital.

"I'm not all the way there yet, but I'm working on a supposition that the bank robber was Mickey Doyle, or Michael Doyle, who had ties to your father's family. His family had a little rocky farm up north of Belleville, he served in the war under your father, and now he's shown up in Toronto. I think his showing up is what set the events of the last couple of days in action."

Abbie wasn't giving much away. All my pause could produce was a terse "Go on."

"I'm speculating, but I think both Johnson and Doyle made their way to Ayscough's church — whether they were just looking for a free lunch, or maybe they bought into having their souls saved I can't say. Or maybe Stanley was a believer, and Mickey was looking for something to eat. Or were they looking for each other? I don't know at this stage.

"I keep looking at the bank robbery and trying to see it as anything other than a tragic accident. It doesn't look like it's something that was planned. I haven't talked to Johnson or Doyle — so I can't say — but I think you have, and that's where you can help out."

There was another long stretch as she stared out the window, looking at the city's outer suburbs: new subdivisions in farmer's fields; muddy construction sites; road-building crews starting for the day; gas stations — their signs giant lollipops thrust into the blue sky; diners and fast-food joints;

cloverleafs and on-ramps; commuter traffic. The sprawl co-alesced, the traffic thickened, the road widened.

"My mother was murdered," she said into the silence.

"So tell me about it."

"I'm serious."

"Of course."

"Nobody believes me. I thought Nanna might, but she didn't."

"I told you what I think — I don't see how it could have been pulled off. Did someone pay both men to make the hit? It doesn't make sense. If you're doing murder for hire, you want to keep the people who know to a minimum: to one, the person who pulls the trigger. In this bank job you've already got two people: Mickey and Stanley. Why would you ever set it up with two and not just one? There couldn't be a worse way to do it."

"Jane killed my mother. I'm sure of it. I don't know how, but I'm sure of it."

"You're saying it's your stepmother. That's always a good choice for a suspect."

"You're making fun of me."

"Why don't you tell me what the two eyewitnesses told you. Let's start with Stanley. What did he say?"

She shifted in her seat and gave me a fierce glare that was either one last stress test on my loyalty or perhaps the withering hatred she felt for the naysayer. But she spoke: "Stanley's a mess. I met him first. I got his name out of the paper — it's a common name, but I had a bit of luck and was able to find him. Even though he's the one who pulled the trigger and killed my mom, he never did a day of jail time. He killed her and he's come out of this as the victim of this story — not her. It's bullshit."

"But that day was a disaster for him too. He lost everything."

"Not his life."

"So you think he's a cold-blooded killer who conspired to kill your mother?"

"Okay. I'll give you that," she said. "Stanley doesn't seem like he could make a plan to save his life, and he really does feel bad for what he did. To hear him tell it, it was an honest mistake. And you're right: the day he killed my mother has become the centrepiece of his life, and he's never recovered from it — and now he's in the gutter. It's not good. He's broken."

"And so when you talk to him, can he tell you anything?"

"He's hard to talk to, because every time I question him, he falls apart. He can't handle the memories."

"So you asked him?"

"I tried, but I never got much sense out of him. In getting to know him and learning what had happened, I ended up at the church and saw his public confessions — and that's where I got most of the information, from what he said in front of the congregation."

"Yeah. I saw one of those last night and it seemed like he was referring to the shooting. If you already know the story. Your dad was there when we heard the confession, and he didn't flinch — at least he didn't let on that he connected it up with the past." I paused, but she didn't bite so I continued: "I'm no head-shrinker, but it seems to me that the amount of guilt Stanley displays, and the downward spiral of his life after your mother's death, make it look like an accident. If he was a hired killer, I think he'd have a little more holding him together. It seems the reaction to a tragic mistake — not the remorse of a paid gunman."

"I've thought about that too," Abbie said, surprising me. "You can look at it from the other side as well. If you make a big mistake, if it's an honest one, you can shrug it off and say 'whoops' — a big whoops, but a whoops all the same; but if you plan something, and do it on purpose, and then once it's done, you see what you've done, I think it'd be possible that you could have some sort of breakdown that forces you to confront it, and it just rips you in half."

"So, if we follow your theory, do Stanley's confessions ever give any indication he was part of a plan; that there was a level of premeditation; that he was thinking about murder — that the whole thing was anything beyond a stray bullet?"

"No."

"It's hard to see, knowing what we know about what a mess he is, how fragile he is, how he could have held up to police interrogation. It would seem that if he had something to hide, he would have spilled it pretty quick to the investigators," I said.

"But the detective died just months into the investigation."

"Tong. But months still would have given him plenty of time to ask Stanley questions."

"Detective Tong, that's his name."

"Killed by the Boyd gang on Dundas at the bridge over the train tracks."

"Do you think that's connected?"

"No."

We sat in silence as I followed the stream of commuter traffic that jogged through the streets of the newly constructed suburbs that connected the 401 to the top of the Don Valley Parkway. We turned south into the heart of the city. "And what about Mickey Doyle? Have you ever talked to him?" I was conscious that the last time I'd seen him he'd been staring at the ceiling and not seeing it.

"Stanley helped me there. I'd given up getting anything useful from him, and was resigned to hearing more of his rambling confessions when one day, just over the weekend, he was in a panic because the bank robber had shown up at the church."

"And you saw Mickey there?"

"From a distance. And then he came knocking at our door on the Sunday afternoon. That pretty much confirmed everything."

"That's what prompted you to run?"

"Yes. I wanted to talk to him — and I was scared to be in the house. I couldn't live in a house with my mother's murderer. The more I find out, the more I'm sure she'll kill me if she knows what I know."

"Jane?"

"Yes."

"It's where we're going now. I'm taking you home."

"You worry about you; I'll take care of myself." All grown up at sixteen. She threw her attitude around pretty well; she had a sharp temper and could roll her eyes with the best of them, but her fears were real: Mickey Doyle was dead. The gun was missing. And here she was telling me she was sure Jane was a killer and here I was busy playing delivery boy, taking her home to the hands of the woman she thought was a murderer. It didn't seem so smart, and it didn't seem so safe, but the wheels kept turning and the car kept moving, bringing us closer and closer to the house on High Park Boulevard. "When did Stanley introduce you to Doyle?"

"Not introduce, but pointed him out to me in the food line. Stanley didn't want to have anything to do with Doyle. He'd spent his whole life running from the memory of his one encounter with Mickey; he wasn't about to strike up a friendship with the guy."

"So did you get to talk to Mickey?"

She paused. We were passing the tanneries and pork-processing plants in the elbow where the DVP curved onto the Gardiner. The stench of dead meat swamped the vehicle. "Not at first. But I did talk to him, yes."

"And what'd he say?"

"He said — I don't know how to take it — whether he was serious or not — he said. Oh, I don't know. He's so awful: swagger and stupidity. Ignorance and confidence. He's gross." It was a long time coming as we sped up the curve of the ramp and tried not to breathe in the foul air. "He said he was my father."

XXI

"WHAT?"

"He said he was my father. But I didn't believe him. He's a braggart. He has that kind of bluster to him that makes me question everything he says. I hate him. He made it sound like he owned me. Everything he said ended up sounding like stuff he'd just made up."

"When'd he say that?"

"Just — oh, I don't know. All the days are running together right now. Yesterday or the day before. I introduced myself and explained why I wanted to talk to him and he kind of sneered and acted like he knew lots I didn't — which I suppose is true; it's why I wanted to talk to him in the first place. But all his answers seemed to hide what he knew, rather than telling it to me."

"Oh?" I tried to pull her along without interrupting the flow.

"After a bit, I got frustrated and said, 'She was my mother. I need to know how she died.' And he said, 'Ask Stan — he's the one that shot her, not me.' I kept trying. I can't remember everything. I asked if he was in partnership with Stan. He just laughed and said, 'How could you plan a bank robbery with Stanley? You've seen what he looks like at that crazy church.' I begged him one more time to say something that could help, that he must know something about what happened. It couldn't have just been a big accident. But he gave that awful look he has, like he thinks he's so much better than you when he doesn't even have two dimes to rub together, and then he said it: 'I'm your daddy. How do you like them apples? Was that what you're looking for?' And I didn't believe it. But he wouldn't stop: 'Your mother — she was a looker, I'll give her that. But you look like me, not her,' and then he laughed like he'd said the funniest thing ever, and I felt like I was going to puke smelling his stinking breath."

And I could see Doyle's handsome face and dark hair in my mind. There was a resemblance, but I kept a poker face.

"And that's why you went to see your grandmother? To check on who your dad is?"

She started to cry. "I don't know. I didn't even ask her that. I couldn't ask her. She might think I wasn't related to her. I didn't want her to think that. I already had plans to see Nanna because there were so many questions I had about my real mother and where she came from and what we know about her. And about Jane as well."

Was this the explanation of Linklater's rush to get his daughter back? We'd come off the highway at Jameson and driven up between its rows of low-rise apartment blocks that had followed fast on the construction of the highway. On an impulse, I turned left onto King Street so we'd have the opportunity to go by the intersection where it met with Queen and Roncesvalles, the corner that had been at the centre of so much of this sordid mess.

"And where'd you meet up with him?"

Abbie didn't answer and I shot a glance over at her, in her tears and desperation, and she looked younger than she had yet. "You don't quit, do you? You don't ever stop? You pretend to be my friend, but you just want what I know — that's what's important to you: the truth, the truth, the fucking truth, whatever the cost. But you don't care for me or anything else."

I felt like a bully, but it was too late to stop. "Isn't that what you're after as well? Isn't that what those days at the library, the chasing down of Stanley and Mickey — isn't that what it's all about? The truth. We should be on the same side; I think we're the only two who care about what really happened."

"I don't know." She sniffled. "I don't know what I want anymore. And it's nothing to you. It's not your life. You can walk away at the end of this." Maybe she'd gone too far, found out too much, scared herself, and now, like the rest of her family, was ready to step back and close the closet door and let the skeletons sleep the sleep of the dead.

We pulled up to the red light at Queen Street and the Edgewater loomed, kitty-corner across the intersection, its sign hanging off the roof and sliding down the corner of the building. Since I'd already been called a bully, I had nothing to lose. "You ever been there, then? To the Edgewater?"

She reached for the door handle as the light turned green; I jammed my foot on the gas, and the car jumped forward, and she turned and said, "I hate you, Bird. I trusted you, but you're just like everyone else. You say one thing and do another." The door was open, but once the car started moving, she slammed it shut, and a fresh wave of sobs interrupted any words that might have followed.

I was going to impress Linklater, with his need for discretion, bringing home his daughter in tears, screaming the family secrets up and down the street. "Steady now," I said. "We're almost there. We'll get you home."

"I keep telling you," she gasped between tears, "I don't have a home. I don't have a family. It's been taken from me."

"Your father and your mother —"

"She's not my mother!"

"— think you have a home, and want you home. Your father is the one who insisted I come and get you in Belleville —"

"And she killed my mother."

We were just a block or two away, rolling behind the streetcar heading north. When it stopped at Pearson, I was afforded a few more seconds. The sun was climbing in the sky, and shadows grew shorter as it reached over the top of the businesses on the east side of the street. "This is your chance, Abbie. Tell me what you can now and maybe I'll have something to run with. If you walk out of this car with all your secrets, I don't like the chances that we'll have another opportunity to put our heads together. Come on. I played fair with you."

"I've told you everything."

"No, you haven't. You're still holding out: What did Doyle tell you?"

The streetcar made its exchange of passengers, off and on, the doors closed with their trademark sigh, and it began the long climb up the gradual incline to Bloor Street.

"Stop and think about what's in your best interest. Do you want the investigation to stop once you're home — or are you hoping it keeps going? We're almost there. We need to work together. We're the only two who actually care about why it all happened."

"Why don't you ask Mickey yourself? He's only too happy to talk to anyone who'll listen."

The car was moving, but I took my eyes off the road and glanced across the seat at her. Was she serious? She had the cunning coy look that only a teenager — not even halfway to wisdom, busy knowing everything and nothing at the same time — can conjure onto their face. There was no way to tell whether she was playing me: Did she know about Doyle's death? She couldn't have if she was in Belleville. I couldn't tell, but I held what I had. I set the signal, waited for a stream of traffic to pass, cranked the wheel, and turned left onto High Park Boulevard.

"Stop," she said, reaching across the seat and grabbing my arm.

"I'm taking you home."

"Stop." The tears sprang back. "I have things I have to tell you."

I pulled over, two blocks from her home, parked on the side of the street and waited.

"I don't even know if he's my father. How can he order me home? Why couldn't I have stayed in Belleville?" It was a fair question.

"Did you have something you wanted to tell me?" I asked now the car had stopped.

She nodded her head mutely, the tears streaming down her face. She sniffled loudly and pulled the back of a sleeve across her nose, saying, "I told him I couldn't be his daughter because my mother was Belinda, and he just laughed some more and said, don't think he didn't know that. And then he said he knew Belinda too. And the way he say 'knew' was totally ick. And then he said, 'Yes, Trent likes to think he's a big shot, but I don't think he's got any bullets in his gun. At least he's never had any luck getting any of his girls up the family way.' And I called him a liar and he shook his head — for once he wasn't laughing, and said, 'I should know. There was a time when Belinda wanted a child more than anything — and that's why she came to me.'"

"What do you think?"

"I don't know what to think."

We sat staring at the ghost of our reflection in the windshield.

"I didn't like him. I didn't want to believe him. I don't want to believe him. I wanted Nanna to tell me it wasn't true. That's why I went to Belleville."

"And?"

"And she proved him a liar."

"Really? She knew?"

"Well, she told me that Mom and Dad had planned to marry in Canada, but had to get married in England because Belinda was pregnant. So, Dad — Trent — is my father."

If only life were so simple. "That's good," I said.

I must have left my poker face on the pillow in Port Hope because she picked up on my doubt immediately.

"You don't believe me?"

"I believe you."

She took me at my word, even if I didn't. The trees overhead shimmered in the breeze and a couple with a dog walked toward us. I recognized the woman from outside the Boulevard Club the day before.

"Let's go," Abbie said. "Take me home."

I hesitated, looking at the woman with the pixie cut, caught between two thoughts, and Abbie screeched, "Now."

Jolted back to the confined space of the car, I turned to her. "You want to go home?" The closer we got to the house the more I worried about the danger of the return.

"Take me home," she said.

I put the car in gear, checked my mirrors, and pulled out from the parking spot and rolled up in front of the stone house, the morning sunlight dying on the grey slate of the roof.

"We're here now." I opened my door and hopped out of the car. Trent hadn't organized a welcoming committee on the front porch — I wasn't surprised — he would keep this locked up tight and away from the neighbours' curious eyes.

We went up the steps and as I reached out to the bell, she pushed past me and swung the door inward. I followed her into the hall.

XXII

"HELLO," CAME JANE'S voice down the stairs.

Linklater emerged from the depths of the hallway, checking his watch as he walked toward us. "Abbie, I'm so glad you're home. We were so worried." He wrapped his arms around her, and she broke out in a fresh bout of tears. Looking at me over his daughter's head he said, "You've made good time, Bird. Thank you for this. You've done exactly what we asked."

I made a sharp, wordless nod, my neck bending under the yoke of his praise, while the domestic reunion, the floods of tears, and the bittersweet tang of return echoed in the hallway.

Jane came down the stairs in a red print dress, her hair still wet from the shower. She tousled Abbie's head and said,

"The little one that came back. We're so happy you're here. I love you, I love you." Abbie froze at the touch, staying pressed into the shelter of her father's chest.

Abbie was home. I'd done what I was paid to do, but I couldn't help worrying about the girl inside the stone walls of that grey mansion with Doyle's killer still busy trying to erase the past. A part of me wanted to grab her arm and drag her out from the house and away from the danger. But it seemed that once the door to the mansion had opened and the threshold crossed, all my will wilted in the face of the family.

Linklater, still with his daughter in his arms, looked over her head. "We have some catching up to do here, Bird — family stuff — you can see — so I'll say thank you again. I'll follow up with Sid Cowan at the agency and let him know how happy we were with the help you provided us. Thank you." It was as gracious as he could be.

"Yes, thank you," said Jane, moving around the pair in the hallway to hold the door and shuttle me out of their home. I felt Abbie sliding away, into the cold house with its secrets and lies.

And so it was: Still early in the morning, case closed. All solved. Prodigal returned. The sun shone through the trees, dappling the asphalt beneath; the breeze blew, the leaves danced in the wind, and the pattern of shadow and light on the road shifted, and everything was different, and at the same time, everything was the same. The case was wrapped up and I didn't feel good about it; there wasn't an ounce of good feeling in my whole tired body.

Back in the company car, I weaved through the side streets on the other side of Roncesvalles and found a place to park on O'Hara. At Queen, I turned the corner and there was the Skyline. I'd already had one big breakfast today, and I was ready for another.

In a booth near the back, close to the pay phone, Rosie came down the aisle, looking prettier than ever. Something twanged inside; a realization that the facades and games I'd played in the past were child's play — it was time to grow up and say how I felt, almost as if the charade with Victoria had taught me something when nothing else could. I reached out to pull her close so I could explain everything that was happening inside. She slapped my hand away. "Bit early for that, Frisky."

"It's different today."

"It's different every day. That's what they call life."

"I'm serious."

"Good for you. Spare me the soap opera and let me know your order — we're busy."

"You know what I order."

"Don't kid yourself, I got plenty of customers. Plenty."

"You don't have to be so tough with me. That's not you."

"You're going to tell me who I am? You don't know anything about it. You got to be tough to work in a place like this with all the spare hands floating around. Yeah, I'm tough. Let's have your order. I've got work to do."

"Black coffee, three eggs over, white toast, bacon."

Her pen moved on the pad. "Got it. Want the coffee now?"

I nodded.

"Give it up, wounded doe," she said over her shoulder. She was back quickly and set the coffee down with a clatter, some of the liquid jumping over the lip of the cup and into the saucer. I picked it up, retreated to the pay phone, and dropped my dime into the machine. Sid answered on the first ring.

"Patrick?"

"Sid."

"Where the hell have you been?"

"Linklater sent me to Belleville to pick up Abbie. She was with her grandmother. I just got back into town about half an hour ago. I dropped the girl at home. Lots of tears and Linklater gave me the big 'thank you very much — your services are no longer needed.'"

"That's it? All done?"

I intended to say something about Mickey Doyle's body in Room 307, but a lot had happened already that morning. Inside the confines of the phone booth, glassed off from the world, I watched the moment slide by. Mickey Doyle was dead. Nothing could change that — not all the questions and solutions and detective work in the world. The case was closed and suddenly, like everyone else — like Abbie who pulled away when the truth got too close; like Linklater, satisfied now his daughter was home; like Jane, the stepmother who still professed her love even when it didn't seem reciprocated — I was done with the case. We could all live happily ever after, if only I could stop yanking at the door to the family closet. I stood in the booth and time passed and the opportunity went with it. I gave Sid one final chance: "There are a lot of loose ends. Still a lot of things that don't add up …"

"Customer's happy. I'm happy. Not our problem."

I had a last impulse, a final flop, like the fish in the bottom of the boat clinging to life before the paddle came down on it. Abbie had been right about me and the truth. "But I have worries about —"

"You'll always have concerns, Patrick; that's part of the job — but when the job is finished, it's over. If you're going to make it in this work, sometimes you just need to walk away with the cheque. You have to find the balance between caring enough and not caring too much. It sounds like you did good, and that you've been running non-stop for the last twenty-four hours. Go home, rest up, give me a call in the afternoon, and we'll figure out the plan for tomorrow. I've got a juicy divorce coming up. Sound good?"

"Yeah." It sounded like something, but it didn't feel good.

"You did all right. That's my boy. Now get some sleep."

"But you don't —" There was a click and then the monotone of the dial buzzing in my ear. It was my secret now.

I ate my food without tasting it; Rosie passed back and forth in front of my booth and my eyes followed her without focus. The drive home was without thought, like a migrating pattern. The whole time my mind was humming with the terrible secret I hadn't been able to share — the look on Doyle's face: peaceful and not peaceful — the marks on the pillow like the strange characters of an cave painting waiting to be deciphered — the final dreamless dream as he drifted in eternity.

I opened a window in my third-floor apartment, stripped down to my boxers, and went into the kitchen to make a last call before crawling into bed. Standing on the linoleum at the sink with a glass of water in my hand, I dialed long distance. It was answered on the third ring. "Hello, is this Mabel Linklater?"

"Yes?"

"This is Patrick Bird."

"Oh, hello, Mr. Bird. How are you?"

"I'm fine, thanks. I just wanted to let you know that Abbie and I made it home safely."

"That's good. Thank you for calling to let me know."

"No problem," I said. "And I had one other question. I just wanted to check what time Abbie got into Belleville yesterday."

"Late. A little after nine thirty last night. She called me from the station. Is everything all right?"

"Yes. Abbie's home with her parents. Everything's good."

"Okay." Mabel was cautious in her acceptance of my explanation, and I was quick to wrap the conversation up.

"Great — I just wanted you to know that we made it home safe."

"Thank you for calling." We said our goodbyes. And there it was. Abbie must have taken a train later than the one Paul had said she'd been on. Maybe she missed the first one. Maybe. Or she could've given him the slip and been in the city as late as about seven o'clock last night. It wasn't a good look.

More information I wished I didn't know. If I'd had any thoughts of calling in Doyle's death to the police, this was another sharp curve in the road. Things had changed again — I didn't like what Mabel had told me. I could always make the call to the police when I woke up.

It was exhausting to care. I lay down on the bed and the images poured over the edge of consciousness, a waterfall cascading into my mind. I was lying on my back on the beach at Sunnyside, watching great white clouds bob in the sky. The clock had been turned back and the old amusement park was open; the Flyer rattling on its wooden frame, the teenagers screaming in delight and the yahoos in the front car had their hands in the air, not holding anything, showing they just didn't care. A fat cloud, blindingly white, came down from the sky and enveloped everything in its shadow. I panicked and tried to sit up as I saw a giant Jane behind the cloud, emerging from the water, holding the cloud-pillow in her massive hands, her tennis whites streaming with lake water, her bronzed arms intent on sealing the bolster over my face. The heavy cloud was pushed onto me, thick and suffocating; the terrible white of the pillowcase filling my world as it was pushed into me. I thrashed for air.

And then I heard it, the old police bell, as some old-fashioned cruiser came rushing through the city streets to my rescue. Ringing and ringing. Coming to save me before the deadly pillow closed off life completely. Louder as it approached, the bell ringing and ringing. And then my eyes opened in the daylight and I could hear the phone.

And I was awake and moving through the apartment to the kitchen, where I picked it up and Jane said, "I got your number out of the phone book. Abbie's gone again. You have to help me."

XXIII

I MET JANE, as she'd asked, a few blocks from her house in a small parking lot at the southeast corner of High Park. Standing in her red dress, leaning on the hood of the car, looking like she was posing for a cigarette ad in a glossy magazine, she waved as I pulled into the empty spot beside her. I wasn't sure why we weren't meeting at the house, but I was happy to avoid Linklater and his impatience and recriminations.

"We're looking in the park?" I asked, stepping from the Ford.

"No. Abbie isn't here. She's done a bunk. But she'll be back; I think we can hold off the panic button."

I was sweaty and dishevelled: not enough sleep and no time for a shower, just a fresh shirt and a slap of water across the face. Still, every time this family snapped their fingers, I jumped.

"Come for a drive." Jane opened her door, sat on the upholstery with her knees together, and swung her legs under the wheel like she'd been to the same etiquette school as Victoria; leaning across the bench, she popped the lock on the passenger side. I circled behind the car, and slid in beside her. She turned the key in the lock, revved the engine, and reversed out of the parking spot.

"Well, this is nice." She turned south on Parkside and passed under the new highway.

"Is Abbie really missing?"

"Yes. I'd still be in the house acting as jailhouse matron if she were home. But when she left, there was the chance for me to escape too. I said I'd go out and look."

"Except you aren't."

"Well, we're driving around and our eyes are open. And I've got the detective beside me." She patted the leatherette between us.

"And so ... we could look —"

"Really? Do you think that would make a difference? She's made her little teenage demonstration. She'll be back. But I forget, you found her once already."

"What about the others? Are they looking?"

"Trent's looking. Through the bottom of a glass, sitting on the couch and feeling sorry for himself." But he wasn't calling the agency again. He'd already been down that road once. "And Nelson went to work. Eileen's putting lunch together. She found her key — that's our news. Another Wednesday at the Linklater residence."

"So where do I come in?" We turned onto Lake Shore and passed the pool and pavilion, where the amusement park used to stand before they tore it down and built the highway.

"You don't know where you come in? Don't play games with me, Patrick. We need time to talk and …"

"And …?"

"And …" she paused again, and then the words tumbled out, "I've never been with a gumshoe."

I was tired of playing peekaboo with this family with their mercurial moods and shifting demands, their need for me coming and going like the waves on the shore, and I came back hard: "You ever been with a bank robber?"

And she came back just as fast and hard with a back-handed slap across the side of my face to let me know what she thought about my response. Maybe she was left-handed — I don't know — but she wore her wedding band and engagement ring on the right side, and the rock caught me on the cheek; diamonds are sharp, and I felt it when this one dug in. My hand jumped to my face to catch the pain and when it came away it held a trickle of blood, bright red in the daylight.

"Jesus," I said. She looked over and the car swerved; she wrenched it back into its lane, and we bounced over the bridge at the Humber River.

"You broke my ring." She held the splayed webbing of the setting riding up against her first knuckle for me to see. It was true, the leather of my cheek had ripped the rock right out. "We'll have to find it. Trent'll kill me if it's lost. Here" — she passed me her purse — "there's a tissue for your cheek in there, somewhere."

The bag landed on my lap, and I wondered, when I popped the clasp, if I'd open it to see Doyle's missing revolver. At least I'd know where I stood. I rooted through the contents: a tube of lipstick, a ravaged emery board, a ball-point pen, an empty change purse, sunglasses, a tiny address book, loose bills, a laundromat's worth of loose coins, and a small package of Kleenex, but no gun. She put on the left-turn signal and pulled into the parking lot of the Seahorse Motel: a fading icon, middle-aged and prettied up as best it could be, pretending the years hadn't passed it by. Memories of a more innocent time: my mother had taken me there for a vacation on the shoreline one summer when we couldn't afford to leave the city. It was where I'd learned to swim. The motel hadn't reached the age when, like a flattened version of the Edgewater — this time it really was beside the water — the tourists had deserted and the only people who came knocking were those looking for a fake honeymoon in a cheap room on a short clock. But the slow slide down the hill of decrepitude had started. I'd done a divorce stakeout with Sid there in the off-season. In his encyclopedia of useless facts, he'd let me know it was a strange name for a house of hanky-panky: "Seahorses are monogamous."

"Yes," Jane said. "I thought we needed to talk, and it seems I was right." She pulled into a parking spot and killed the engine. Leaning across the bench seat, she put her hand on my face, next to where I pressed the tissue against the scrape. "Sorry about that." She stretched over and kissed it better and her lips lingered longer than necessary. There was no revolver in the purse, but the waves of anger and the determination of her desire still scared me.

"We need to find that diamond," she said. "But since you ask: yes, I slept with Mickey — that's who we're talking about, right? — but that was before he became a bank robber. Not after." She moved her hand down my front, smoothing the creases in my shirt. "Here it is." She perked up, holding the rock up in the light of the front seat, and it sparkled just like a diamond should, but the depths of its magic, twinkling in the motel parking lot, did nothing to help me forget the mess I was in.

"You knew Doyle?"

"Of course I did — do — that's why we're here. Because he's back and he's threatening to take everything away. Everything. I need your help. Why? What did you think was happening?"

She dug into the purse and came out with a piece of paper, dropped the rock in, slid the band off her finger, and added it to the cache. Folding the paper into a square so nothing could escape, she dropped it back into the bag. "I won't be needing that," she smiled in conspiracy.

I shook my head. It was dizzying the way she moved from needing help, to flirtation, to hard pragmatism.

"You look so surprised. You ask a question and I answer it honestly and yet your mouth's hanging open. Careful, or you'll be catching some flies." She laughed. "Isn't that what you do in your business?"

I scowled.

"You'll need to work on your interrogation techniques."

"Maybe."

"The Doyles lived down the road from me when I was growing up; I've known Mickey since before I can remember. If you must know, Mickey was my first. Truth or dare?" She kept me off balance, unabashed, sharing the details, testing me with her honesty.

I fought the impulse to tell her my truth — that he might have been the first, but never again — Mickey was no more. "Isn't this nice?" I said. "Everyone knows everyone. And Mickey was in your husband's battalion in the war."

"You've been talking to Mabel. Of course, it was all local boys. Why would you expect anything different?"

"And she told me your maiden name is Smart."

"Oh, yes. Well, that's true. I doubt she thinks it's descriptive. Not my biggest fan. But yes, I was born Jane Smart. What does that have to do with anything?"

"Someone was sending cryptic notes to the Smart party earlier this week."

"Well, I never got one."

"No, I chased him away before the postman could knock."

She nodded her head and said in wistful voice, "Mickey." Her tone changed. "I need to thank you for chasing him away. We had our time, but it wouldn't be fun to see him now."

"So did he know the first Mrs. Linklater?" I asked remembering what Abbie had told me.

"Well, yes and no. I don't know whether they were acquainted in England, but once they were all on this side of the pond, of course, they knew each other. Mickey was their odd job man — mowing the lawn, and shovelling snow. If you want to know about what happened in jolly old England, you'll have to ask Trent. I wasn't over there."

"I don't think it was so jolly. My dad went over and never came back."

"Are you trying to make me feel old?"

Part flirtation, part investigation, the parry and thrust of our banter hit the wall and there was a pause. I wasn't trying to make her feel old, but I was trying to make the situation make sense and wasn't having much luck. My head spun in the fog of fatigue, and I failed to come up with a response.

"Are you going to help me or not?"

"Help you? What do you want? I'm listening, aren't I? I'll need to know the whole story — what I'm getting into."

She shook her head, flipped the hair out of her face, and tucked a loose strand behind her ear. "If you're going to help, let's at least have somewhere to talk in comfort. Go get us a room." She took her hand off my chest and slid it into the open purse.

I frowned as she dug for money and heaved myself up from the seat and into the parking lot before she could offer any. Maybe I was fooling her, but I wasn't fooling myself with this fake gallantry, crossing the lot to make the payment with her husband's bills in my pocket. A hot wind blew into the office through the carport window as I registered us for a room with a tired bed and a view of the highway they hadn't finished building. It was early enough in the day that the housekeeping service still pushed their carts of bedding and towels and little beige rectangles of soap around the bungalow horseshoe. Plastic bucket chairs on metal frames stood like a kindergarten lesson on primary colours, two outside every door. A splash, followed by a scream of excitement came from the unseen pool. I crossed back to the car; the key in my hand dangled from a plastic orange diamond; a door painted a pale shade of teal had the number eight hanging by a screw above a peephole.

She stepped out of the car and came close to me at the entrance to our room, giggling like a girl, shocked at her own audacity. Or was it all an act for me? Maybe, but she didn't need to act. The attraction had been there since I first saw her on the tennis court at the Boulevard Club, and later on the couch in her home, and again as she stood beside her stiff-shirt husband, and now here we were, standing at the door to a room of our own. It was coming true, and I had a twang of disbelief and doubt and the flash of terror that pops in your head when you get what you really want.

We entered the shade of the room and in the close hall-way that led to the bed she turned to me; her mouth found mine and she pushed me against the wall and it didn't seem so terrible to get what you wanted after all. She started un-doing the buttons of my shirt. Her nose hit the scrape on my face; the pain jolted me and I remembered that first flash of anger in the car and Doyle dead at the Edgewater.

"But what about Mickey?"

She disentangled herself from our embrace against the wall and as our bodies came apart I sucked in a breath, see-ing her in the half-light of the motel room.

"That's what you want to talk about right now? Is that it?"

"I'm just trying to figure out what happened."

"I see why Trent treats you the way he does."

"How would he feel if he could see us now?"

She smirked. I wasn't half-sure, but she wouldn't like that; nothing seemed to scare her. "You know Abbie thinks you're responsible for Belinda's death."

She stepped back from me. "I've already slapped you once. I guess you didn't get the message. I keep telling you: I haven't lied to you yet — and I'm not about to start. I'm honest. I haven't always been good, but I'm honest."

I wasn't so sure.

"Come and sit down." She took my hand, now the chaste sister, and led me over to the bed — she did everything but pat the space beside her. We sat apart, wary, on the coverlet and she began to speak: "It's a long story, but if you want to hear it, I'll tell you. God knows, there's better ways to spend our time, but since you need to know, we'll do it your way.

You're the same as Abbie, fixated on Belinda's death. How did she die? Who was responsible? I'd hoped this was all in the past."

"Abbie thinks you're responsible."

"So you keep telling me, and it's killing the mood. You ever been with a ...?" She let it hang in the air.

"I'm just the messenger."

"You might want to work on your delivery then." I could feel the chasm opening between us on the bed. "You want the whole story? I'll give it to you. It's all old history. Gone and done."

"Doyle told her he was her daddy."

Jane laughed. "Oh, Mickey! That's just the kind of thing he'd say. So full of half-truths and confusion and arrogance. Such a terrible mixture of ignorance and self-assurance. I thought we had wars to take boys like him away."

Maybe I'd upset her with some of the things I'd said, and this comment was just payback. But I don't think it'd even registered when I'd told her I'd lost my dad over there. Was he one of those boys fed into the mill of war? Never mind: I still held one trump in my hand — what I knew about Mickey, and she didn't — or maybe she did, in which case, I was already in too deep. I looked over at where Jane sat, bending over to slip off her shoes and there wasn't much to see except the nape of her neck and her hair falling over her shoulders and the red of her dress pulled tight across her back, but it looked good from where I was sitting. She sat up and caught me staring; her teeth shone in the darkness and some reflex in me smiled back.

"To understand, you need to go back to the war," she said. "Did they even spend any time fighting? I don't know. While the boys were whooping it up over in England, one thing led to another, and Captain Linklater found himself an English girl: Belinda. She's dead now, so, of course, everyone believes she was a saint, the greatest thing since sliced bread. But she was a bitch, misery incarnate with that dour face and a personality to match. I don't know the details of what happened in England because I wasn't there, but when the troops came home, Trent and her were already man and wife. The story is she was pregnant before they even left. It's one explanation as to why Trent married her. I'm sure there were plenty of wartime romances that never amounted to anything. But he'd gotten her pregnant — and that forced the issue and he did the right thing and married her. He likes to be the hero.

"But Belinda never had that child; the way she told it, there was a miscarriage on the boat over. It goes some of the way to explaining her state of mind later — because she wasn't well, not at all."

It was hot in the little box of the motel room, and I waved the open flap of my shirt, trying to create a breeze.

"Mickey had known the family for a long time and served with Trent, and once they were back, he mooched around and did the odd job here and there, maintenance, yardwork, manual labour, picking up the odd piece of change where he could. He fancied he was my boyfriend because he'd been my first, right on getting back from the war. There was lots of celebrating going on then and the soldiers thought that was the way to do it."

And Doyle had still had the photograph of young Jane on a fence rail all these years later. Right to the very end.

"But Belinda didn't take to Canada. She was falling apart, so they decided to hire a maid to lighten the load of housekeeping. Mickey suggested me, and I was as desperate as could be to get off the farm and head to the big city — Belleville seemed like a metropolis back then. So I moved to the Linklater house. I had a room at the back above the kitchen and was responsible for cooking and cleaning and keeping the fire going in the winter and shopping as best I could."

"How old were you then?"

"I was probably fourteen when I started there and had a hell of a lot to learn. But I wasn't going back to where I came from, so I did what I could to make it work."

I looked into the circular mirror hanging above the TV and angled to point back down on us and there we were, two lonely shadows sitting together and apart in the darkness on the motel bed.

"Belinda and I didn't click. I don't think she clicked with anybody. She scared me with her moods, her loneliness, and her unpredictable anger. I kept my head down: I learned to cook and worked hard. At least the house was clean and there was food on the table. Trent was unhappy too. He was home from the war; he'd been a hero of sorts and he had it in his head that he should've had a hero's welcome. And instead, he had this bride who never seemed happy and was nothing like the person he'd known in England, a big empty house, and a loveless life."

"And so you decided it was up to you to solve his problems?" I said, looking at the two of us on the edge of the bed in the mirror.

She shook her head. "You make it sound so terrible when two people get along. It's just about the only thing in life worth anything and you make it seem cheap and awful. Maybe I had to help move it along, but it's what we both wanted. You tell me you want to know what happened, but you don't make it so easy to tell."

I did want to know the story, but the way I remembered it, she was the one asking for my help and not the other way around.

"One morning I came down to the kitchen to start the fire, and found him sitting at the table with a bottle of whisky in front of him. He'd been up the whole night trying to drown his sorrows, but it hadn't made him any happier. He reached out for me. He wanted me and I liked him well enough, and that was when I started to get an idea of what could be."

XXIV

JANE SLIPPED ACROSS the bed, closer to me. "And that morning, in the kitchen, I jumped back away from Trent and said, 'Mr. Linklater!' like I was shocked, but also in a quiet voice because I didn't want to wake Belinda. And, of course, I wasn't shocked. I knew Mickey — I'd had my education and learned a thing or two."

She reached out a hand and took mine from where it lay between us, and the words I was about to say died on my lips as her fingers played with mine and the electricity passed from her to me.

"So Mr. Linklater didn't have his way that morning," she said, "but now I knew what he wanted. And then one night when I was clearing the table, I heard him and Belinda arguing. He wanted children, but she kept saying, 'But I can't, I can't do it.' She was crying. 'You know I can't. You know what the doctor on the boat said.' And Trent said what did a stupid quack doctor at sea know about women and babies and he wanted her to see a proper doctor — a gynecologist — and see what was possible. And she kept crying and said she couldn't do it; she couldn't go through that again — it didn't matter what any doctor said. Trent was angry. He wanted children, and what was marriage if there were no kids and no family? And she said they could adopt, but he said, 'I don't want any child, I want my child. This isn't a shopping expedition; this is about me.' Men make me laugh. 'This is about me.' It was more education; I was at finishing school now. Learning."

She rose from the bed and pivoted to stand over me. The strength of her will radiated through the thin dress. "It's hot. Let's put on the air." She crossed the unlit room and fiddled with the box in the window; the drone of the air conditioner sounded in the darkness. When she came back to where I sat on the bed, she didn't sit, but stood before me and put her hands on my shoulders. They found the back of my neck and her knees forced mine apart as she pulled my head toward her and pushed my face into her body. My hands climbed her back and held her tight.

"That conversation showed me the path I was searching for, that could lead me to a better life. Mr. Linklater wanted a child; Mrs. Linklater couldn't have a child; I was there in the house, and I was young, and I have to tell you, I felt pretty fertile. Couldn't we all just get along? Everyone could get what they wanted if we played it right. But it couldn't be my idea. I had to figure how to put it into Trent's head without him ever knowing where it came from."

It was coming now. The mystery of the past emerging from shadows of the room. Her hands fumbled with my hair as she brought me closer against her. A horn honked in the parking lot and the air conditioner whined as it fought its losing battle against the heat.

"That's nice of you," I said. "You're the neighbourhood Good Samaritan."

She laughed her brittle laugh. "Yes, I used what I had. And it's not as if I made the idea up by myself — it was taken from me at the age of thirteen and given value — and after a bit, I began to figure it for what it was worth. And if I used it to get somewhere in this world — good for me. You don't need to say it, I know what you're thinking. I'd hoped you were different, might have a little more understanding, but …"

I pulled her closer and in the crush as we met, I felt myself falling into her story. It was hard to argue with someone who admitted to everything.

"But you want to hear the rest of the story." She pushed me away, and my hands fell to the side as she stood looking down at me, a smile playing on her face.

"I had nowhere to go but back to good old Mickey. He was a friend when I needed one. Mickey was not Trent's pal, but he was around the house a bit, doing the odd job here and there. And he talked to Trent; and men are men, and you know what they talk about. Well, I set it up so they were talking about me. Mickey isn't so smart, so I had to script his lines for him, and then pray he didn't go freelancing. I told him to start talking me up to Trent; to say me and him were going to get married; that we were going to have kids; how great I was — to do a real PR blitz. To put the idea in Trent's head that if he wanted a child, there was a woman who could give him one under the same roof; and if he wanted me, to figure out the path to getting me, then he better move fast before I became someone else's wife. It was up to him to square it with Belinda. That wasn't my problem, or Mickey's. And Mickey went to work.

"Then one day it happened. After dinner, Belinda disappeared somewhere up the stairs, and as I was cleaning the table, casually brushing against Trent when I picked up his plate, strutting back and forth to the kitchen, giving him an eyeful, he called to me, 'Jane, come and sit here at the table. I have something I need to talk to you about.' And I piled the dirty dishes in the sink — Belinda had barely touched her food, but she'd done a good job of pushing it around the plate and making a mess. I didn't sit in her seat, but chose one a good distance from him, the full table between us. There weren't going to be any free samples. I sat down and he asked me how old I was. I told him sixteen and it was close enough to the truth; my birthday was coming soon. 'Jane,' he kept repeating my name like a halfwit; that's what I'd reduced him to. And he told me that him and Belinda couldn't have children and asked me if I knew that. I hadn't planned on saying anything, but as the silence extended, I saw I needed to help him out. That's how it usually is."

She smiled down at me and pulled at the drawstring on the waist of her dress and the knot came undone. The fabric hung in a shapeless cylinder and she still she looked beautiful. "God it's hot in here. Is that air conditioner doing anything?"

It was hot. My mouth was dry and all I could manage was a grunt of agreement.

Her mouth formed her smile of conspiracy, and she returned to her story. "I acted surprised and told him how sorry I was to hear that. He nodded, looking morose and trying to find the right words, and then he put it on his wife. 'Mrs. Linklater isn't able to conceive. And yet, we want children; we want to have a family.'"

I remembered what Abbie had said Mickey told her. Things were making less sense, not more.

"There was another awkward pause before I jumped in to help, and agreed, of course, a family needs children. And, buoyed by my eagerness, he continued, telling me about their ideas of adopting a child and how he didn't like that idea so much, that his real dream was of having a little Trent running around the house; his own flesh and blood, who he could shape into the perfect likeness of himself. Doesn't that sound like Trent? Arrogant even in his humility.

"He said that he and Belinda had discussed it and thought about what might work for them, and they'd come up with a plan. He was struggling, trying to figure out how to say it: it was only an idea, he told me, but one he thought might work for all of us. It could be a chance for me to earn some extra money and for him to father the child they'd always dreamed of. They were wondering if I'd consider taking on the position of a surrogate mother. 'Surrogate?' I asked. I really didn't know what the word meant. I mean, I could guess, but it was new to me. 'We could make the baby,' he said slowly as if explaining to a child. 'You and I could make a baby.' And once the baby was born it would be Belinda's and his. And I'd get paid for my services."

She leaned into me, where I sat on the bed and took the back of my neck again and drew it into her. I felt myself falling backward and put my hands behind me to brace against the pressure and we held the position for a second, pushing into each other, before the tension lessened.

"I didn't say anything. It seemed the wrong time to ask about the payment. And he seemed like he was spent with the energy of trying to explain it to me. He asked if he'd scared me. I told him no, so he asked if I was surprised and I said yes, that it was a strange idea. He interrupted me to tell me that it wasn't so strange. In Genesis, he said, Hagar is brought to lay with Abraham; men have been using women for thousands of years to bear their children. I'm not sure if he thought this was a selling point — that I was being used by him in his little process. No matter: it was how I liked it to be; he thought he was in control and using me when really the plan was mine all along. I asked what would happen when the baby was born; would I ever get to see it again? It was smart of me, because once it came to pass, the pain of separation was more than I could have imagined. I wish I'd paid a little more attention to my Bible study because while it's true that Hagar bears Ishmael for Abraham — it would've been helpful for me to know what happened to her afterward.

"When pressed, he had to admit that once the baby was born, it would belong to him and Belinda. The plan was I'd never see it again. I asked what would happen to my job; and he answered me like I was a child, not a woman when he told me that surely, I could see the baby couldn't have two mothers. I'd need to leave the baby with its family. He explained to me the miracle of formula and how nursing could be done from a bottle, like he was an expert. I said I'd need to think about it because it'd mean losing my job. And then he named a figure that was more than I could dream of and said half could be paid right away; and the other half when the baby was born. Still, I didn't jump at the money. I knew what my answer would be, but I didn't want to seem too eager. I wanted him to have to convince me.

"So it began. Trent thought what he wanted was to get me pregnant, but he was wrong. What he wanted was me. He'd been miserable with Belinda for too long; he'd forgotten what love was. And I showed him. I scheduled our attempts to conceive clear from my time and made sure that whatever happened, in those early months, I wouldn't get pregnant. I was playing a long game. He was trying to play the dutiful husband; meeting with me just three nights a month — when he thought it was my time — and only those three nights. But he wanted me all the time. I could feel his looks playing down my back; I could see the frustration in the clench of his jaw, and I loved it."

I believed it. She stepped away from me and my arms slid down her back and came to rest on the curve of her hips. She looked down at me from her height, and returning her gaze, up through the darkness, a tremor ran through me.

She bent at the waist, breaking free of my grip. Her head came down; her tongue darted in and out of my mouth; she straightened, laughed, and continued, "And then he came to me one night when it wasn't one of his nights; he was desperate, he was begging me, and there were tears in his eyes. He told me he couldn't go on with Belinda. And I put him off and sent him back to his loveless bed. I was feeling good about myself. Really good. I had him where I wanted him, and it would only take a small push and Belinda would be gone and I could take my place at the head of the table.

"But Belinda must have sensed where we were headed because something changed in her. I was too busy celebrating the success of my plan, the joy of being wanted and loved by Trent, to worry about her. Already I was trying to figure out how to get the idea of divorce into his head — another idea that couldn't come from me. Could I get him to bring it up? The closest I got was that he once told me he and Belinda were tied for eternity because she was Catholic. So it was only death that could them part.

"But I'd underestimated Belinda. She was planning too. One day I was called back into the dining room after dinner, and this time they were sitting together, and she held his hand in her lap like it was her possession, and I was asked to sit across the table in the same chair I'd taken almost a year earlier when I'd chosen that seat to provide me with the distance needed. But now they sat united, a partnership against me. Belinda said, 'Jane, dear. I know you have a contract with us to provide a child. And I know you have received the first half of your payment, and you have been' — she had a hitch as she searched for the right word — 'fulfilling your duties of the agreement faithfully, but things have changed. I have wonderful news, for all of us, that I need to share. Trent already knows. But I was at the doctor this afternoon, and by some miracle, I'm pregnant. I'd been told that it would never happen again but I'm pregnant. The doctor confirmed today.'

"'Congratulations,' I said, feeling anything but congratulatory."

XXV

STARING UP AT Jane, as she stood above me, I'd heard just about enough; the picture was coming clear, and, although it didn't feel like the AC was doing anything to the air, a chill ran across the back of my neck, cooling the sweat that greased my collar. "So, she had the twins and then you killed her in a bank robbery. Nice."

"Patrick, be quiet and listen." She put her finger on my mouth to shush me, but soon enough it was tracing a teasing circle around my lips. Looking into the dull glint of her eyes, I ached for her, and understood how even as a teenager she could have overwhelmed the unsuspecting Trent. "And shut your mouth." She bent her head down, her hair falling over my face, and closed it for me with a long kiss. Straightening back up, she leaned into me and threatened to collapse us onto the bed. "I like you. We might come to an understanding yet. We'll see." I held her waist and arched back to pull her down onto the bed on top of me, but she slipped away and I fell back onto the mattress on my own.

Jane laughed her short sharp laugh. "Belinda thanked me, called me 'dear,' and said my services were no longer needed. I'd been paid. She and Trent had decided I could keep the first half of the surrogacy fee, even though I hadn't fulfilled my end of the contract. She might have thought she was tiptoeing around it, but it sounded like she was calling me a whore.

"'We've asked Mickey to come and pick you up tomorrow and to take you home. Thank you for what you've done. It's been' — she looked like she might choke on the word — 'appreciated.' And Trent sat beside her and took it; his hand, which I'd known greedy on my skin, held captive between two of hers. If the carving knife had been lying on the table, I might have killed him then and there. I'd never been so humiliated.

"In the moment, words failed and I couldn't figure out how to claw my way back into the family picture. But the next day, the sun rose, the world hadn't ended — it just felt that way — and I picked myself off the bed, determined to find a way to make it work. I found a spare moment when Belinda was occupied to say my goodbye to Trent, and I let him know how happy I was for him and Mrs. Linklater, and how sad I was to be leaving, and how if he ever needed anything with Mrs. Linklater in her condition — cooking, cleaning, anything — he should let Mickey know and I'd come and help. And he grunted and sweated and said yes and no and he was sorry too and put out his hand to shake goodbye. And I held it and looked in his eye and saw fear and desire, lust and misery, and I knew there was still a chance."

I sat up, but she turned, her back to me, so now both of us were looking at our reflection in the round mirror on the wall beside the television. My hands rested on her hips as I saw the glow of excitement shining in her face in the unlit room as if telling her story after all these years still stirred something inside.

"Mickey came in his old pickup to drive me and my possessions back home. As soon as we were beyond the town limits, I told him to pull over and said I needed him then and there. He was never one for asking questions or wondering about the why of things and we had a time of it on the side of the road across the dusty seat of his truck. At the end of the week, I got him to drive me to town and I waited around outside Trent's office. When Trent came out, I was there. He saw me standing by the car and said, 'Jesus, Jane, what are you doing here?' He looked all around the parking lot, fearful of who might see. I said I was stuck in town and needed a ride; I hated to bother him, but I didn't know anyone else. I was apologetic and in need and pretty much telling the truth. I'm an honest person at the core."

Jane took a step backward and pushed my legs aside with her knee. "Move over. Give a girl somewhere to sit." I did what I was told, and she landed in my lap before I could catch her. She wriggled on my knee, got herself comfortable, and continued: "Trent agreed to give me a lift. This time it took a little more finesse than my ride with Mickey, to convince him to give me what I needed; but it was what he wanted too and so, once the idea was in his head, it didn't take long for him to agree. And I got home, my legs trembling and his seed inside me."

I wondered how much finesse she needed with me. Not too much. Abbie believed she'd killed Belinda. I believed she'd killed Doyle. And now she was sitting on my lap asking for my help. She leaned back and nuzzled into my neck and my hand came up her rib cage and she held it there. "There's more to tell." The truth looked distant and oblique as my hand struggled half-heartedly in hers.

"There was just one last step. It was bold — but after that time with Trent in the car I really believed I was pregnant. It's not lying if you believe it, is it?" Her laugh was loud and harsh inches from my ear. "I got Mickey to take me back to their house and I made my humble entrance. 'I'm so sorry to come bothering you, Mr. and Mrs. Linklater, but something has happened and I think I'm pregnant with your baby — and I know things have changed and you've let me go, but now I'm having a baby, I just don't know what to do.'" Jane did a convincing imitation of a younger self, mumbling and contrite, but steeled with desperation. "I broke down in tears at their dining-room table. What can I say? I was emotional: young, alone, without anything, with a child inside me — or at least I hoped so. It was up to them to make it right.

"Belinda couldn't hide her fury. This time it was me who was glad the carving knife was safely in the drawer. Trent felt it too; he was afraid to speak. At last, Belinda spoke and gave me the brush-off — it wasn't their problem. I'd been paid. She was a cold bitch. There was no acting now; my tears and curses were real. I raged: they'd promised, they'd promised to take care of me when I was pregnant. But Belinda was immovable: she said that was then, and this is now, and things had changed. I turned to Trent and tried to appeal to him, reminding him of the agreement we had. He managed to get a syllable out before Belinda swept her glare on him and he was silenced. Things had changed. The baby inside Belinda had galvanized her, given her a strength she hadn't had before. I was dismissed but not before I made a scene, yelling they better be in touch and that if they weren't my father'd be down to solve it with his rifle. I let them see what it would mean if I walked into the world shouting their secrets for everyone to hear."

My hands got loose again, and Jane was slower to capture them and hold them tight. But after a time she found them and settled them in her lap.

"But there's more," she said. And the terrible thing is, I knew there was.

"That was the beginning of our war. I went home and stewed and waited and prayed that my period wouldn't come, and each morning I woke without its arrival was a moment of relief. And before the week was out Mickey showed up and told me to pack my bags — the Linklaters wanted me back. I was returning to the home I'd been turned out of."

Jane pushed my hands away and rose to her feet. "This air conditioning is doing nothing." Her manicured fingers came up to the hook on the back of her sundress. "Help me here."

I stood, unclasped the catch, and pulled on the zipper. She shook herself a little, the dress dropping off in one motion, and I didn't even remember Victoria in the Royal York two nights before. "That's better," she said, down to her undergarments, steering me back to the bed, sitting me down, and landing back on top of me. Now the dress was gone, I felt the heat radiating from her skin.

"And this time Trent led me to the front parlour, where Belinda sat stewing on the couch; things had shifted in their dynamic. I wasn't on a hard-backed chair in the dining room. This time Trent did the talking and he welcomed me back and said what an awkward situation we were all in. But we had a deal — and they'd keep their side. I was carrying his child — and of course, they wanted the baby, just as they had at the beginning. They wanted to take care of me during my confinement to make sure I was safe and healthy. They'd decided they'd have to leave Belleville; all three of us were going to Toronto. Trent had a new position down there. And when we got there, they'd find me a doctor. 'And,' he said, looking at Belinda, 'as we agreed the first time we discussed this, once the baby is born, you'll be paid your second payment and return to Belleville, and our family will begin its life with two children: we'll call them twins.'"

So here it was. The beginning of the unwinding of the spool of secrets; the disparate threads finally fitting together. Abbie could find out plenty in the newspapers at the library and listening to Stanley's meanderings, but she couldn't find out everything. At least not until Mickey showed up. Jane reached behind her back and unhooked her bra. She lifted herself off me and I helped to slide her panties over her thighs and down her legs. And then she was sitting back on top of me and she wasn't hiding anything.

"The next weeks were a whirlwind of packing and cooking and cleaning, managing Belinda's cravings and moods, and catching the odd moment for a knee-trembler with Trent, who was as desperate as ever in that house of two pregnancies. And then one morning, just before the move, I threw up. I'd never been so happy to be sick. Things were beginning to feel real. We moved into some rooms in a house on Heath Street and I saw a doctor who pronounced me a perfect pregnant specimen. Trent worked. My belly grew. Belinda and I grew heavy together, wary, hating one another as our time approached.

"I went first, even though I'd conceived second. Trent took me to the hospital and dropped me off. I'd never felt as alone as I did in that delivery room and then he came: a boy. I remember my joy. I'd given birth to a little man — the mini Trent he'd always wanted. But, also, this was the end."

Jane had manoeuvred herself so she was sitting side-saddle on my thigh, one arm around my back, the other working on the final buttons on my shirt; her hair tickled my cheek as our heads hung together. "Three days later," she said into my ear, "Trent showed up at the hospital; he had some forms to fill out and had me sign a few places. He wrote his name and Belinda's name on the birth certificate. To this day, I don't know how he fudged it all. He called the boy Nelson after Belinda's father. What could I do? By the time the three of us went home, Belinda was at the hospital having her child. Trent arranged for a nursemaid to come in to care for the baby, and Mickey's muddy truck showed up just on time as always. I could see him trying to figure things out in the front hall of the house as the baby unleashed a scream offstage.

"The whole way back to Belleville I ached for Nelson — my whole body ached for him — and I started plotting my revenge. Mickey asked about the baby he'd heard crying in the house. At first I tried to put him off, but then I got the idea that by telling him the baby was ours, I could find a friend in my fight. I mean, it might have been ours, who knows? I could convince myself of it, if it could help me out. Mickey didn't care one bit for children — it's hard to imagine anyone more poorly equipped to be a parent — but he had a keen sense of justice, aware of every wrong that'd ever been done to him. And so I told him it was my child and I showed him the bulge still there in my middle. And he got to feeling like someone had taken something from him.

"I could see his mind trying to count the months backward since we'd had our moment on the same seat of that truck. He asked me who the father was. I said that Trent thought he was the father. Mickey thought about this for a moment, then he opened his mouth to say something, but before he could, I jumped in and told him it was important that Trent thought that. We didn't want to be telling him anything different. I told Mickey they'd paid me for the baby, and I showed him the second payment from Trent and Belinda in my purse. He drove and I counted the bills, all of them, so he could see the total and then I counted them again halfway and made two piles and gave him one and he whistled a low, happy whistle and he laughed, and I laughed. I'd had a deal with Trent, and now I had one with Mickey.

And although I was laughing, I was miserable, away from my baby, alone, going back to nothing on that hard-scrabble farm."

XXVI

MY SHIRT WAS unbuttoned now and she was trying to pull it off my back, but it was caught under us. With my arms around her, I rose off the bed, lifting her up with me, so she could pull it loose; halfway up, I tottered and we both fell back onto the mattress with her on top and the shirt in her hand.

But it didn't stop her story; she put her lips to my ear, bit the lobe, and said, "We're almost there." I knew there was more, because we still hadn't gotten to the mystery of the bank robbery, but maybe that wasn't what she meant. "Back home on the farm, I spent six months wearing baggy dresses, feeling miserable, and thinking about ending it all. I'd never thought I had maternal feelings, but I did. My whole body ached for Nelson. I felt it. I was desperate to see him — and worried too; thinking of him living in a house with that woman who hated me. I had their money in a shoebox under the bed, but it couldn't make me happy, couldn't get me to see my baby, and couldn't get me back into Trent's arms."

I wasn't thinking too much about Trent's arms as her hands travelled down my back, hooked under the elastic of my boxers, and pushed them down my legs. Lying at her side, the two of us there with nothing between us, in the murky light of the motel room with the noise of others' vacations, the splashing and yelling coming through the closed window, feeling her fingers on the back of my neck, hearing her younger self's loneliness, my mood swung again, and I pulled her closer. Our eyes met and locked, and she held where she was, resisting coming any closer. I stayed my hands as we looked at one another, our eyes so close it almost hurt, and a smile played across her lips.

"You're surprised," she said. "I'd plotted and schemed to get Trent. I'd done him dirty behind his back, but I loved him too. He loved me. He treated me not as an equal, but as someone to be cherished. He could be a pompous windbag, a stuffy old man, too fond of the sound of his own voice, but we all have our faults. And I knew I could make him happy; and making him happy made me happy.

"I was so desperate that I went up to Toronto on the bus and back to the house on Heath Street and rang the bell. I didn't even know what I'd do when I got there. A stranger answered; they'd been living there for the last four months. Who was I? I went to the phone directory, but the new address wasn't listed, and I wandered the city alone and miserable and cried the whole ride home."

I leaned into her and this time she met me and we shared a kiss. A slow kiss with the promise of more and I wished I'd never asked for this story that went on forever, explaining the complicated Linklater family bramble. Jane pulled away; the more she felt my desire the more determined she was to tell me everything.

"And then two things happened," she said.

"Forget all that."

"You're the one who wanted to know."

"I changed my mind."

"Me too." The smile flashed again; she was as contrary as me. "The first one was when Mickey showed up and told me —"

I groaned.

She laughed her harsh laugh in the darkness. "He told me he wanted to show me a good time. He had some money and was throwing it around and wanted to throw some of it at me. I'd sworn off him: he was the past, not my future — and if he became my present, it would be a long, unpleasant life on one of those rocky farms I'd grown up on. Still, he was one of the last ties I had to Trent, and I wasn't willing to lose that connection.

"I let Mickey take me out on the town, and I asked him where he got the money, and he told me he'd robbed a bank. He was pretty proud of himself; he told me how easy it was. All you needed was a gun and some nerve — he'd smuggled his service revolver out of the army — and had more than enough gumption. You're not supposed to blab your exploits, but Mickey did, at least to me, and I believe that if he ever had a vocation, something he was born to, it was robbing banks. He had the all dumb courage, the unthinking luck to make it work."

We were moving at a slow pace on the bed as the story ground to its end. But even as we enjoyed our tumble down the incline to love's sweet ending, hearing Mickey's name, and about the gun he'd taken from the army — probably the same one that was missing from his room at the Edgewater; the one that matched the bullet wrapped in the envelope addressed to Miss Smart — brought back the memory of him, lying on another bed, alone and unmoving.

But Jane didn't notice my hands stop their movement and my body tense at the memory. "The other thing that happened that year is I got a letter from Trent. He was missing me. He loved me just like I'd grown to love him. He sent a ticket for the train and put me up at the Royal York for a few days during the week. He had a job and a family he went home to in the evening, but every other moment he was with me, and we were catching up on old times and he made me believe we had a future. He was ready for love, and I was dying to hear news of Nelson and to see pictures and figure out how we could all spend the rest of our lives together."

And look at you now, I thought, from the Royal York to the Seahorse Motel — and from Trent to me. And although I was as desperate for her as ever, I said, "And you figured it out. By staging a murder disguised as a bank robbery."

She laughed, a nervous tinkle, like icicles breaking, and said, "We're getting there. You need to know my side before you judge so harshly. And I need your help, now Mickey's back in the picture."

"I don't imagine he's too happy with you."

"I'm asking for your help. Try to take my side, won't you?"

The air conditioning was working now; the room was cold and a chill passed over me as dead Mickey, his face too peaceful and too still, stuck in my consciousness. But she didn't feel it, at least she didn't act like she did, and that bothered me as much as anything. I rolled onto my back and groaned at the stucco ceiling.

"Patience." It wasn't clear what she was talking about. "I need to tell you everything so you understand. You were going to figure it out soon enough — I realized that last night. I decided I'd save you the work and just tell you. But promise me you'll help me; that you'll come to my rescue, because I need that now. Promise."

"Help you with what?" I peered through the dusk of the motel room, trying to read the expression in her eyes and failing.

"Your help. Your protection. Your ..." She left it un-finished, the suggestion between us, and I felt the scrape on my face where her ring had caught me. Her cascade of laughter sounded again. She was on top of me now. What a fool I was for falling for her, like Trent, and before him, Mickey. The frost crept over my skin as the stucco ceiling swam behind her smiling face.

Looking down on me, she returned to her story. "And so it went on, living on the farm, milking a half-dry cow, picking berries, snapping rabbits' necks, and skinning deer. And occasional weeks in Toronto, playing at being Trent's mistress. Fending off Mickey. Trying to figure out a plan. I wanted Belinda dead. I wished her dead. I prayed for her death before I got into my cold bed in that old farmhouse with the wind rattling the windowpanes. I dreamed of her death through the long nights. I dreamed of sitting at the breakfast table and Nelson waking up and calling me

Mom. But I never dared to say those words aloud; I never dared to even write them in a diary. I never spoke them to Mickey. But it's true: I told him of the bank she used; I let him know when she went there — what time and what day. I'd taken to stalking her on my trips to Toronto, learning her movements and routines. I got Trent to tell me: asking when she was out — when she did her shopping and banking — making him think I was looking for a time when me and him could be together. I let Mickey know that she was what kept us from our child. I let him believe he was the father — maybe it was true — and I let him think about the rest: How could he solve the problem? And then fate stepped in and solved it for me."

I didn't know what to believe anymore. There was a part of me that wanted to believe her, to believe her innocence, to believe that it had been luck or fate or something that couldn't be explained; that it wasn't her fault; that all that really mattered was me and her and this moment between us; that she could be mine.

"I couldn't make a death out of nothing, but maybe if I could align enough pieces, get Mickey riled up enough, put him in the bank with her, with a gun in his hands, maybe it would break my way. My only hope was to trust Mickey's genius for that sort of thing, and he came through. I couldn't have planned it better if I wanted to."

But as much as I wanted to believe it, I couldn't. The freeze tingling on my skin began to seep into my insides. It held me in its vice and I shivered beneath her touch. I don't know why I was surprised — the story had been leading to her for two days. I can't pretend that some variation of what she was telling me hadn't already crossed my mind, but to hear her tell it, cool and calm, was what I wasn't prepared for.

"I worked on Mickey. He'd only ever robbed small-town banks, and they were a little different. In the country, he made his escape in a car and if things ever got too tight he just disappeared into the woods and lived rough for as long as needed. But I worked on his hatred of Belinda — how she'd stolen our baby. I primed him: he was to follow her into the bank, line up behind her, and when she got to the teller he'd make his move, and pull her in front of him. I never told him to pull the trigger — and he never did — but I made her the problem that stood between us and Nelson. He could worry about the details. He had an intuition for mayhem that never failed, and he didn't let me down. He had that magical power to come through chaos with the answer he needed and not a hair out of place. In the war, he must have been a hellion, charging through a spray of bullets, impervious to them all. And he made it work here. The gods were smiling, because better than Mickey having to pull the trigger, or dragging Belinda out of the bank, the teller pulled a gun out of the drawer and shot her dead. I can't help it if I'm lucky, can I?"

She smiled her smile, showing her short, sharp teeth as she looked down at me. And then that crescent of lips came down and met mine; beneath her, in the closeness of our embrace, I remembered the pillow coming down on my face in my dream. She lifted her head and put her finger back on my lips to quiet any thoughts I might have.

"It scared Mickey, though, holding her body and feeling the life drain out of it like that. Not that we talked after, because it wasn't two days before Trent was on the phone to me, asking for help — he had two toddlers who needed care — and suddenly we were picking up where we'd left off and my dream to be off the farm and in his arms and queen of that big house with my baby and his sister had come true."

It scared me too, holding her, hearing what she'd done. "So you did kill her," I said, wishing I was elsewhere; wishing I didn't know.

"I didn't kill her. Didn't you hear anything I said? I had the thought, the idea." She pulled away from me. "What's the saying? The road to heaven is paved with bad intentions?"

"I haven't heard that one before." But I had.

The teeter-totter of our desire shifted again. She lowered her head and hair brushed my face. Our lips met again. It was getting hard to care too much about what had happened so long ago.

She was running on her own momentum now. "And then the genius of it was that Mickey went and got caught trying to hold up the bank in Lyndhurst before three months were done. Something had changed in him after Belinda's death; his luck had run out, and he got the job all wrong. He roughed up a cop and got himself caught. They pinned plenty of bank robberies straight across Eastern Ontario on him, and because of his tussle with the officer, they really threw the book at him and he was put away for a good long time. And I was lucky again; they never looked to connect him with the robbery in Toronto."

Our bodies were closing in now. I knew Belinda was dead. I knew Doyle was dead. Approaching the end of her story had brought her to one place and me to another; the cold feeling inside wouldn't leave. "That must have been convenient for you," I said, trying to roll out from under her.

"I'd be lying if I said it wasn't. But, honestly, I don't know how you always manage to think the worst of me." She pushed my shoulders back into the mattress and hung over me, her eyes holding me on the bed. She made one of those sudden changes of direction that continued to leave me dazed: "Enough of all that. I've told you everything you want to know. Now let's forget about it for a bit and ..." She dipped her neck and lowered her head to mine. I closed my eyes, but the kiss didn't come. She needed something more than my kiss and her lips slid to the right and whispered into my ear, "Patrick, you've got to help. Doyle is back."

This time my escape was more determined and I struggled out from under her and rolled to the side of the bed. "Wait," I said, clarity emerging as I disentangled myself from her. "Sending Doyle into the bank wasn't good enough. You weren't trying to scare Belinda — scaring her solved nothing. You were always planning on killing her. You just got lucky that Stanley pulled the trigger first. If he hadn't, Doyle would have done it for you — and then you'd have to find someone to solve that problem for you."

"Is that how you figure it?" Her tone shifted as she reached for me even as I could feel the breath from her words hot on my cheek.

"You really are something. You set up the hit."

"It doesn't make any sense the way you tell it," she said. "I told you, I'm lucky. That's the truth. Mickey wasn't going to kill her. He's not like that. And there's lots he'd do for me, but not kill Belinda. And not in a bank."

"What was he doing there then?"

"What he always does. Creating chaos."

"No," I said. "You made it about the kids. You fired him up about Nelson. That he couldn't see his son." I was up out of the bed now, putting distance between us, sure now of who I was talking to.

Jane rolled over and sat on the edge of the bed as I stood next to window where the air conditioner rattled the glass pane.

"You used that. You stoked his anger. You convinced him of his fatherhood, what was rightfully his, and sent him into the bank with a plan that didn't make sense and him mad as hell."

"I never told him to kill her." She was so sure of herself, it was hard not to believe her. "I've told you everything and this is what I get. You act like you don't believe me. Why would I tell you all this if it wasn't true? It's not like it reflects well on me."

"But you're so deep in this you don't even know what's true and what isn't anymore. You believe your words. You're happy to tell me your truth."

"It's the only one I have." She looked down at the floor and maybe she'd never looked so beautiful. "All this talk is getting me down. I told you, I need help. Mickey's back — I thought you could help me."

"And that's another answer. Find the next helper. Someone to carry the can if something goes wrong this round. They can do the next stretch of jail for you."

"You're impossible." She stood and came toward me across the motel carpet.

"I don't know. You don't have a great track record with the people who help you."

"This time is different. You could help me. That's what we came to talk about."

"Help you how?"

"Mickey's back. I keep telling you. He's out of jail and I'm scared."

"You have to do better than that. We all know he's back. It's not news. You knew yesterday morning when I told you I'd found someone snooping in your yard — except you didn't tell me then. And I found a note for Smart in his pocket, but no one bothered to tell me that's your maiden name. And you're telling me all this now because you're in a jam. Perfect."

"That's not nice. This isn't about me. It's the children. If Mickey catches up with them, God knows what he would do. They're more fragile than they look."

"It's too late for that too. And you know it. What do you think Abbie's been doing all summer? She's stuck on Belinda's death. Who do you think she's been talking to? And why do you think she disappeared this weekend. It's all tied up with Doyle's reappearance. Everything. It's why she went to Belleville to talk to her grandmother."

"Oh. God help us. Mabel. Pretends she's everybody's best friend, but is just here to outlive us all."

"You want to blame the bank robbery on her?"

"Don't be stupid. I understand things are catching up. Closing in. It's not looking pretty. I've made some mistakes, but I've fought too hard for everything to lose it now. I had some luck and I just need a little more. And I thought you were the one who was going to help me. It's not too late." She caught up to me at the curtained window, and pulled my face down to hers. In that last embrace, as her hands travelled down my chest, and the light leaked through the window, I felt her need, and it was possible to see a world where maybe she was right after all, and she and I could salvage something out of the mess swirling around us.

"You could help scare Doyle off. Maybe do something to get him off my back and keep him from the children."

Mickey kept coming between us. I stepped back and snapped the air conditioning off. The room was cold enough. After the drone and rattle of the machine, the silence was loud.

"He'll always be coming back. He sees that big house and comfortable life and he just got out of jail. It can hardly seem fair to him."

"Can't you arrange a way to pay him off?"

"Is that what he wants? He'd be back. You pay once, you'd be paying again and again."

"It'd buy us time."

"Us?"

She reached a hand out to me, but I knocked it away.

"Isn't there anything we can do?" Tears sprang to her eyes and reflected the half-light leaking through the drapes.

They seemed real, but I'd had enough of this charade: "Here's something for you," I said, pulling my head back so I could see her clearly. "Doyle's dead. He was killed in his room at the Edgewater last night."

She stepped away from me and the thin strip of light that came through the part in the curtains crossed her body. Her face was alive with surprise. I knew she'd killed him, there was no other answer, but everything about her reaction told me different.

XXVII

"YOU KILLED HIM and you know it," I said, to say it aloud, to convince myself as I felt the belief draining from me.

Her voice shifted again: "It's one thing not to show me a good time, I suppose I can forgive that — although I don't know why I should — but now you're accusing me of murder."

She crossed back to the bed, found her bra in the tangle of the sheets, hooked it over her shoulders, and reached both hands behind her back to fix the clasp. There was still no ice pick, no hidden gun, no poisoned drink, no pillow closing out my world. Jane picked up her panties, sat on the side of the bed away from me, slid them under her heels, and pulled them up as she stood. "Get dressed if you want a ride back to the city." She dropped the dress over her head just as Victoria had at the Royal York thirty-six hours earlier.

"You knew Mickey was in the city," I said.

"We already talked about this. Talked and talked and talked. You can't accuse me of murder and then come back with a few clarifying questions. That's not how it works. Especially not with the woman you're trying to bed."

I hadn't thought it'd been quite so one-sided, but held my tongue. I found my boxers on the corner of the counterpane and reached for my pants, remembering the pathetic old man in the Royal York, scooping his clothing off the carpet, before hiding behind a closed door. Her hands wrestled with the zipper on the back of her dress. She didn't ask for help, but disappeared into the washroom for a minute. Running water sounded behind the closed door; I pulled on my shirt and straightened it out as best I could.

She appeared back in the bedroom. "Let's go."

I left the key on the bureau, under the television, and followed her out into the sunlight. It wasn't the longest day of the year; it just felt that way. "He was staying at the Edgewater Hotel," I said. "Conveniently close to where you live. He came by your house on the Sunday, the day Abbie disappeared. I don't know if she spoke to him that day, but Eileen did. Abbie talked with him yesterday, sometime before she left for Belleville. He told her he was her —" Jane turned quickly and hit me again, this time with her open palm. There was a loud clap and a couple sitting outside in the sun in the colourful plastic chairs, bouncing a baby, stopped their conversation and stared. A teenager crossing the parking lot looked, looked away, and changed direction to avoid us. Jane opened her door, slid in behind the wheel, and reached across to unlock the passenger side. I dropped onto the bench beside her, my face flushed and smarting, more humiliated than hurt.

"You can slap me this way and that and pretend I'm to blame for this, but I'm telling you the truth. I found Mickey dead last night; someone put a pillow over his face and suffocated him. Those are the facts. And if I look at who has anything to gain from this, it's you and Trent, who might want to keep the past silent. Especially you. Maybe Trent didn't know, but maybe he guessed it. Maybe Mickey was trying to blackmail him and his solution was to protect you — to protect the whole family — by getting rid of the loose cannon who holds all the secrets of your past. Maybe. But he didn't have a chance to go to the Edgewater and put the pillow over Mickey's face. He had the best alibi in the world: he was with me."

She turned the key and the engine roared to life. "Stop."

"I'm trying to help you so you'll have had a minute to think about it when the police come calling, because at a certain point they may put it together and figure something out. It strikes me as too much coincidence that this guy gets out of jail, comes knocking on your door — not once but twice — and now he's dead."

The Coupe de Ville screeched out of the parking lot, lurched onto the road, and we were off; she drove recklessly, her foot heavy, alternating between the gas and the brake, changing lanes aggressively, and daring the traffic to challenge her.

"I hate you," she said. "I thought I liked you. I thought we could make each other happy, if only for a moment. I thought we could help each other. But I was wrong. Enough talking. It's time to stop."

We rode in silence, the wind streaming through the windows, chafing the welt where she'd hit me the first time, cooling the sweat under my shirt, all as the heat pushed up from the tarmac, and the sun beat down through the windshield. No radio sang about the summertime; no announcer talked about the change coming in the weather; no hack tried to sell me the same cigarettes he smoked.

We took the left turn off Lake Shore too fast and I was thrown against the door. She roared into the parking lot and only slowed slightly to slide into the shaded spot next to my car before braking hard. My head snapped forward and back. "Thanks for the ride." I stepped out of the car.

She sneered in response. But before I could slam the door shut and put a final piece of punctuation on our afternoon, I looked up and saw the woman with the pixie cut — the same woman I'd seen talking to Mickey Doyle in the parking lot of the Boulevard Club — crossing the lot toward me. "Don't look now," I said through the open door. "We've got a welcoming committee." Pixie Cut had a big German shepherd straining forward on its leash as she made a beeline toward us.

Jane looked into the rear-view mirror. "Shit. Someone else I hate." She tucked some of her hair back where it belonged, opened her door, and stepped out of the car. "Hello, Bridget."

"Jane," said Bridget. "You're aging backward! You look so young and fresh, even in this heat. It must be the company you keep," she turned her eyes, big and round in her small face, on me.

"Oh," said Jane, as bored as could be, "this is Mr. Bird. He's the private detective Trent hired. I think you might know we've had some problems with Abbie. She disappeared and ended up in Belleville at Grandma's house. Mr. Bird helped us out and picked her up there. And then Abbie disappeared again today, so we've been out looking for her." Jane had shifted again; her ability to slide between the roles of life, to camouflage the anger I knew was there, only made her more dangerous.

"*Enchanté* to meet you in person." Bridget proffered a slim hand. It was cool and dry and held on to mine a trifle too long. "We spoke on the phone yesterday. You were looking to interview my daughter, Lena."

So here she was, at last, the fabled Mrs. Moore, neighbourhood lending library, *Peyton Place* parent, mother of a fast-talking teen. I was about to jump in and tell her I'd seen her yesterday at the club, but she spoke first: "So sorry to hear you wasted your time, driving around looking for Abbie; she showed up at our place a short while ago. I'd already had a call from Trent, so I just walked her home before coming out with Moxie." The dog barked at its name. "But I'm sure a drive with Mr. Bird was no waste of time." She gave me a once-over with her twinkling eyes and turned to flash her smile at Jane.

"It's good to know Abbie's home again. Thank goodness. What's gotten into that girl? I can't think?" Jane could lie so calmly and naturally. I remembered the surprise she'd shown at Doyle's death and replayed it in my mind trying to determine where my gullibility began and her deceit ended.

"Oh, to be young again!" said Bridget. "So much energy and emotion and restlessness and passion. It's not easy, but it sure beats getting old."

"Thank you for the good news about Abbie. I best get home if she's there." Jane turned back to the open car.

"I saw you yesterday," I said to Bridget. "In the late afternoon at the Boulevard Club, talking to a boy in a cardigan and a man who looked like he was living rough."

Bridget wrinkled her nose. "It is nice to be noticed, isn't it?"

Jane paused with her foot on the sill of the car's door, her body twisted in an awkward pose. "Don't worry about Mr. Bird: he only notices you if you're carrying a smoking gun. It's the detective in him."

"I won't believe that for a second." Bridget turned to me. "The boy seemed nice enough, but the man stank to high heaven — sweat, alcohol, hot weather. Yuck. And he'd been drinking. Not a pretty combination. They accosted me in the parking lot of the club, but you know this already, Jane." I snuck a look at the woman at the centre of it all; both her feet were back on the ground; she stood steady and unflustered. "And they were asking for Jane — did I know Jane and they needed to talk to Jane. It was the drifter who did the talking; I'm not sure where the boy fit in. They insisted I get a message to our friend Mrs. Linklater here: and the message was that there was someone who needed to see her who was staying at the Edgewater" — she did a fake exaggeration of a shudder at the mention of the hotel's name — "in room three oh seven. And sure enough, I phoned Jane when I got home yesterday afternoon and passed the message on."

"And I," said Jane, "told you I had no idea what you were talking about or who this man could be and I wouldn't be visiting any room in that dump." Maybe she hadn't lied to me yet, but she could play pretty fast and loose with the truth when she chose, and she could deliver her lines straight and clear.

"And so ends the mystery. But if you do find out the answer to who the man is that's looking for a visit to his hotel room from our friend Jane, you must tell me," trilled Bridget with her unerring knack for getting in every possible dig.

"I should get home and see Abbie," Jane said for the second time.

"Bye now. Great to meet you, Mr. Bird."

"Likewise."

Moxie barked; Bridget yanked on the leash and dragged him off. Jane started the engine, her mask coming off behind the windscreen; her scowl flashed, and she pulled out of the lot. I fumbled in my pocket for the keys.

Two men in suits rose from a parked car and started toward me, and before I could open the lock they were upon me. "Patrick Bird," said the first one, not as a question, but as a matter of fact.

"We'd like you to come downtown with us," said the second.

"What for?"

"That's not how it works, shamus. We ask the questions." Here it was: the plainclothes coppers had caught up with me.

"Come quiet," added the second.

"Let's see your badges."

"He wants to see our badges."

"Everyone's suspicious."

"No one trusts law and order today."

"We're here to serve and protect and all we get is questions and stalls."

The first one flashed his badge at me and I trailed the two to their Crown Victoria. "Frisk him, Lefty." Wordlessly,

Lefty guided me up against the car and gave me a once-over with a professional hand.

"He's clean." Number One lit a cigarette and Lefty opened the rear door and put me in and closed it behind me. And there I was in the back of the cruiser; no door handles, the grill between me and the front, the beginning of the lock-up.

Lefty took his seat behind the wheel and we were off, crawling across Queen Street, no rush at all. "This look familiar to you?" asked the one in the passenger seat as we passed the corner where the Edgewater stood.

"Yeah, it looks familiar," I said.

"Good. Save it. 'Cus there'll be plenty of questions about that when we get where we're going."

The sidewalks and shops and restaurants passed by outside the window like the scenes of a movie seen far away on a silent TV. They were detached from my life now, distant, a memory, not reality, and I felt the cold trickle of regret at the path that had led me here. I was determined not to speak, not to give these two goons anything that could count against me, but I couldn't control myself. "I didn't do it." Could anyone sound more guilty? I was a rank amateur of the worst kind.

"You hear that, Mike? He didn't do it." Lefty laughed.

Mike pushed his hat back farther on his head so that all I could see from my seat was a roll of flesh on the back of his thick neck. "Didn't do what?" Mike thought that was pretty funny and laughed at his own joke. "Tough guy, hold your chatter 'til we get to the station. He didn't do it." He laughed again, a pleasant-sounding chuckle that didn't sound pleasant from where I was sitting.

Lefty stopped at a light and picked up the radio and called in: "Jansen and Jones bringing in a certain Bird. ETA two forty-five."

The radio crackled some words and numbers that meant nothing to me. We passed the Skyline and I remembered my unsatisfactory breakfast there earlier that morning. I was hungry again. I was tired. I closed my eyes, drifted, and let out a sigh.

"Sounds good," said Mike. "Sounds like we softened him up already. I tell you, Lefty, this might be the easiest pinch we ever made."

Lefty grunted.

"What about these, Birdie? See what we found in the back of your car?" I opened my eyes and saw Doyle's boots and jacket being waved back and forth on the other side of the screen. Mike's profile sneered at me. "Explain those, Mr. 'I didn't do it.'"

"I —"

"Shut up," yelled Mike. "I told you to save it until we got to the station."

We rode in silence for a bit longer, past the turn to St. Matthias's church where Ayscough had reunited Doyle and Johnson with the daughter of the woman killed in that fateful bank robbery. I remembered the body twitching with shame on the floor, spouting the unknown language, begging for forgiveness, and wondered if that could be me after this was all finished.

"And this," said Mike, flourishing my business card from the other side of the grill, "buddy, I got to tell you: next time you go to murder a guy, don't leave your card at the front desk." He laughed again, and this time his chuckle expanded into a joyous guffaw.

Lefty laughed too.

I closed my eyes and felt the car roll across the city, slipping in and out of the trolley tracks. We passed the building site where the city hall Linklater was working on was almost finished and swung south on Bay to police headquarters. I rode in the back of the unmarked car and did my best not to think: not to think of Jane and her perfidy, her daring and dangerous game, her credible surprise and show of innocence when accused; not to think of Linklater and his cold superiority and ultimate alibi — he'd been with me at the time Doyle was killed; not to think of Abbie and her confused teenage dreams and heightened sense of justice and the fact that she'd missed the afternoon train to Belleville; not to think of Stanley and his broken-down body writhing in repentance on the church floor as it seemed impossible that he could pick himself up off the dirty ground and make one last response to the man who'd shattered his life; not to think of Bridget Moore, her pixie cut, her probing eyes, her faithfulness in the role of messenger and faithlessness in the role of wife and friend. I tried not to think of them as the city passed by outside the window. I told myself I wouldn't and I did.

Doyle's body had been found. So what? I didn't kill him. The two main suspects, the two with the most to gain, were Jane and Linklater. And unless Linklater had managed some time machine miracle, I couldn't see how he'd worked the trick. I'd been with him more or less continuously from about 6:30 p.m. until I found the body. And then there was Jane: she had the means, the method, the motive — she had it all. But there was something in the natural surprise and ferocity of her response that convinced me it hadn't been her who'd pushed the pillow down on Doyle's face and cut off his last breath. She was a lot of things, but I wasn't so sure she was the murderer.

Lefty pulled into the underground parking garage.

XXVIII

THE THREE OF us rode up in the elevator to the fourth floor. The doors opened, and Lefty prodded me in the back to let me know this was it. We stepped out into the middle of a big room with desks littered with loose paper, cigarette smoke, crewcuts, shirt sleeves, and the endless ringing of a phone. "This way." Lefty guided me down a lane between the work stations to a door. "In here," he grunted. "Have a seat."

Three chairs, one table, and a window, less than a foot square, cut into the door. White paint on the wall scuffed black above the baseboard, like the dirty collars on TV commericals. "Your wallet and your watch," said Lefty with a smirk. "You want to give 'em over, or should I wrestle you for 'em?" I passed them across the table and Lefty took them and went out. The door closed behind him. I sat and waited. And waited some more. I started counting my breaths in my mind but lost focus somewhere after ninety-two. I closed my eyes and tipped my head back. I stood up and tried the door. Locked. I paced: three steps forward, three steps back. I sat down. I stood up. I looked out the window into the narrow world of the homicide division: a man with his tie loosened cradled a receiver on his shoulder and listened; another phone rang unanswered; the crackle of the intercom came muffled through the door; a smouldering butt lay unattended in an ashtray, its smoke rising in a vertical line. This was the life I'd once wanted. I'd been in training at the police academy and planned to start as a patrolman and work my way up to detective, but it hadn't gone like that. I'd put it behind me now; I'd found a job in the same spirit, in some senses better — and now I'd fucked that up as well. I put my head on my arms on the table and tried not to think, but couldn't completely hold back the waves of self-pity. Boredom came and went and came back and stayed. I sat and I waited some more.

Voices sounded on the other side of the door. The lock clicked and the man with the loosened tie that I'd seen on the phone entered the room. The familiar face of my boss, Sid Cowan, followed close behind. If the cop looked calm and determined, Sid looked flustered and haggard. Maybe it was the day's heat that made his light hair curl a little more than usual and made his face shine with a little more dampness than was the norm, or maybe it was the jam I'd put him in. I felt it too, the heavy oppression in the atmosphere pushing down and squeezing me tight.

"Let's skip some of the preliminaries and get right to the nitty-gritty. A lot of time has been wasted and time is of the essence here." I'd been waiting forever and he was telling me about lost time. "I brought Sid into this because he's an old friend and a former colleague — as a favour to him and a favour to you. You should listen to him and stop pussyfooting around and freelancing and, frankly, fucking things up: come clean and tell us what the hell you know about this situation."

I waited a beat, and Sid jumped into the breach. "Listen, Pat, this is Detective Manning. He's going to cut you the breaks he can, but you have to play ball. This isn't the time to clam up."

After another beat, Manning looked over at Sid before continuing, "I'm going to play straight and tell you what we know: Mickey Doyle, Michael Doyle, formerly of Prince Edward County, formerly resident in Kingston Penitentiary, is dead. Rap sheet: bank robbery (multiple), assaulting an officer of the law, and resisting arrest. Sounds like a real piece of work — still, murder is murder. He was suffocated in room three oh seven of the Edgewater Hotel last night at some point between five in the evening and midnight. We can't narrow the time down any closer because we didn't find out about the body until about eleven this morning when housekeeping opened the door. Nice work for them. Go to change the sheets and find a stiff lying on the bed. Coroner confirmed the cause of death — asphyxiation — rough outline of the handprints are still on the pillowcase, which is still over the face. No questions there: it's a homicide. No way to do that to yourself, and just about impossible to do accidentally. You need to press hard and hold down a good long stretch. And like I said: it doesn't happen when you're sleeping alone in your bed.

"So we got going. We have a report from Dexter Manifort, night clerk at the hotel, that you were there yesterday afternoon looking for Doyle. You left your card."

Sid's eyes met mine and there was a level of emotion and accusation that made me uncomfortable. There was something in me that wanted to please him — and something else that rebelled with fury at the idea.

"My boys who went out to pick you up found some boots in the trunk of your car and an old jacket; they belong to Doyle. Belonged. It's time to come clean and tell us what you know. Sid, you got anything to add before we let your young maverick have his say?"

"Patrick, you were on a case, chasing things down. Okay. There's been a murder now, that escalates this up and out of our range. Tell the inspector what you know; we co-operate with the police. Detective Manning is on the same side as us."

"I'll put it to you clear," said Manning. "You fuck with us now, it's Sid's licence. Tell us what you know. Tell us everything you know. Don't jerk us around. I don't like that it took us two plus hours to find you. I'm smelling something that stinks. I'll tell you straight out: you know things you haven't shared."

I don't know if it was Sid's patronizing talk, acting like he was my dad, or Manning coming in heavy, but I'd been teetering on the edge of coming over to their side until those last lectures, and then I felt the imp inside calling me to come out and play: the determination to swim against the tide, to fight the easy path every inch of the way. I wasn't giving these assholes anything. It was the same anger, the same self-destructiveness, the same boiling rage at the injustice of everything that had overtaken me at the academy and

caused me to nearly kill their star recruit — the son of someone famous on the force — which had ended my chances
of becoming a cop. The sluice gates opened and the anger
flooded into me, the acid rage on the raw wounds of life,
the sullen child, petulant, tantruming; and it came to me
then, at that moment, sitting in the windowless room with
those two, both old enough to be the father I never knew.
Seeing no way out, no way forward, no path to anything, I
realized what had happened and how Doyle had died. And
with that knowledge came the cold understanding that this
wasn't over; the killer was still out there, angry, reckless,
dangerous, and I had to get back and stop more carnage
from happening.

I looked at the window into the squad room and tried
to gauge the time by the grey light filtering into this inner
cube. There was no way I was helping this bastard, Manning.
I would tell him what he already knew, but the rest could
stay with me and to hell with him and Sid and everyone else.
I sucked some of whatever filled the airless room into my
lungs and said, "You've got it straight. There's not a lot more
I can tell you. Doyle was a person of interest in the case that
I was working. I'm sure Sid told you that. Missing person:
Girl did a bunk. Ended up in Belleville. I went and picked
her up. Brought her home. Case closed. I reported to Sid this
morning — and he told me as much himself. All done and
finished. Wrapped up and tied with a bow." I was taking a
risk, hoping that Doyle's neighbour at the Edgewater was
keeping herself out of sight; it wouldn't take ten seconds
before she gave me up to scrape out of a jam. I didn't blame
her — I just prayed she'd made herself scarce.

"For god's sake, Pat," said Sid. "They're giving you a
break here and helping you out. Give the man what he asks

for. Where did Doyle fit in the case and what were your interactions with him? You keep inching farther out on your own shaky limb. It's going to break and there isn't going to be anybody to catch you when you fall."

"I first saw Doyle snooping around the back door of the house. I gave chase down to High Park. He lost his boots and jacket; I stopped to pick them up and gave up trying to catch him. He could go. Later I saw him outside the Boulevard Club and tried to run him down there, but got knocked down by a car, and when I came to, he was gone. I found out he was staying at the Edgewater and went there to try and see him. I met Dexter at the desk and he wasn't overly co-operative, so that didn't lead anywhere. I left my card there, so he'd give me a call when Doyle showed back up, but I didn't have much hope in that."

Manning blew a cloud of smoke across the table at me. Here it was: the moment I put my heels in the ground and held on. I was thinking of Jane when the detective said, "You look like you got your face a little roughed up there. How'd that happen chasing Doyle from afar?"

She'd slapped me twice and didn't want to have anything more to do with me. Something sour and uncontrollable inside had seen to that, twisting my response to every approach she'd made. But she'd seen something in me — even if it was just a young body to counterbalance her wayward husband, and a hired hand to scare Doyle off — and she'd treated me like she'd cared, which was more than these tough guys in suits had done. I didn't owe her any allegiance — she'd thrown me out of her car when we'd last parted — yet still there was something inside that held on to what she'd told me, to protect her from what was coming. "I told you," I said, checking my mood as best I could, "I was hit by a car yesterday. I rolled on the front end and caught my cheek on the hood ornament." It sounded unlikely even to me.

The inspector stood. "Show me how you managed to roll on the car and catch your cheek like that. I don't see how even a rodeo clown could pull it off."

"I don't know how it happened; all I know is it did. One minute I was running across Lake Shore, the next I was rolling into the windshield and looking through the glass at a couple of old ladies: Myrtle and Phyllis, members at the Boulevard Club. They carpool together; check with them if you don't believe me."

"Testy," said the big man, coming around the table.

Sid looked unhappy, but he didn't say anything. There was nothing to say.

Manning's face came up to mine. "Tough guys make me sick. And I don't even think you're tough."

Sid shuffled his feet under the table and brought an arm up like he was going to say something, but Manning got there first. "You make me sick. We treat you fine. Sid's in here pleading your case, but you got some axe you got to grind. Grind it, son. Grind it. See where that gets you. If it wasn't for Sid and our friendship and owing a favour or two, I'd lay into you. Guys like you ..." He trailed off, seeing if his hard stare and silence might have more effect than his threats.

The room was frozen in time. The trail of smoke from the butt in the ashtray straightened up and stood to attention. And I was all shut down. Sid shifted in his seat. Manning pulled his face away from mine as he stood; I was glad his sweaty mug and hot breath had retreated. My blood was reaching the boiling point and it was all I could do to restrain myself, to not get up and go at him and get both my hands around his bull neck and my thumbs on his Adam's apple and push like hell until they came through the other side.

"Get the hell out of here. Get the hell out of here, you cheap bastard. You may think: Mickey Doyle, what the hell, he didn't matter to anybody; what can the world care about one more death. And you're right. Nobody cares. This doesn't get solved. No one cares. But I do and I hate your cheap punk attitude that thinks you're better than the next guy. A couple of years down the road it's going to be your stinking corpse I'm worried about in the alley behind the Gladstone. See if I care then. Take your Linklater money and your pay and Sid's licence and get the hell out of here and hope you never meet me again."

I pushed my chair back and stood up.

He wasn't finished: "But I'll tell you now; I know you're holding out on us and when we figure it out — we're coming for you."

I held his gaze and we had a silent stare down like two wolves trying to see whose tail sticks up higher in the wind. "Get the fuck out of here," he said as he turned to open the door. "And, Sid, this is the last time I cut you a break. Friends or no friends."

I stood and followed Sid into the bullpen. I picked my wallet and watch off Lefty's desk and made a show of thumbing through the billfold to see that my money was there. Sid didn't bother trying to go after Manning, his old friend; he pulled on my elbow like a little boy. In the elevator, he turned and said, "What was that? You might've cost me my licence. You've cost me plenty of goodwill. I can't afford that. No one can in this business. You're going to ruin me. I depend on guys like Manning — our model is to eat the scraps off their table. Those scraps add up. Who the hell do you think referred us this case?"

I exhaled an invisible plume into the elevator, feeling the release after the tension of the standoff. "If he referred it, what does he need me for? He can just drive on out to High Park Boulevard and ask them what they know about Doyle."

"The police aren't ringing the Linklaters' doorbell without a say-so from somebody: not the Linklaters, not in that neighbourhood. No. That isn't how this works. They need someone to tie it together for them. That's where you could help."

"Well, I didn't."

"You could have."

"And so could you. Everyone's so righteous until it comes to upsetting the Linklaters. You and Manning are plain weak. You knew about the tie-in with the bank robbery in '51 and Belinda's death. You were free to say something. And you chose not to." The elevator doors opened, and we stepped into the lobby. We were both silent as we walked across it to the plate glass door. I reached it first, pulled it open, and stepped through; Sid followed me out onto the sidewalk. "But that wasn't how you wanted it. You weren't giving up your client's precious privacy to the cops. You'd be okay with me doing it — you could always blame me after — but you wouldn't do it yourself." The barometer was dropping, and a hot wind howled through downtown. We stood in silence and I held on to my hat as a gust coughed.

"You're going to blame me?" asked Sid. "It's one thing — and not the right thing — to have that kind of attitude with Manning; it's another to pull this stunt with me. And I need to let you know, Manning wasn't joking about holding you, about sending you over to the Don. I talked him out of that. Manning is my friend, and, I should add, a friend of your mother's — and your father's — and it was for their sake he agreed to cut you some slack. So don't get so tough and angry at the world when it's trying to do you a favour. It would have broken your mother's heart to know you were held in a murder case."

"Fuck you and your favours."

"Hey, I'm your boss." And then realizing the score. "Oh, fuck it. We're done. Find another job."

I fumbled in my pocket and came out with a key chain and worked the one for the Ford off the ring and tossed it at him.

"You really are a piece of work. Manning was right and I'm the fool. What the hell's got into you?" There was a part of me watching from above that could see the wall coming between us and what I was throwing away; this job might have worked. There was a part of me that could even see what I owed Sid, but that feeling of indebtedness only made me angrier.

"I've got to go," I said, checking my watch. It was half past four.

"What the hell has got into you?" Sid said once more to my back as I stepped onto the street. The last of Linklater's expense money would do for what I needed. I hailed the first cab I saw, but it had a fare in the back and passed me by. The buildings created a wind tunnel and the warm air whipped through the concrete and glass and the hand that had been hailing a taxi reached up and grabbed my hat, which was about to go for a ride. The second cab coming across King stopped for me, and I piled into the back seat.

"The Boulevard Club," I said.

The driver nodded and started off. "Fast, fast," I said, seeing the clog of rush hour starting up and remembering the gun missing off the top of Doyle's dresser. The cabbie grunted something that made no sense to me and swung south to the highway. Emerging from under the downtown towers, I could see the sky: it was grey and massing over with big thunderheads in the west — the direction we were heading. The air had gone from hot to heavy and it had the feeling of a late afternoon storm. The driver's grunt must have been in the affirmative because he was making time; he ran a red at Front and accelerated up the on-ramp onto the Gardiner. The city was a blur outside the windows as I sat back and gulped a lungful of air. It felt like I'd only had time for a couple of breaths when we pulled into the club's parking lot. Behind the building, the storm was already raging, and the lake and the sky had merged into a grey in the distance with no line where one met the other.

XXIX

I BURST THROUGH the door of the Boulevard Club and the first thing I saw was the goon in a suit at the front desk who'd welcomed me as Linklater's guest the day before. His thin moustache straightened out, his dull eyes came up and took in the raw scrapes and wild look on my face. Muzak played in the background; a woman who might have been Myrtle passed through the vestibule on her soft-soled tennis shoes. "May I help you?" he asked.

I was opening my mouth to say something when Thad emerged through a door deeper in the building. Ignoring the doorman, I rushed forward, calling his name. Thad looked up, like every other person in the lobby, surprised to hear my urgency echoing within the sedate confines of the club.

"Excuse me, sir," said the man behind the desk, coming out from his aerie and following after me.

"Thad, I need to talk to you."

"This is a members-only club," said the voice behind me.

Thad approached from across the lobby. "Hello, Mr. Bird. How are you?" His eyes settled on the fresh wound on my face on the opposite side from the one I'd received courtesy of Phyllis's car. "Are you okay?"

Security in a suit and tie caught up to me and gripped my arm with a hairy hand. I didn't try to shake it off. "I need to see Nelson."

"Buddy, like I already said once, this is a members-only club —" Some of the veneer was peeling and the bouncer hidden beneath was starting to show through.

"Save it." I turned to him. "I'm here on Mr. Linklater's business. You call him if you need to."

"Nelson left early today. He wasn't feeling well," Thad said, looking anxious as the vortex in the lobby threatened to engulf him.

"What time'd he leave?"

"Let's go back to the desk and check in with Mr. Linklater and make sure you're who you say you are," said security, squeezing my arm in his big hand.

"Just about an hour ago. He looked fine to me, but he was insistent."

"Thanks, Thad." And turning to the doorman I said, "Get your hands the fuck off me." I saw a woman I thought was Myrtle make a face like a she'd swallowed a wasp. The piped-in muzak, a bouncing vibraphone, faded to be replaced by the lugubrious wheezing of a pan flute. The help ushered me to the door. Thad receded into the distance. I didn't put up resistance to the short goodbye: no fussing and fighting, no grabbing on to door frames, no hopeless uppercuts or rabbit punches — my feet moved in lockstep with my handler.

The hack who'd driven me from downtown was still waiting, hoping to pick up a fare at the club; he might have been happy to see me again, but he didn't show it. A peal of thunder rolled in the distance and a fat teardrop of rain splatted at my feet, leaving a spiked circle on the asphalt. I took shelter in the taxi and gave the driver Linklater's address. He flipped the meter and we were off: the lake on one side, the rise of land up to Parkdale on the other, the blur of buildings and trees, traffic and headlights flashing by the windows. The whole world had lost the light of day as the rain drummed on the roof and an impenetrable gloom cloaked the city; a jagged line of light cut the sky in half. The windshield wipers picked up speed, pushing the water on the glass back and forth.

We turned north on Parkside and pulled away from the lake and now there was the verdure of the woods on one side and red-brick houses on the other, both melting through the rain-streaked windows. We came onto High Park Boulevard and stopped opposite the big grey house under the big grey sky. A boom of thunder detonated in the distance. Water ran down the dark slate roof and into the eavestroughs. The mansion was monolithic, unmoving; the windows, unseeing eyes cut into the facade. Not for the first time, I wondered how anything lived inside that cold mass of stone.

I gave the cabbie the last of Linklater's expense money and stepped into the storm. The wind had died and the air was still as the rain pelted down; I ran across the street, getting drenched in the process, and pounded on the door.

There was no awning on the porch and no answer at the door; I turned the handle, stepped inside, and stood dripping in the unlit interior, listening for a sound of life.

Abbie appeared out of the gloom, from the archway of the living room. "Patrick, you're drenched."

I tried to smile, but imagine it looked like a grimace to her eyes.

"I'm glad you came," she said. "I wasn't completely honest with you. There's something Mickey Doyle told me that might be important. I didn't think so at the time. No, that's not true: I didn't believe it before, but I guess —"

"Where's Nelson?" I said. Her face stiffened against the harshness of my interruption. There was still time left to destroy any last vestige of goodwill the family might have for me.

"You don't want to know about what Mickey said?" There was a noise behind her in the hallway and she whispered as quickly as she could, "He told me he was Nelson's —"

The girl was interrupted again, but this time it was June who came into the gloom of the hallway, still in the red dress I'd seen her pull over her head at the Seahorse Motel. "What the hell are you doing here?"

"He said that Nelson —" Abbie persisted.

"What are you talking about? Abbie, go upstairs and let me speak to Mr. Bird. And let's leave Nelson out of this. You see where your digging up the past has gotten us."

"Not upstairs," I said. "Where's Nelson now?"

"But I need to talk to Patrick," said the girl.

"Abbie. Don't talk back to me."

It was my turn to interrupt. "Where's Nelson?"

"Patrick?" Jane asked Abbie. "Isn't this cozy? All of us together again. And no, you're not talking to Mr. Bird right now. Not ever, if I have my way." She turned to me. "And you, Mr. Bird — or is it Patrick now we're all friendly and close — get out. The case is closed."

She was in charge, and my urgency threatened to melt under the strength of her will. "Where's Nelson?" I asked for the third time.

"Honestly, Mr. Bird, your behaviour is just too much. I asked you to leave. Told you to. Trent was right about you. You're rude. You don't know your place. The last I checked, no one invited you in. Get the hell out."

Lightning interrupted Jane and we all flashed in its strobe for a second. Something new, harder, and vicious, showed in her face — she'd told me everything and still there was more I didn't know about her — and then the crack of thunder crashed on us.

In the vacuum of silence and darkness that followed the echoing boom, Abbie looked from one adult to another, confused by the hostility and conflicting directions. "I'll go and help Eileen in the kitchen," she said.

"That's right. You do that," said Jane.

"And you'll be okay?"

Jane's face twitched in the darkness. She recovered with a harsh laugh. "I'll be fine. Just fine."

"Goodbye, Patrick."

I nodded my head in farewell and a pool of water slid off the brim of my hat and landed on the tiles of the front hall.

"Nelson came home early from work," I said.

"Weren't you told the case is over? All done. Finished. Why are you still snooping around? He wasn't feeling well, so he went upstairs to lie down."

"He's lying down?"

"That's what I just said."

"I'm asking if you've been upstairs to see him. Are you sure?"

"He's sixteen. He works hard. This is the first day he's been sick in two summers. Thunderstorms give me migraines — I wouldn't be surprised if he ..." she caught herself and paused.

"You know that isn't what this is about."

"I hate you, Bird. No one loves a hero. You need to get that through your handsome head. I hate heroes. Go and have your own little war somewhere else — so tough and brave: you were born just a little too late. At least Mickey had the decency not to pretend to be what he wasn't. Go now. Get out of my house."

Some of the raw intimacy of the motel was returning as we stood too close in the darkness of the hall and all the love for her boy was funnelled into a hatred of me.

And then it came: a massive crack rent the darkness, the lightning strike and the peal of thunder right on top of one another as the storm exploded overhead. The flash froze time and held us in our ragged pose. In the silence that followed, a muffled "No" was shouted from the second floor. I pushed past Jane and bounded up the carpeted stairs.

She raced behind me, shouting and cursing. "Look what you've done to my family. Look at it, you bastard! All I ever wanted was my baby and my family."

At the top of the stairs, a line of yellow light showed beneath a door in the back of the house. I approached it and paused for a second, listening; I knocked softly — no surprises — and pushed it open.

Nelson stood with the revolver held in two hands, extended at arm's length, straight in front of him, its barrel pointing at the man who might have been his father, who sat in an overstuffed armchair on the other side of the room with his head in his hands.

Trent lowered his hands and raised his eyes to meet mine, and seeing me, interrupting their family business, seemed to wake him from his torpor. "Bird, what are you doing here. Didn't I dismiss you? The case is finished."

"You call this finished?"

Jane pushed in behind me, and the bedroom became crowded with bodies and the terrible presence of the gun.

"Nelson, baby." Jane addressed her son, his face set, his focus complete, his eyes locked on his father. Keeping my gaze on the scene before me, I reached my hands back for Jane, to wrap her up and slow her down, but she slid through my grasp and passed into the room toward her child.

Trent, now the audience had arrived, pushed himself up from the chair and stood, intent on taking charge. "Nelson, put that gun down, right now. This is absurd. You might have questions for me, you might be confused, but you don't point a gun at anyone, certainly not your father." He began his determined walk around the frills and fluffs of the marital bed toward his son.

"You're not my father," said Nelson. "You're lying."

That stopped Trent. I followed his gaze as he turned to look at Jane, who failed to meet his eyes, and then back to the boy he'd thought was his son. The confidence on his face dissolved and he lunged at Nelson.

"No …" I dove to intercept the attack.

This time when the crack of the explosion and the flash of light came it wasn't thunder and lightning from the outside world. Trent's head snapped back. His body collapsed and he sank to the ground, revealing the crimson spatter on the wall behind him. An impossible lull washed over the room. The rush of water pouring down the gutters and into the storm drains could be heard. A glob of red slid from where it had landed on a mirror and dropped onto the thick pile of the carpet. Nelson leaned against the wall, the gun still in his hand. It wasn't five steps from where I'd landed to where he stood, but it sure looked like a long way. Something, at last, had slowed Jane down, and she too stopped in the no man's land between the boy and the door.

XXX

NELSON WAS THE first to move. He lowered the revolver, almost as if he was surprised at the results of pulling the trigger: the explosion and recoil, the bullet, death. Abbie appeared behind me, in the open doorway, pushing her way into the room. "What happened, Patrick? What's happening?"

I didn't answer — but she had eyes and could see for herself. I kept my focus on the boy; he'd lifted the gun back up and tried to rest the end of the barrel against his temple. His hand was shaking so much he was making a bad job of it. But even bad jobs can go right some of the time — the blood on the wall was proof of that.

Abbie, like her mother — who wasn't her mother — stepped into the bedroom, drawn to where she could see the full extent of the carnage. She made a truncated animal sound as her intake of breath was strangled by the image in front of her. "Dad? No. Mom, what's going on?"

Jane, still standing in the middle of the room, turned. "You call me Mother now? Now? After fourteen years of pretending I wasn't? After months and months of trying to prove I was something else. All your snooping and digging. You call me Mother now? You little bitch."

The outburst diverted Nelson, and without his full focus, the gun slid down his cheek to point at the floor.

Jane approached Abbie, who stood just inside the door. "You stupid busybody. Look at what your amateur snooping has done. Look!" She raised her hand to hit Abbie, who stood frozen as if lightning had flashed once again.

Their conflict held Nelson's attention and the arm holding the revolver slumped further. This would be the time to tackle the boy and wrestle the firearm free. Keeping my eyes on him, I pushed up and off the carpet to standing. Abbie retreating from her stepmother, and Jane pursuing, crowded into the centre of the room, and, caught in their own dance, were moving too quickly for my liking. Nelson's focus faded; he seemed oblivious to it all, his expression weary, petulant, and afraid was reflected in the triptych mirrors of Jane's vanity; three different angles showing three different faces.

Jane swung her open hand at the teenage girl, her red nails a blur in the air. I caught her wrist before she could make contact. She hissed and a spray of spittle landed on my face.

"Here he is, Abbie. Your knight in shining armour's arrived." Jane's wrist twisted out of my grip and she spun away from me. The violence woke Nelson out of his slumber; the gun came up again, and this time the hand that held it on his temple was steadier, committed.

"Nelson!" screamed Abbie.

The barrel of the gun remained still, even as his eyes lifted to meet his sister's. Abbie's face was lit with emotion, begging her brother through a wash of tears to put the gun down and come back, but Nelson might already have been dead for anything that showed in his expression.

But Jane, that magician of human emotions, conjured him back. She stepped to the side to reveal me and made another appeal. "Nelson. We can beat this. We can do it. Only Mr. Bird stands in our way. You can go free. I'll take the fall for both the deaths. I'll say I shot Daddy. I'll say I killed Mickey in the hotel. The only thing that stands in our way is Mr. Bird. You have the gun. You can solve everything. If you kill him, I can say I killed them all. You don't need to go to jail. You're too young. Your whole life is before you. The only thing that can stop us is Bird and his perverted need for the truth. We'll make our own truth. You can do it. Oh, my baby. You can do it. Shoot him. Shoot him and you'll be free and Mommy will say she did this all. I killed them, Mickey and Daddy and Bird. I killed them all. Let me save you. I will."

A low roll of departing thunder sounded in the distance. The gun moved again, slowly this time, the stock coming away from his head, the deliberate straightening of his elbows to horizontal, the elongated arms swinging in a slow arc across the room as the boy rearranged his position and the barrel foreshortened and then disappeared and all that was left for me to see was the empty circle at the end of the gun as the sights lined up.

"Yes," said Jane. "Yes, you can do it. This is your chance. Save your life. We all make mistakes. You don't need to pay with your life. You can do it. Baby. Oh, my little boy. They took you away from me before and now they're going to take you from me again. It wasn't until I met you that I knew what love was. You can do it. Shoot him."

Nelson appeared transfixed by Jane's words, and the barrel pointing at my head held steady as she poured her love into his ears. There was no sliding surreptitiously across the soft pile of the carpet now that I was in his sights. I stood still, not calm, not frozen, but resigned and careful, my hands at my side, my palms open toward him. My eyes found Jane and her desperate bargaining as she tried to ne gotiate her son into one more death. We formed a triangle: he training the gun on me, me looking at Jane, and Jane begging him to accept her love. I looked back at the boy. His face again became that mask of hatred that I'd seen in the moment before his father died. And then the gun shifted as he reset his sights on Jane's streaked face. I jumped for him. The explosion sounded. We landed on the floor, the gun still in his hands. There was no resistance when I wrenched it from his hands. I rolled and looked up. Jane still stood in the centre of the room; a chunk of plaster had fallen from the ceiling and a fine mist of dust floated in the air.

I released the cylinder and knocked the bullets out. They bounced on the pile of the carpet; I scooped them up and into my pocket.

"What happened to us? What happened to our family? What happened?" asked Jane without expectation of an answer. "My baby. My boy. What happened?"

Nelson tried to back away from her approach. Crowded into the corner, he pushed past her and knocked her onto the bed. She fell back, and lay staring at the ceiling, the hole where the bullet had entered, the white powder flitting through the air, her hands wandering and worrying over her eyes and mouth. Gone was the laughter of the tennis court, the coy smile of the motel room; gone was the confident lady at the dining room, the anger and power she'd shown in the car and the front hall: her face collapsed on itself, hardly recognizable.

The brother and sister, not twins, not even sure if they shared any blood at all, stood immobile in the centre of the room.

"Downstairs. Let's get out of this room." They obeyed and we trooped through the dark house, down the dark stairs, and into the living room where the lamps' pale pools of yellow light failed to chase away the shadows. Abbie first, Nelson second, me with the revolver, held by the barrel, bringing up the rear. And Jane, alone on the marriage bed she'd fought so hard for, without her prize husband, and without her only child.

Nelson sat on a big soft chair out of the light, a silhouette against the darkness.

"I didn't mean to kill him. I just got so mad."

With the echo of the gunshots still in my head I assumed he meant Trent lying beneath the quilted counterpane, but it was Abbie who got it right. "You mean Mickey? In the hotel room?"

"Yeah, that's who I mean," he said, as if there weren't a body with only half a head lying in the room above us.

"I didn't like him either," she said. "The way he talked to me. Like he owned us, but Dad?"

Nelson, still staring at the floor, didn't answer.

After the silence had gone on too long, Abbie turned to me. "So Jane did kill my mother. That's what I told you this morning."

"Stanley killed Belinda," I said. "It was an accident of sorts. But Jane helped it all along. She sent Mickey into the bank with a gun and trusted her luck."

"She killed her." Abbie wouldn't be swayed from what she knew to be the truth.

The unearthing of the past and the saying of Mickey's name seemed to bring Nelson back from the depths he had sunken into. "That night. Last night. When I left the house, I saw you" — his head moved marginally to indicate me — "as I was going down the street. I ran into Mickey on the corner. I didn't know his name then. He said he had to talk to me. He told me he had something he needed to tell me. I thought he was a wino looking for a nickel and told him to leave me alone, but then he said, 'I know your mother. I knew Jane, way back, when she was Jane Smart, and I have things you should hear.' And I said, 'She's not my mother. She's my stepmother.'"

He'd said the same thing to me when I met him at the bowling alley the day before. It seemed a long time ago now.

"And he laughed. It was a horrible sound, his laughter — hoarse and hollow. I don't know whether he was laughing at me, or whether there was something he thought was funny — but he had a horrible way of laughing when there was no joke. It was awful, but it made me understand he was telling the truth. And I was angry. How did he know more about my life than I did? So I listened and he said, 'Smart boy — not so smart. She's your mother. But the question you have to ask is "Who's your daddy?"'

"So we went back to his room at the Edgewater. He was drunk, and he got drunker. And he told me the story about how he was my father and Jane was my mother. That she'd been a maid in my parents' house — I don't even know who my parents are — and she'd been asked to leave for some reason and he'd picked her up to take her back to her farm — and on the way back in his truck she'd made him stop and they had ..." He searched for the word. "Sex on the side of the road. And he said, 'That was February 1949, and you were born that November. Work it out. Count it up. Your mother was something else.' And then he lay back on the bed and let loose his horrible rasping laugh and I needed to stop it, and I grabbed the pillow and put it over his head and pushed it down on his face and held it there to stop the laughing. And I stopped it. I stopped it, but I didn't stop pushing the pillow. I just kept on so he wouldn't laugh again. And when I let go it was too late.

"His gun was lying there. He'd already shown it to me. Told me he was coming to our house to ask questions — that you could always get an answer if you asked a question with a gun in your hand. I thought I could get an answer that way as well. So I took it."

Abbie moved across the room and put her hand on his shoulder. "But Dad," she said. "You didn't have to do what you did to him."

The emotion pierced the numbness, and tears began to roll down Nelson's face. He took it without comment and just kept on with his mumbled monologue, trying to make sense of what had happened. "I thought if I could come home and if Dad could explain whose child I was, maybe I'd feel better. The gun was supposed to make him tell me the truth. But it didn't seem to work with Dad — with Trent. He just kept repeating the same thing over and over, telling me the same lies. Even when I had a gun on him. He knew the truth; he could tell me. But he never explained anything.

I'd had enough of his lies." Nelson's tears stopped him from talking for a moment. And we sat there in the gloom listening to his distress.

The swing door to the kitchen pushed open and an oblong of light stretched into the room. Eileen's wrinkled face appeared, and the door closed noiselessly.

"He didn't have to die. If he'd just told me the truth. If he'd just said he wasn't my father then I could've forgiven him. Did your dad ever lie to you?"

I could tell my own untruth and say that he had, but Abbie knew I'd never met my father and I didn't want to get caught in lies of my own. "I never knew him."

"Yeah, I wish I'd never met my dad."

I didn't know which of the two he meant.

XXXI

OUTSIDE, THE RAIN had stopped, but there was still the sound of water running down the streets and into the sewers. Through the thin curtains, the sky was lightening before the evening faded to dusk. I told the maybe-siblings I was going to phone the police, took the gun with me into the kitchen, and made my call. Eileen, seeing the revolver in my hands and the look on my face, watched silently from across the room.

Back in the living room, I stood while Nelson and Abbie sat; time passed in the yellow glow of artificial light. Nelson had had his say and now he sat immobile, his spine straight, his expression flat. Jane was out of sight, upstairs, but her presence in the room above weighed on us all, pushing on the ceiling and making our space that much more cramped and claustrophobic. Abbie avoided my eyes. The sirens moaned in the distance and grew louder; the rotating lights, red and white, swept their beams across the curtains of the front window. The cavalry had arrived to sort through the ashes of the twisted family tree and rescue me from this house where love had gone so wrong. I exhaled a long breath, trying to get rid of all the fear and failure clogging up my insides; I got rid of some, but there was still plenty left. I opened the front door and Abbie followed me out into the hallway; she looked like she hated me too. It was me: I was the one who'd brought death into their home.

A patrolman came up the walk as an ambulance stopped in front of the house and its siren's wail died in the air. I told him about the body upstairs and the boy on the couch and gave him the empty revolver and the loose shells.

More cars were arriving all the time. There was a lot of activity: the crackle of the two-way radio, the wet imprints of the ambulancemen's shoes on the stairs, the bagging of the murder weapon, doors opening and closing, the command centre set up in the back den.

They talked to Nelson; they talked to Abbie; and then Manning called for me. I sat back down on the L-shaped couch where I'd joined Jane in her tennis whites just the day before. Manning's questions were factual and so were my answers. He didn't say anything I hadn't already said to myself. He didn't accuse or yell, or tell me I was an amateur, but his dull professional's eyes, inured to death, emotionless, scudding over the carnage without being tainted by it, were enough to make me understand why he was him and I was me and how that could never change. And when all the words were said and all the story shared, he told me to get out, go home, and wait for their phone call. I didn't hang around to see Jane come down the stairs to meet with Manning, to see what she might look like entering that room where explanations were demanded and her grim pragmatism and fast schemes would hold no sway, where the game was over and all that was left was the answering of questions.

I drifted back into the kitchen away from the bustle of the crisis. The swing door shut itself behind me and Eileen said, "Oh, no. A bird in the house never meant any good."

I failed to smile.

"Fly away, Birdie, fly away." She made a shooing motion with her hands, driving me out the back way. I realized I'd never taken my shoes off when I came in from the storm. I opened the kitchen door and stepped onto the back porch, mere feet from where I'd first seen Doyle just yesterday. And now he was dead, in the morgue, staring at the roof of the refrigerator room's sliding drawer. I started to walk. A lot had changed in two days. A lot had changed in the stone mansion — its hatred coalescing to a focal point. And I'd been the magnifying glass that had bent the sunlight into the crucible and started the fire that tore through those rooms and burned everything under the grey slate roof until now the family was no more and all that was left were the cold stones. Trent was dead, his brains staining the wallpaper, and Nelson would go away somewhere for a long time, his youth wasted in a dusty yard, in the tough company of the range, already broken, only to be broken more. And the stone house would be home to Jane and Abigail, with not an ounce of shared blood between them, and no love either. Just the two of them in that mansion, watching each other, thinking of their loss, and blaming the other, and after this, the hatred would still be simmering, waiting for one more flare to start it over again.

My feet led me through the streets as the clouds cleared and the sun sent its oblique rays between the big trees and off the glass windows. My steps were leading me back to Rosie and every thought that crossed my mind was just a rehearsal of what I would say when I saw her; how I would explain myself and what I did and what I didn't do and how it was all my fault. Mistakes were made. Things went wrong. People were hurt — and not just the dead. If I could just talk to Rosie — to someone who wasn't a part of it — maybe she could understand. She could tell me it was all right; it wasn't my fault. Things could get better.

I turned onto Queen and saw the neon sign that said SKYLINE RESTAURANT with an arrow like a shooting star pointing to the doorway. It hung over the sidewalk glowing in the falling dusk. I noticed the flickering dissonance between the easy cursive of the neon SKYLINE and the block capitals of RESTAURANT, between the fixed background of the words painted on the wooden board and the shimmering lettering of the lighted tubes. And in that space, vibrating between the soft glow of the light and the permanent paint job of the sign, it seemed like there was some hidden mystery — and if I could just find what it was, I'd understand something. Anything.

I pulled on the glass door, swung it out, and stepped into the darkness, my eyes adjusting to the inside. I nodded to the man behind the counter in his white apron, stained with the days' work, and started walking back into the dining room: the leatherette booths that lined the wall on my right; the short stools at the Formica counter on my left; the tables up ahead; an ugly landscape painting hanging on the wall; a big mirror making the room look bigger than it was. There were people inside, talking, eating, smoking, living their lives, worried about their children, their taxes, the rent on their apartment; they worried about leaving the job they hated; they were trying to remember to pick up a quart of milk on the way home for breakfast tomorrow. There were people with french fries speared on forks, rice pudding on a spoon, lifting coffee cups to their mouths, folding a newspaper in half, sitting alone at a booth, pouring an Old Vienna into a glass, holding a flame across the table as their best girl placed a cigarette between her lips, opening the menu, searching for their glasses, digging in wallets for cash to pay the bill. There were people, loud in their talk, laughing, sitting with their heads tilted back to watch the silent TV above the counter, ears cocked to the side listening to the song on the radio that played in the background and could only be heard when a lull came in the waves of conversation that ebbed and flowed across the greasy air. There were people with eyes and mouths, with thoughts and feelings, with pain and happiness — a whole world of them, and I could just see those squeezed into this little diner. But I couldn't see Rosie.

I felt unsteady on my feet as I stood in the centre of the room, looking for her and not seeing her anywhere. A middle-aged waitress used a forearm, her fist already clasping cutlery pre-wrapped in a paper serviette, to nudge me to one side as she passed with two dinners — the fish and chips and the hamburger platter — running up the other arm. I took another step deeper into the restaurant, past where the counter ended and the tables began, seeing the pass-through cut into the back wall and through it the grease and haze of the kitchen; the white chefs' uniforms moving above the dining hall, a pair of tongs snapping in the light, a platter placed on the ledge for pickup. To the right of the opening was the swing door and behind the door, three steps up and into the kitchen. I stood in the centre of the room, a traffic pylon on the road. The door swung outward and Rosie walked down the stairs wearing her street clothes — a pair of jeans and a gingham shirt — looking more perfect than ever.

I saw her before she noticed me and stepped forward. "Rosie."

"What are you doing here?"

"I came to see you."

"You already saw me today."

"That was a long time ago now."

"A long time for me too."

"You're going?"

"That's right. My shift is over. That's what happens when the day is done. I'm not sticking around here. That's —" She paused, realizing she was in the middle of the dining hall.

"Do you want to do something?"

"I've done something with you before. Thanks, but no thanks."

"I had a bad day," I said.

The older waitress, her hands free on the return trip to the kitchen, pushed on my back. "You're blocking traffic. Take a seat or take it outside. Help me here, Rosie."

"You're in the way."

"Should we go outside?"

"I don't know where we should go; I'm going home. You can figure out where you're going."

"But I want to do something."

"You told me that already." Somehow, she'd gotten around me and was walking to the door, saying a goodbye to the guy in the apron behind the counter.

A couple stood up in the aisle; I squeezed between them and got a dirty look. "I know. I'm telling you again. I had a bad day."

She had her hand on the door to the outside; she turned halfway around so I could hear and said, "You told me that as well. Everybody has bad days. Maybe I had a bad day too."

"So can't we do something?"

"Not tonight. I told you: I'm going home. I'm tired."

She stepped into the dusk, half dark, but across the street the last of the sun's rays were reflected bright bright in the glass of the grocery there, shining and reflecting, almost blinding us.

ACKNOWLEDGEMENTS

SO MANY PEOPLE to thank for so much.

Thank you to my first reader, Hugh Box, who stomached my earliest work and provided me with a few cautions, as well as the encouragement to keep going; Chris Forbes, my first writing partner, who really awoke me to what good writing could be; Jenny Manzer, who took a great deal of her time to provide me with the kind of honest and professional feedback that made me understand that I wasn't there (yet!) and encouraged me to continue; Andrew Steinmetz, who provided encouragement and a much needed and well-timed email; Peter Sellers, who was so kind as to provide me with some very important words of wisdom, and a reality check of how far off I was; Eva Wisting, for welcoming me into her community and encouraging me to submit my work for publication; and Stephen Luscomb, who helped me a great deal with *The Man Who Went Down Under*, which was my first success.

Thank you to the two communities I was so lucky to stumble into for their support and encouragement: to Andrew, Bill, Susan, Nina, Cheryl, Brian, Karen, Aveek, and Deborah; to Eva, Jeffrey, Aaron, JingShu, Kat, Katherine, Irene, Jaclyn, and Ninu; and especially to Ted Fines, who read an early manuscript of *The Road to Heaven* and provided me with his invaluable copy-editing eye, his insight on plot and pacing, and also some much-needed fact-checking on my Toronto of the 1960s.

Thank you to my parents who brought me to Toronto in 1969, and were kind enough to read an early version of *The Road to Heaven*.

A huge thank you to my partner, Lara, for all her support, encouragement, and honest feedback. I am so lucky to have a partner whose aesthetic choices I trust so implicitly. Thank you for reining in all my worst literary impulses ("too much!"), for providing your perspective on all aspects of my work, and for helping me to be the best I can be in life and in writing.

Thank you to the team at Dundurn: to acquiring editor Megan Beadle for believing in this book and fighting to get it published, for all her kind words and encouragement, and for all her suggestions and edits to make the final version the best it could be; to Erin Pinksen, Shannon Whibbs, Meghan Macdonald, Laura Boyle, and Rajdeep Singh, without whose support this book wouldn't be possible.

Listing people to thank is never a good idea. It is inevitable that I have forgotten someone. My apologies. There have been so many who have helped me on my way, and I have nothing but gratitude for the support I've received.

ABOUT THE AUTHOR

ALEXIS STEFANOVICH-THOMSON WRITES a wide variety of crime and crime-adjacent fiction. *The Road to Heaven*, featuring detective Patrick Bird, is his first published novel. His novella *The Man Who Went Down Under* won both the Black Orchid Novella Award (2021) and the CWC Best Crime Novella Award (2023). He also won third place in the *Toronto Star*'s Short Story Contest (2022) for his story "The Unfinished Book." For many years he worked as a special education teacher, primarily with students with intellectual disabilities and autism. Alexis lives with his partner and their two children in Toronto. He is currently working on the next Patrick Bird mystery.

BOOK CLUB QUESTIONS

1. The author has described this novel as "maple-noir." What features do you think make it "noir"? What parts seem distinctly Canadian?

2. The artless Patrick Bird solves the mystery despite making many missteps throughout the story. What are some of the mistakes he makes? Do you think he should continue as a detective, or should he quit while ahead?

3. All the action in this novel takes place in less than forty-eight hours. Were you conscious of the compressed time when reading? What did you think the advantages and disadvantages of this technique were?

4. The title of the book, *The Road to Heaven*, is an ironic twist on the common aphorism. Do you think this was the right title for the book? How did you judge the *intensions*

of each of the characters, and did that change how you eventually judged their actions?

5. *The Road to Heaven* is written in the first-person; we see the world through the eyes of young Patrick Bird. How does this limit what we are able to see? Is there a scene that we miss that you would have liked to be present at? What does first-person narration allow a mystery author to accomplish that third-person narration would not?

6. At the heart of this story is a family and their secrets and lies. In what sense are the Linklaters typical of many families, and how are they different?

7. As you were reading, who did you think was responsible for Mickey's death? What lead you to that idea, and were you surprised when you learned the truth? Were you right?

8. Private investigators seem to live only in the pages of novels and on screens. Why do you think characters like the Linklaters often choose to hire a PI instead of going to the police? Can you think of a situation where you would consider hiring a private investigator?

9. This book is set very distinctly in Toronto. Have you been to Toronto? Were there any buildings or settings that were recognizable to you? What benefits and drawbacks are there to using a recognizable location rather than one that has been invented?

10. L. P. Hartley's *The Go-Between* starts with the line "The past is a foreign country, they do things differently there." What is different in Toronto of 1965 from the present day, and what is the same? Do you read books about the past to see and learn about the unique features of that time; or are you more interested in seeing the universal human characteristics that transcend time and place?